ENTER PORTAL 3:

WORLDS ASUNDER

Printed in Australia

First printed October 2025
Paperback ISBN 978-1-7637872-4-7
eBook ISBN 978-1-7637872-5-4

Cover design by Jessica Chaplin
Typeset by Jessica Chaplin

A catalogue record for this work is available from the National Library of Australia

ENTER PORTAL 3:

WORLDS ASUNDER

A. J. ELKSNIS

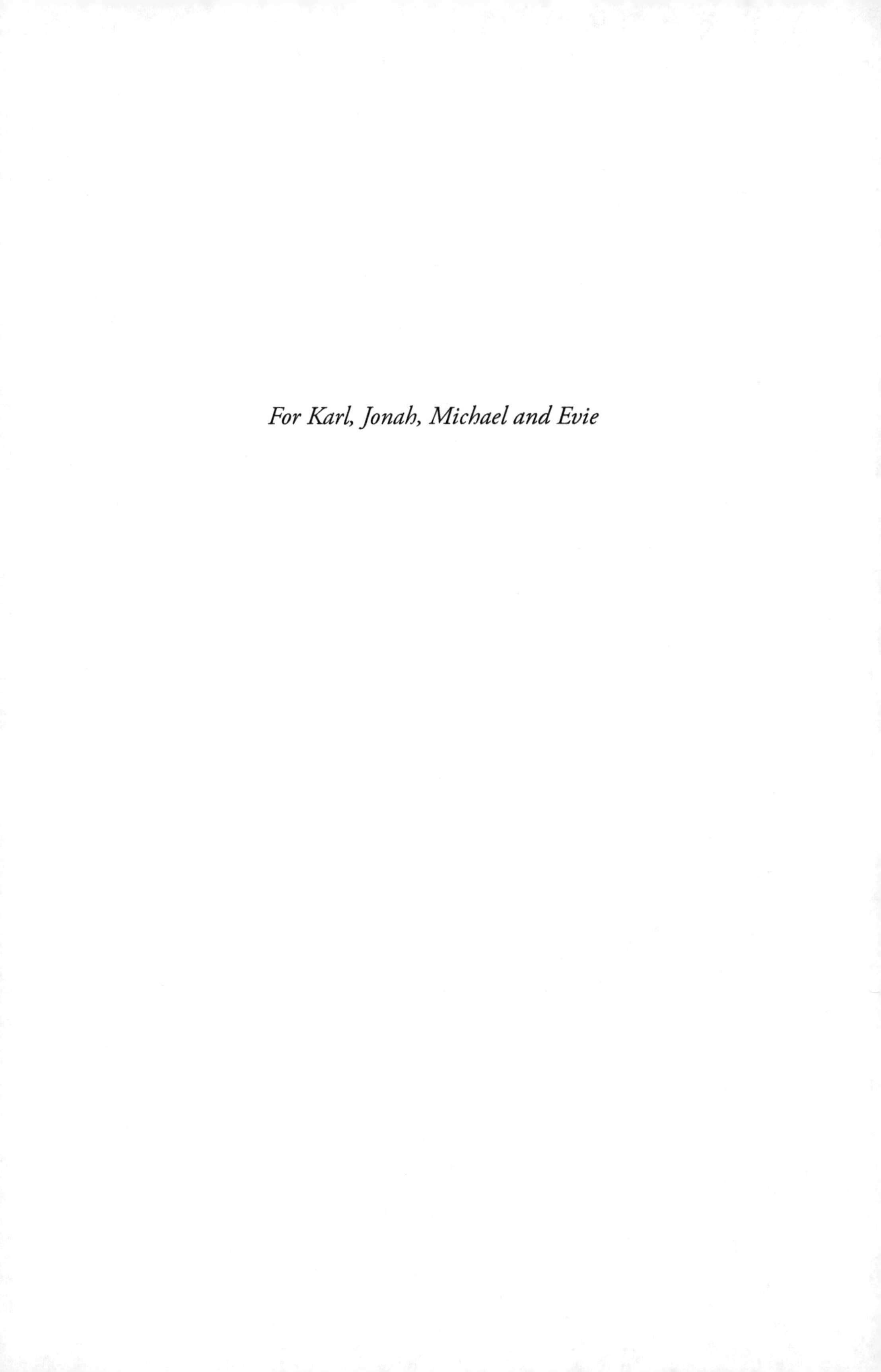

For Karl, Jonah, Michael and Evie

Chapter I

Before Lana. Before Sabre Company.

Pablo and Andula Casal woke to the sound of the ship engine powering down to orbit entry speed. The window shutters rose, and Andula gazed out at the frozen moon, Glacier II.

The star ship descended to the Genesis Lab hangar. The doors opened, and the pilot taxied them in. Enveloped by swirling snow, the craft powered down while the hangar closed. The white haze fell, revealing supply crates stacked against the walls. Security guards were posted on the catwalk above the elevator to the lab, radioing in the new arrival. Pablo and Andula were greeted by a grey-haired man wearing a lab coat when they disembarked.

'Welcome. I'm Professor Peter O'Conner.' Pete introduced a pale woman propped on a walking stick, wearing an orange bandanna. 'You've already spoken to my wife during your interview. Professor Lucile O'Conner.'

'Lucy,' she offered with a welcoming smile. 'Call him Pete.'

The four made their way to an elevator. 'If either of you have any doubts at all…' Pete began.

'None, thank you,' Andula assured him. A beep sounded from a console in her purse, and she took it out to check the notification. 'Pablo, we're clear.'

'Here is the thing,' Pablo began in a frank tone, pronouncing his vowels short and sharp. 'We told you in our interview that we were unable to accept the Migration Grant within the time frame that was offered, and are struggling financially to join our families on a new colony…'

'We *are* departing to start a family on a new colony,' Andula added, distinctly rolling her 'r's, 'and we do intend to donate to your project, but the rest we told you was a cover story.'

Lucy raised a finger. 'I'm confused. You lied so you could enter our facility?'

'I will explain,' Pablo assured them. 'We told you we are diplomats. We are actually Peace Keeper Operatives.' He gestured to Pete. 'We served with your friend, Captain Henry Drake, during the Unmasked War on Earth. Andula and I assisted with peace talks all over the Middle East and in Russia at that time.'

'We were also gaining access to soft target schematics, military communications, drone surveillance.' Andula made flowing hand movements to indicate a lot more espionage was involved.

Pablo gave Pete and Lucy a reassuring glance. 'Don't worry, you both have clearance to know this. We arranged it with the Council before coming here.'

The elevator arrived at their lab floor, but Andula pressed the hold button. 'You must never speak of our involvement, of course.'

'Of course,' Pete replied, dumbfounded.

Lucy echoed confirmation, and leaned conspiratorially on her walking stick to ask, 'Was it you and your fellow operatives who revealed which nations were supplying and supporting extremist groups?'

'We identified leaders and their subordinates who were culpable for war atrocities,' Andula confirmed.

'We linked irrefutable evidence to those responsible,' Pablo added. 'Much of what we were able to achieve would not have been possible without community support in every country we travelled to. Every population of people, the warring and the invaded, wanted peace.'

'Only the powerful wanted conflict,' Andula agreed. 'Only they had something to gain from war.'

'Andula and I were not involved in combat operations,' Pablo clarified. 'Crews led by thousands of different Captains like Henry performed all of the captures, sanctions and unavoidable wet work.'

'Unavoidable what?' Lucy queried innocently.

Pablo pressed his lips together before letting out a sigh of regret. 'Unfortunately, the very same methods our predecessors used to achieve global nuclear disarmament had to be employed again. The powerful who would not see reason, even when their own advisors begged them to capitulate, to stop their invasion and resource theft, had to be put down.'

'Let's discuss the reason we are here,' Andula suggested.

'Yes, why *are* you here?' Lucy asked, perplexed. 'Why do you want to help us?'

Andula opened the elevator doors. 'Pablo and I read your proposal to the Council and your ultimate reason for wanting to start the Augmented Human project: to explore alternate universes in search of a "cure for conflict". We financed a search for candidates while you two were conducting your own.'

Pablo chuckled. 'After a week of poor results, our team turned to us and requested the necessary tests. We agreed, and lo and behold, our genes are what you are looking for.'

Andula beamed at them both. 'So here we are.' They arrived at the lab, and one of Pete's staff handed him a report to check. Andula's tone shifted completely. 'The very generous credit you have offered will pay for everything we need to join our families and start a new life.'

Lucy played along. 'I hear all of the colonies are doing well.' She turned their attention to a small pod. 'This is the machine we will be using to accelerate the growth of the baby you give us. The child will receive early development learning through a neural link.'

'Where will they live?' Pablo asked.

Lucy ushered them to a service elevator, and explained during their ascent that there was a gymnasium built into the mountain about fifty metres from the Genesis Lab. The elevator arrived, and Pablo and Andula explored the gym and the loft above it, which was to be the child's quarters once he or she reached an independent age.

'We are grateful that you're doing this,' Pete said. 'The few prospective donors we've invited here changed their minds. They didn't trust the science behind neural learning. And the fact that the big purple Parabola is on its way to destroy Glacier II didn't help, despite our assurances that the project will be finished and all personnel will be evacuated well before the light band arrives.'

'You are obviously good people,' Andula said. 'You have prepared every necessity for the child's upbringing. We are confident that you will raise him or her with the best intentions.' She locked eyes with Pete. 'The child must never know who we are. You must lie when asked.' And she turned to Lucy. 'Can you do that?'

The gym comms beeped an incoming call.

'Professor, a Kiyol vessel is on approach and is requesting permission to land.'

Pete exchanged a look with his wife that said "We don't have a choice".

'Yes. Yes, we can.'

An egg-shaped Kiyol vessel taxied into the hangar above the Genesis Lab, tilted its nose, extended three legs and landed deftly. A ramp descended from the rear, and a female warrior emerged, stopping half-way to scope out the waiting humans.

The hangar doors closed, and the last gust of chill wind blew over Hodge Franko, head of Genesis Lab security. Being a middle-aged Alaskan man, he was no stranger to cold. The snow that had blown in settled around his boots, and he nodded to the Kiyola on the ramp. Hodge had only ever seen televised footage of the Kiyol. They were shorter than he thought they would be, although he understood the males, called Kiyolo, were larger.

The Kiyola warrior noted that Hodge's side-arm and those of his two security staff were holstered. She spoke an alien word to her protectee, and Ambassador Jainon descended the ramp and greeted Hodge.

Lucy arrived in the meeting room to join the discussion held with the Kiyol to finalise a trade agreement. The Kiyol possessed technology that allowed them not only to teleport great distances, but also to step between parallel universes. With approval from the Universal Council, the two parties had established a partnership, whereby information and technology would be shared.

Ambassador Jainon nodded to the Kiyola sitting beside her, prompting the handover of an ornate wooden box. Anticipation was building.

Pete and Lucy glanced at each other and returned their eager attention to Jainon. The Ambassador opened the box and pushed it across the table to Pete.

'Translated to your language, this device is called a Shifter,' she said, and gestured to the Kiyola beside her. 'My ward will show your people how to use it safely.'

Pete opened his mouth to thank Jainon, but she spoke first, placing her hand on the box. 'This technological path enlightened our scientists and in many ways improved our social and sustainable way of life.' Serious intent sharpened her jade eyes. 'But it also exposed us to many dangers. Proceed with caution.'

Chapter 2

The transition into their new life was made easier for the Raekeem by the forty-one who had come before them. The Lustitians had used a passive weapon to expel all life forms carrying the Warden mutagen. Those Raekeem, and Hal, had been thrust into the Ether Realm. After an arduous arrival, Hal and all those cured of the mutagen were now comfortable in their new environment, and in their new way of life.

Miri had moved out of her sister's into a tree house of her own. Lana came to visit as often as she could, so often that she felt that the Ether Realm was her second home.

Woken by morning light, Lana slipped out of bed while Miri dozed. She descended winding stairs and pulled aside the pantry curtain in the kitchen. She was nosing about for breakfast ingredients when a shadow fell over her and she could feel a hostile presence.

Lana turned around and saw herself. Her other self was standing right in front of her, wearing her usual combat gear: leggings and a cropped tank top. Before Lana could utter a word, her double took her by the throat, shoving her against the pantry shelves. She stared in horror at this person who looked like her but couldn't be. And before her throat closed over, she woke with a gasp.

Lana swung her legs out of her top bunk bed and waited for her senses to guide her back to waking life: the hum of engines, the sterile scent of a star ship interior. She was aboard Talon's ship, the Black Heron, flying to their first aid mission. Lana's heart rate settled, and she felt her neck. She was uninjured. Just a dream. She dressed and walked out to the loading bay, passed the armoury and headed to the cockpit.

The Black Heron was a ship that Talon acquired during the fight against the Raekeem. Lana said good morning to her, dropped into the co-seat, and peered out at the streams of light from stars stretched by her perspective of space travel. She and Talon had been travelling to different planets, interviewing prospective crewmates. None were promising, but they had a lead on a man who happened to live on the same planet they were headed to.

Lana was a Captain now, but the title didn't feel real to her. Not yet. She thought once she and Talon found a good crew, she would feel more like a leader. Like her friend and mentor, Rachel Navara. Lana thought to call Rachel, to relate her dream, ask her what being attacked by a double of one's self could mean. Rachel was still working with her partner, Sam, and Sam's father Pete, investigating alternate worlds.

Lana touched the woollen bracelet on her wrist, a gift from Miri, a traditional Fyrst Born weave that Miri wore as well, symbolising their joining. She had only been away from Miri for a day, and she already missed her. *Focus on the mission*, Lana told herself.

First on today's agenda, ahead of seeking out the possible recruit, was a request for assistance at a colony called Stone River. Second was a mission she and Talon accepted from Lincoln, the decorated AM who was only recently promoted to General. A "secret mission".

'Coffee?' Lana offered Talon.

The pink-haired AM, Cambodian in appearance, gave her an appreciative glance, but signed *No thanks* with her free hand while tapping a holo display of engine output readings. Talon's voice box had been damaged during combat. Repair would have been easy enough, but she refused, instead opting to design her own sign language. A language she taught only to Lana.

Back in a tick, Lana signed and left for the kitchenette in the bunk room. She made a coffee, boiled some eggs and took sips and mouthfuls while putting on her gear, holstering her trusty axe on her left hip. She picked up an M9 pistol and pushed it into her right thigh holster.

Lastly, she tied her long fringe back Fyrst Born-style, into a ponytail, to rest on her loose, shoulder-length hair.

The engine tone changed, and the walls of the Black Heron vibrated. Lana guessed that she and Talon had arrived at the Outer Rim planet and were entering the upper atmosphere. She smiled when she heard heavy metal music start and left to re-join Talon in the cockpit. The band Talon put on was a female-fronted group called Follow. The singer entered harsh vocals and completed an impressive extended roar. Then the chorus, soulful and melodic.

The Black Heron dipped beneath the clouds and flew over rocky canyons. Talon followed a snaking river until the gully opened up, and they saw the colony that had been settled during the Great Migration. Stone River was established on both sides of the water, with two bridges connecting east and west. Both were a mix of small businesses and residences. Lana requested permission to land, but there was no reply.

'Set us down,' she said to Talon. 'We'll walk from here.'

They landed a hundred metres from the town, next to the river. Talon programmed security, and a gun turret popped up from the roof. She set it on sentry mode and left for the armoury. There, she equipped herself with a side-arm and a grenade, and she joined Lana on the down ramp.

While the two of them strode toward the nearest building, Talon pressed a lockdown command on her console. The wings of the Black Heron extended and swung around to meet at its beak. Lana noted the ease with which she used the new personal console. Wrist consoles were being phased out, so it had been redesigned by a Japanese company into a ring that could be fastened onto the wearer's index finger, between the first and second knuckle. The navigation pad was operated by the thumb. By tapping to bring up a holographic screen and swiping in different directions, the wearer could navigate menus, send messages and access comms.

Lana peered through the first shop window they reached. No sign of movement. She took point, her boots crunching on the gravel road leading to the bridge. The second Lana noticed that it was barricaded, bullets kicked up rocks a few feet in front of her. She and Talon took cover in a clothing store.

'Hold your fire!' Lana shouted. She stepped out with her hands raised. She saw two AMs standing poised to shoot. Their eyes were shifting, looking out for something that wasn't Lana or Talon.

'What's going on here?' Lana called. 'Where is everyone?'

Talon arrived at her side and tapped her arm. She turned to see that the gravel beneath their feet was vibrating. The store windows were rattling, steel verandas shaking. Lana and Talon backed onto the bridge and aimed their weapons at a rising bulge moving through the road. It split into three smaller mounts, creating ridges in their wake. Dirt exploded into the air, and three giant black beetles leapt through the falling dust.

Lana and Talon were knocked down by the weight of their carapace bodies. How many, neither could tell, blinded by dirt. Though Lana was able to engage her silicon-carbide ability to armour her skin, she cried out when serrated pincers sawed rapidly against her arms, ribs and legs. The dust finally cleared enough for her to see. She pried, kicked and elbowed the creatures off of her, and fired her gun at the beetles climbing all over Talon. Covered in cuts, Talon shot them at point blank range, while wriggling away on her back. The two of them rolled to their feet and ran for the barricade, firing blindly behind them. The AMs killed the remaining creatures. Wind blew away the beige cloud hanging in the air, and there was silence.

'They never cross the water,' a soldier told Lana. 'Everyone on the west side of Stone River has been evacuated to the east.'

Two more soldiers arrived, and one spoke to Lana. 'Ma'am, we saw you land. Sorry we couldn't warn you. Our communications are down. The best we could manage was Morse code.'

'We received your distress signal,' said Lana. 'We heard reports of Warden stowaways hitching a ride on supply carriers–'

'It is a Warden, ma'am.' The soldier showed Lana acid burns that ran the length of his arm. 'It gave me this last time it attacked. It's been spawning more of its kind since it arrived.'

'Sorry for shooting at you.'

Lana turned to see the AM who apologised had also suffered an acid burn. His left eye was gone, his cheeks looked boiled and his ear was missing.

'Can't see very well,' he said.

'If the two of you will follow me, I'll take you to the Mayor,' the other said. 'He'll fill you in on the details.'

The Mayor, a forty-year-old man, was tending to an injured senior lady when Lana and Talon arrived. He glanced up at them while tying a bandage around the woman's arm, took her hand and spoke to her gently before standing to greet them.

'Thank you for coming.'

'We might not look like much–' Lana started.

'I know who you are, Lana,' the Mayor said with a gleam in his eye. 'If everything they say is true, you and your friend are all the aid we need.'

A soldier handed the Mayor a pair of binoculars, and they all climbed the stairs of the building to get a better view of the settlement from the balcony.

'The support we receive from the UC Migration Division arrives on the west side of Stone River, over there, every six months.' He passed Lana the binoculars and pointed to a large container sitting on a landing pad. 'We found a hole in the last shipment. The Warden had eaten all the food in transit and burrowed through the landing pad into the ground when the container was delivered. There was no activity for two nights, until the Warden's spawn started popping up all over the west side.'

'Talon and I will go in with two of your security,' said Lana. 'We'll need ground-penetrating radar to give us warning before the bugs resurface.'

The Mayor nodded to the soldier for him to make it so and cautioned Lana, 'Be careful out there. Some of the buildings are sinking.'

Talon and Lana returned to the beetle-infested side of Stone River, stepping lightly on their approach. Their ring consoles displayed activity beneath their feet the second the ground radar was active.

Lana stepped up onto the deck of a restaurant. There were still plates of uneaten food on some of the tables. *The people here must not have had time to return home and gather their belongings before being evacuated.* She saw her reflection in the window tremble when the building shook. The veranda tilted ten degrees, and the back of the restaurant started to sink.

Dirt exploded into the air. Lana shielded her face against pelting rocks. She saw a figure through the dust. Lana raised her palms at the beetle Warden when it strode toward her.

'Woah, woah, take it easy, big fella!'

It stopped and leaned, ready to charge her.

'You're Raekeem,' Lana continued. 'And in case you didn't hear, we saved your asses.'

'I heard,' it said in a throaty rasp.

'We can help you too. Call off your spawn and we can get the mutagen out of you.'

Rapid thudding sounded in the Warden's throat, as though it was laughing. 'Why would I want it out of me?' Its words started deep, but warped into a shrill screech toward the end. 'The mutagen has given me the ability to multiply. This town is ours!'

The hulking beetle charged and rammed Lana. The air left her lungs, and her body crashed through a window. Light-reflecting shards spun and rotated inches from her face. She landed on a table, rolled and hit the floor.

The glass settled. Lana rose and staggered back toward the veranda, pushing aside chairs that were sliding across the floor. The restaurant seemed to be fighting her efforts to leave. The building was groaning and cracking loudly. The chandelier directly above her hung from the ceiling at forty degrees. Pots, pans and utensils were falling against the back wall of the kitchen. Lana scrambled up the floor toward the rising volume of gunfire outside. She climbed out of the front door, braced her feet against the exterior wall and jumped to the edge of the rising deck. She heaved herself over it and landed on the road, while the restaurant disappeared into the ground.

Giant beetles were scattering, making themselves difficult targets to hit despite their size. The Warden backhanded one of the AMs, sending him through the door of a pharmacy. Talon fired on it, but was unable to find a weak point.

Lana ran at the Warden's rear, kicked the back of its knee and round-house-kicked it in the chest, throwing it on its back. Lana drew her axe and drove it down, the blade halting an inch from its face when one of its arms caught hers. It screeched and clicked until four of its spawn shot out of the ground, drove Lana back and helped their master back onto its feet. Dozens more sped toward it.

'Everyone on me, on my signal!' Lana called out. 'We need to draw them to the ship!'

Talon shot three of the giant bugs to pieces, and the Warden screech-signalled six more at her. She backed up onto a deck, ran forward, jumped and gripped the veranda roof above her. Using her forward momentum, Talon swung her legs and flipped herself onto the roof before the bugs could reach her.

'Frag out!' the recovered AM called, before tossing a grenade from the pharmacy into the middle of the grouped beetles.

Talon ran to the edge of the roof and leapt at the Warden. The fragmentation grenade exploded, sending shredded bugs in all directions. In mid-air, Talon gripped the Warden's head, threw her legs to complete a summersault, and slammed it flat on its back. Lana hit record on her ring console when the Warden called for help.

'To the ship!' Lana called.

The AMs sprinted after Talon to the Black Heron. She opened the bay doors while the engines fired, lifting the ship, and the soldiers leapt in after her. She loaded the recording Lana sent to her console into the ship system, and played the Warden's distress signal at high volume through the ship comm speakers.

Running, but still eight metres from the ship, Lana could hear the Warden's pounding feet gaining on her. She spun around, skidded on one foot and kicked the other, driving her boot under the Warden's chin before it could duck and ram her. Its momentum continued. Lana braced and maintained her balance, her boot sliding. She leaned into the beast, drew her axe under her leg, and swung the blade an inch from her ankle, slashing its throat. Its spawn surged by as though their master were not even there, while the hulking Warden dropped to its knees, gripping its throat. A cloud of dust rose when its body hit the ground, and Lana turned to see the Black Heron flying low across the gully floor.

Talon manoeuvred the ship along the edge of the river to encourage the beetles to form a line. With the bay door still down, the screeching, clicking tones continued on loop. Talon pulled on the steering to swing the ship around, and she fired on the line of beetles.

The Warden's spawn were blown away in one sweep of the Black Heron's gunfire. Their sizzling bodies exploded into the air, pelting the water with shards of carapace.

Chapter 3

Talon and Lana found the Mayor at his home. He was relieved to hear of their success, but so exhausted that he struggled to find the words to convey his gratitude.

'I've not seen to so many wounded since my NATO days,' he said, while they followed him upstairs and to the balcony.

Lana gazed out at the roofs of the west side structures. 'You have a lot of rebuilding to do.' Stores and homes were sinking.

'The Kiyol received word of our situation from their traders that live here. They offered to help, and of course I said yes.' The Mayor looked Lana up and down, concerned by her torn clothing. 'Are you injured?'

'I'm fine,' Lana replied stoically. 'Hey, I didn't catch your name before.'

The Mayor hesitated. He looked to a woman who appeared at the door in that moment, moved to her side and asked her tentatively, 'Are you ready?'

He received a nod, returned to Lana and Talon, and asked them to sit at a dining table. Talon looked from Lana to the woman and the Mayor. There was a definite physical resemblance. She sensed the coming discussion was going to be private, so she signed to Lana, *See you in a bit*, and left them.

'My name is Pablo Casal,' said the Mayor. 'Andula and I came here to join our family after the Great Migration.'

'Lana,' Andula started, hesitantly. She drew strength from her husband when he placed his hand over hers. 'We are your parents.'

Eyes wide, Lana pressed both palms on the table, steadying herself.

'Your biological parents,' Pablo clarified. 'We contributed to Pete and Lucy's Human Augmentation Project.'

Lana's first words were breathless. 'You know who I am. Why… didn't you try to contact me?'

Andula glanced at Pablo, and back at Lana. Her tone was sad, and she could not stop herself from reaching across the table to take Lana's hand. 'Pablo wanted to. I'm sorry, Lana. I wasn't ready.'

Lana could feel her mother's guilt. Even though their part in her existence had been a contribution to science, Lana understood that Andula would have felt as though she had abandoned her child.

The silence was broken when thumping footsteps came up the stairs. An AM followed two girls who looked to be eight and twelve. A tiger brindle staffy shouldered its way between them to take the lead, and bounded straight for Lana to greet her.

'Theresa insisted on seeing you,' the AM explained to Andula apologetically.

'Of course she did,' said Andula, and she raised an eyebrow at the older of the two girls. Theresa lifted her chin at the soldier like a victor and strode with perfect posture to her mother. Andula nodded for the AM to go. 'Theresa, I told you to keep your sister safe on the edge of town with your aunt.'

'The bugs never crossed the water, Mother.'

'Their bodies did,' said the younger girl when she ran over to her father.

'Brody, why are you wet?' Pablo asked, and gave Theresa a stern look.

Brody nodded to the dog, which was being rubbed all over by Lana. 'Toby and I were helping the soldiers pull the beetles out of the river,' she said, as though the reason was obvious.

Pablo smiled supportively. 'I'm sure they appreciated your help.'

Theresa had a sickened look when she remembered the scene of so many dead giant beetles, but her eyebrows rose when she saw Lana. She recognised her immediately and found herself unable to speak.

'Oh, wow!' Brody exclaimed when she locked eyes on Lana. 'You're one of the Silica heroes! Is your friend downstairs a hero too? She doesn't talk. Why doesn't your friend talk?'

'Girls, this is Lana,' Andula announced, and she hesitated again. Pablo took over introductions.

'Lana is your sister,' he said. 'Lana, this is Theresa and Brody.'

'Hello,' was all Lana could manage. She wiped the beginning of tears from her eyes and smiled at Brody and Theresa.

'We're related?' Theresa breathed in awe.

'Girls, why don't you go and bring photos to show Lana?' Pablo suggested, and he turned to Lana, with tears forming as well. 'We have a lot of catching up to do.'

Brody made to leave, and stopped to tug on Theresa's arm. Toby saw this, bit on Theresa's pant leg and pulled. Theresa had seen Lana in media reports, and she had read about the battles Lana fought to protect the Universal Community. She was guided away, dazed and in disbelief.

Andula sighed. 'I had hoped we would meet under better circumstances.' She moved close to Lana and wrapped her in a hug. The two of them held each other and let their tears flow. They cried out the longing that had remained a void inside them for so long.

'I hear you're a Captain now,' Pablo stated proudly.

Lana wiped her cheeks and saw Talon arrive at the top of the stairs. 'I am.' She watched Talon's hands signing discreetly.

'You must encounter many dangers,' Andula stated with concern.

'We were on our way here when we received your distress call.' Lana replied to Talon with one hand behind her back. Talon's boots could be heard as she went down the stairs. 'General Lincoln has been monitoring this planet for Sabre Company activity,' Lana continued.

'The militant group?' Andula looked from Pablo back to Lana. 'But they were defeated. Conroy and Williams are in prison.'

'That's right,' Lana lied. News about the Raekeem abducting inmates from the correctional facility had been kept quiet. Very few people knew that both Jericho Williams and Dennis Conroy were dead, and those few were sworn to secrecy.

'Lincoln found it suspicious that Dennis Conroy would order all colonies to be destroyed,' Lana said, and added pointedly, 'except Stone River.'

'I must admit,' Pablo said, thoughtfully, 'I questioned that too. So the General sent you to investigate.'

'I just asked Talon to send a joint transmission that Lincoln will receive shortly,' Lana said, checking her comms. 'When he gets it, he will release information to the Press regarding Conroy and Williams. That information will make its way here, which should trigger a reaction from any remaining members of Sabre Company.'

'A reaction?' Andula stood abruptly. 'Lana, your trigger could endanger our people. My girls.'

Pablo took her arm gently. 'Any Sabre Company insurgents would likely leave,' he assured her.

'Why didn't Lincoln send troops?' Andula questioned, still standing.

'Because whoever is hiding here would have been forced to take hostages,' Lana answered coolly. 'Our intel suggests there is only one. Talon has a suspect and is watching him closely.'

Andula opened her mouth to question Lana further when there came the thumping of small feet racing up the stairs. Theresa appeared carrying a data pad. She strode to the table with Brody on her heels.

'Let's watch photos,' Brody chanted impatiently.

The girls found their chairs and joined their family. Theresa laid the pad in the centre of the table, chose a file and hit play. A holographic rectangular prism beamed from the pad, and the four outer sides played a slideshow. Lana watched while Brody explained what the images were and who was in each picture. Andula provided the year and what was happening in the colony.

'This was when Pablo was sworn in as Mayor of Vrucht,' she said and added, 'that's what the first Mayor called this place, before we had a river.'

'The population was only around three thousand,' Pablo remembered. 'Thanks to funding from the Council, we were able to install subterranean—'

'Dad, can I...' Theresa whispered.

'Go ahead.'

'Liquefiers were installed to melt the ice in the caverns ten kilometres from here,' Theresa explained, in a confident and academic tone. 'We were dependent on water shipments. Now, we have a river and purified water is pumped to all homes from underground. Since that development, our population has grown to ten thousand.'

There was a photo of Pablo, Andula and the girls by the river. Theresa commented on how hot it had been that day, and how Ian, the AM unit that watched over the family, had run out of coolant by the end of it. Lana saw what looked like a tattoo on Ian's right bicep, partially obscured by the sleeve of his uniform.

Lana reached over and hit pause on the data pad. She zoomed in on the tattoo.

'Ian got that when he went for his service at the Branner Factory,' Brody told her.

Lana stood to leave. 'Sorry, guys. I have to go check on my friend. Thanks for showing me your photos.'

'Girls, you can keep watching with your mother,' said Pablo. 'I'll be right back.' He leaned to Andula's ear and whispered, 'Take them to the roof if you hear gunfire.'

He and Lana walked down to the road and out to a clearing, where Talon had reparked the Black Heron.

'I didn't mean to scare you guys before,' Lana said regretfully. 'I couldn't say anything until Talon had eyes on all of your AMs. We don't know how many could have been reprogrammed. You should go back to your family.'

'Our family,' Pablo corrected. 'And I appreciate your concern, but I need to know what's going on here.'

'Sorry… Dad.' Lana glanced back at him awkwardly. 'It's going to take some time for me to get used to this.'

'You have it. We're not going anywhere.'

Pablo looked over his shoulder when they reached the edge of Stone River. He could hear a news update coming over the announcement speakers.

'I thought if Hutch Branner's programming was tampered with, the AM unit wouldn't survive,' he said. 'It's been years since Sabre Company attacked.'

Lana guessed that Ian, that AM, had been recalled to the Branner Factory under false pretences, and was captured en route by a cell of Sabre Company loyalists.

'Doesn't matter,' Lana decided. 'Once they find out Conroy and Williams are dead–'

'They're dead?' Pablo exclaimed. 'The Council would never allow corporal punishment. Did they try to escape?'

The memory of Lana's fist ploughing through Jericho William's skull played before her eyes. 'In a way,' she answered vaguely.

Lana spotted Talon, and when they reached her, she gestured for them to follow. She guided them down a curved rock formation to a standing boulder. Although the look of the boulder was convincing, it was not made of rock. It was a hard composite that had been moulded over a steel door. Talon nodded to an AM who was standing at the opening to the hidden entrance. She had followed him from Stone River when the Council made their public announcement.

'Ian?' Pablo circled the AM, and waved a hand in front of his face. 'What are you doing out here?'

Ian stood motionless, staring down at the holo display from his ring console. The news update had finished, and other feeds were streaming.

A strong wind blew through the gully, and they all braced themselves and covered their eyes against the rising dust. Ian rocked like a statue, before coming to a rest.

'Pab... Dad, get behind us.'

Pablo turned to Lana for an explanation, and held his breath when he saw that she and Talon were in weaver stance, pistols drawn. Lana stepped around the frozen AM after Talon and in through the hidden doorway. She pulled the side-arm from Ian's holster and nodded to her father to follow.

Talon found a switch and turned on overhead lights. The room was only a couple of feet wider than the door, and three metres deep. The temperature inside must have been near zero. All that was contained in the room was a two-metre-high cabinet of drawers. Talon opened one and a plume of frost obscured its contents. Pablo arrived beside her and took a corked test tube out of a set of over a dozen tubes. Most of them were labelled PABLO CASAL or ANDULA CASAL.

'It's a hair sample,' said Pablo. 'Why would Sabre Company reprogram Ian to collect our DNA?'

'Conroy wanted Professor O'Conner's Human Augmentation research,' said Lana. 'Maybe, by keeping your and... Mum's DNA, they were going to create their own version of me.'

'Human soldiers,' Pablo agreed. 'Their AMs couldn't last, so they were going to make variations of you.' He noticed Lana backing out of the room. She looked as though she was having difficulty breathing. 'Lana, this is just an outpost. There's nothing to indicate that they progressed—'

'I have to go,' Lana stammered. She saw the concern in Talon's brow, but she couldn't begin to explain what was causing her distress. The vision of her double's hands wrapped around her throat flashed before her eyes. 'Burn everything.'

Talon nodded and Pablo left to catch up with Lana.

'You're leaving?' he called after her.

'I'll come back,' Lana said over her shoulder. She strode away without offering an explanation, because she didn't have one. She could feel herself closing up.

She had to get away.

Chapter 4

Lana returned her weapons to the Black Heron's armoury and activated a portal to the Ether Realm. She walked through the mercury sphere and emerged outside an enormous tree in a sunlit forest. Lana stepped onto a flat log and tugged a hidden rope that engaged a counterweight lift mechanism. The portal retracted beneath her, while she rose to a thick branch ten metres above the ground. The mechanism reset as soon as Lana stepped onto the branch. She approached the four-metre-wide trunk of the tree, turned a hidden handle and pushed. The perfectly camouflaged door swung open, and Lana entered Miri's home. She closed the door behind her, leaned against the curved wall, and exhaled out her anxiety as though she had been holding her breath since Stone River.

Miri was standing atop the winding staircase. It was summer in the Ether Realm, and like all Fyrst Born, Miri had been to the Elder Tree to receive the summer body paint. The ochre used was mixed with properties that allowed the bold curving lines of pale orange to stay on the wearer's skin, even after bathing, for the duration of the season. Miri was tying her waist sash, watching Lana with concerned eyes while she descended to the lounge. 'What's happened?'

Lana pushed away from the wall, sitting down on the step as Miri arrived and resting her head against her lover's hip. Miri crouched and held Lana in her arms. They stayed like this for a quiet while, listening to the wind.

'Tea?'

Lana nodded, and Miri left to prepare a soothing herbal infusion. Lana made her way to the dining table in a sleepwalk state. She sank into a basket-weave chair, planted her elbows on the table and held her head in her hands. Miri sat down opposite and slid a terracotta mug between Lana's elbows. Lana breathed the herbal steam deeply, and her muscles began to relax. She told Miri about the dream she'd had, how terrifying it was.

'And just now, we found out an old enemy was going to make clones of me,' she said. She drank deeply and watched Miri's sage expression.

'You have fought in conflict after conflict your whole life. It has taken its toll.'

'I can't avoid it.' Lana shrugged. 'It's my job.'

Miri searched the wooden table in front of her as though the answer were hidden in the grain. 'You have not yet seen the Mountain Folk shaman. We should go to him. He may be able to help you.'

Lana welcomed the thought of visiting the Mountain Folk again. They were humanoid, apart from their legs, which resembled different kinds of hooved animals. Lana knew that Rachel had been to see their Shaman for assistance with her Mitochondrial Memory. Her sight had been polarised from seeing the past to seeing glimpses of a possible future.

'I can delay my duties here,' Miri decided. 'We can pack food and journey to the Mountain today.'

Lana's heart swelled with the love and devotion Miri committed to her. She leaned across the table and kissed Miri deeply, before standing to help her prepare food.

While wrapping chive and garlic buns in cloth, Lana realised that she had forgotten to share her news.

'I found my parents.'

Miri was leaning over her kitchen bench, mashing berries and soft cheese into a paste, when her posture straightened as though Lana's parents had just entered the room.

'That's wonderful!' she exclaimed.

Lana told her about the circumstances of their meeting and about Pablo and Andula's daughters, her sisters, and how Brody was a tomboy, while Theresa was astute like her mother. Lana was surprised at how much detail she had remembered from such a brief encounter. Miri listened, beaming, and she laughed when Lana described Brody coming to meet her, all wet after helping the soldiers in the river.

'How are the Raekeem doing?' Lana asked, placing their supplies in two shoulder bags as Miri handed food parcels to her. 'Good crop yield this season?'

Miri's mouth quirked to one side and she dipped her hand. 'So-so.' She enjoyed using human slang from time to time, to better fit in when visiting Lana's world. 'We have been teaching them agriculture for some years now, but their people have never done anything like it before. They're getting the hang of it. Oh, by the way, they have elected Xera to be their new leader.'

Lana took a pensive moment to remember who Xera had lost. 'Kordin would have been proud of her. And how's Hal?'

'He and Fang have had their second cub.' Miri ducked her head under the strap and rested the weight of her bag on her hip. 'That reminds me: I thought you said Hal was born as you were.'

Lana nodded, lost as to where Miri was going with this.

'He is aging.' Miri stopped at the door when she saw Lana's surprise. 'Not dramatically, but there is grey in his beard that was not there last year.'

Lana thought for a moment, while she followed Miri out and across the thick branch to their elevator. She could only guess that the Lustian particle beam might have caused Hal's genetic kill switch to reset. 'Well, he won't outlive his children.'

Miri watched Lana's sedate expression while they descended. 'Lana, the people you love will grow old, while you remain young. But they will live long, rich lives. Your sisters will have children of their own. You have a unique opportunity to witness generations of your own kin.' Miri sensed that her words were not helping. She looped her arm through Lana's and took her hand. 'And I will witness with you.'

'But for how long?'

'At least another one hundred years.'

Lana thought on that. *One day in Home Realm is anywhere between five and ten days in the Ether Realm.* Why time difference varied was unclear. 'Wait... one hundred years here? That would be over three hundred in my realm.'

'Here, there, you and I will always be together,' Miri stated confidently.

Lana's heart melted at Miri's words, and at the thought of being able to continue what the two of them had for so many centuries.

They left the forest and walked for an hour toward the mountains. They stopped at a stream to cool themselves, and then sat under a tree to eat and drink. Dry leaves blew across the rocky edge of the stream, scratching and tumbling. Two large maple leaves drifted down and were carried by a breeze that pressed them against Miri's chest.

'When Fyrst Born loved ones are apart…' she said, taking a couple of lengths of twine from one of the used food parcels, and a stone knife from her bag. 'When we miss and need each other…' After poking holes in each leaf and feeding through twine, she pulled the first leaf necklace over Lana's head. 'We hold hands with the wind. "The wind will hold you when we cannot," my mothers used to say.'

The two of them walked on, and Miri looked down at her leaf necklace, pleased that the colour matched her body paint.

'I want you to come and meet my parents,' Lana decided.

Miri looked up with a smile. 'I would be delighted. To meet the girls, especially.' She glanced ahead and gestured to the winding path to the Shaman's home. 'We're almost there.'

'What do I call him?' Lana asked.

'His name is Orin.' Miri saw a tall stack of flat rocks. It was the cairn that marked the location of a Shaman. 'His cave is on the next bend.'

'He lives in a cave?'

'It is actually quite comfortable.'

A young Mountain Folk man stood from a campfire when Lana and Miri approached. His hand dropped to a sheathed sword, but he relaxed when he saw Miri, and moved aside for them to enter the cave. Lana was impressed by his physique. His upper body was toned, and his four-legged half looked similar to an alpaca breed, with black, powerful legs.

Miri led Lana through a narrow S-bend tunnel, before they entered a large candle-lit room with a tall ceiling and a small opening at the top. A wood fire burned directly below, and the smoke drifted into the shaft of light the gap provided. Orin, the Shaman, was standing at a table grinding herbs in a mortar. He was half horse; Clydesdale, Lana guessed. Miri greeted him and gestured to Lana. 'I have brought some-one dear to me. Her name is Lana. She seeks your counsel.'

'Anyone dear to our sweet Miri is indeed a friend to this old goat,' Orin said, with a welcome smile. His hooves echoed against the cave walls when he approached. By human years, he looked to be around eighty. His moustache hung down ten centimetres from either side of his mouth. He pointed to cushions on the floor nearby.

'Sit, and tell me what is troubling you, Lana.' His tone was both kind and direct.

Lana joined Miri on the cushions, which smelt of horse, and began by explaining the dream she had. Orin handed her and Miri clay cups of tea. And without warning, he pressed one thumb against Lana's forehead and closed his eyes.

'Your path is a righteous one, though fraught with danger.' He sat, watching her pensively.

Lana reacted to the strength of the herbal tea with an involuntary tremble.

Orin's moustache swayed when he shook his head, pain in his furrowed brow. 'You see much conflict.' His expression softened when he read something else in Lana. 'But you will find a cure. Many years from now.'

'A cure for conflict? How?'

He shook his head. 'Unclear.' And he seemed fearful when he uttered, 'Battles will be fought. Worlds will be torn.'

Lana and Miri exchanged a worried look.

'When?' Lana questioned. 'How?'

Orin turned away, mumbling incoherently. Miri tried to coax more information from him, and when she reached and touched his arm, he turned to her with a smile.

'You look so alike,' he said to her. 'Your mother misses you dearly.'

Lana saw hurt and sadness wash over Miri.

'She is alive,' Orin insisted.

'Where?' Miri took hold of Orin's shoulders. 'Where did you see her?'

'On the other side of the Veil,' he replied weakly, touching his hand to his forehead. And he pointed a shaky finger at Lana. 'You were there.'

Miri was stunned, motionless. Lana had asked about her parents early in their relationship. Miri had said they were gone.

'What's the Veil?' Lana asked.

Miri didn't respond, and she wouldn't move. Lana had to support her as they walked out of the cave. She sat Miri down by the guard's fire, and Miri stared at the swaying blades of orange.

'There is something I have not told you,' Miri started. 'None of us here are from this world.'

Lana glanced at the half-alpaca man, and saw his brow furrow with deep emotion.

'Fyrst Born, Mountain Folk and humans were brought together during the Collide,' Miri explained. 'A powerful force or being took our worlds in thirds and drew them together to form this planet.'

Lana scooched closer and watched Miri pick up a fallen acorn-like nut from the dirt at her feet. She held the domed end upright. 'Over the past decades, we have mapped all of the lands. A great barrier separates one half of this planet from the other.' She indicated the green half of the acorn and turned it upside down. 'We tried to penetrate the Veil, get to the other side, to where we think our loved ones are. But anything that crosses is severed.' Miri looked at Lana with watering eyes. 'Orin saw you there with my mother. On the other side of the Veil.'

'Then I'll go to this Veil, and I'll find your mother,' Lana said, resolute.

Miri wiped her eyes. 'But those who have tried–'

'Hey.' Lana placed her hand on Miri's. 'I fell into your world, and I walked back out...' She drew close, so Miri could only see her eyes. 'With you.'

Fresh tears spilled down Miri's cheeks.

'I'll ask Sam to investigate the Veil,' Lana offered. 'She'll need a guide to take her there.'

'My sister will take her.'

Lana nodded confidently. 'If there is a way through to your mother, Sam will find it.' And she let out a harrumph with a glance back at the cave. 'What good are warnings of battles if we don't know what to prepare for, or when?'

'Orin once told me, "Trying to change the future may cause it to happen".'

'So he knows specifics, but can't tell us.' Lana checked the time on her ring console. 'I should be getting back to Stone River.'

Miri stopped to breathe out her anxiety. 'I will join you. You finding your parents gives me hope that I might find mine.'

Lana programmed a portal that would take them back to the Black Heron, while Miri pulled a cotton shirt from her shoulder bag. She had travelled to Lana's Home Realm many times, and she understood that in most cases, female humans were expected to wear clothing that covered their breasts.

Lana recognised the shirt from when they were drinking at a tavern last week, in one of the human lands in the Ether Realm. Miri had seen the barmaid wearing it, and she fancied it. She proposed a trade, and the maid assumed Miri was drunk. Miri took a gold leaf-shaped clip from her hair and placed it on the table. The maid served the ales she was carrying to the next table, returned to Miri and pulled her shirt off in front of everyone. She took the gold clip and strode out the door. Lana and Miri were promptly shuffled out by the tavern owner.

Minerals swirled around the Black Heron as Lana and Miri walked through the portal and down the loading ramp into wind-blown sand.

'No pressure, Miri,' Lana started, 'but… Talon and I are going to find our next potential recruit on the other side of this planet. Have you given any more thought to–'

'I would be honoured to join your crew,' said Miri. 'I am sorry I did not give you an answer sooner. Helping to settle the Raekeem has made my days–'

'Crazy busy,' Lana prompted. 'I understand.'

When they arrived at Stone River West, Lana found Pablo standing outside the restaurant that had sunk backwards into the ground. Both he and the business owner were staring at the roof, which was at ground level, discussing options.

'The interior can be repaired,' the owner said optimistically. 'We can cut in, lay stairs and build a foyer on top of it.'

'I'll see that you get the materials you need,' Pablo promised her.

Lana arrived next to him and Pablo asked her if she was alright.

'Better.' Lana turned to Miri. 'Miri, this is my father, Pablo. Dad, this is Miri. She and I met in her home world, which we call the Ether Realm.'

'It is an honour to meet you,' Miri said, offering her hand as per the custom she had observed among humans.

Pablo took Miri's hand. 'Pleasure to meet you, Miri. I have been reading the reports Professor O'Conner releases to the Council. Your world sounds fascinating.'

He asked Lana to continue on to their house on the east side of the river. 'Andula and the girls will be happy to see you. Go on ahead, I'll be along later.'

Andula answered the door and welcomed Lana and Miri into her home. Brody came stomping down the stairs. She hopped from the second-last step onto her mother's back. Andula paused mid-sentence to brace before carrying Brody into the kitchen.

'We were of course glad that the beetles couldn't cross the river, but those poor people in the west...' She gestured for Lana and Miri to sit, turned a kettle on and leaned toward a cupboard for Brody to retrieve mugs from over her mother's shoulder. Miri was mesmerised by Brody's big brown eyes, and the two of them made faces at each other and giggled.

'Will you and Talon be staying longer?' Andula asked.

'We need to travel to the other side of the planet. Talon received a tip about a man who lives in Kuru. He has skills I could use.'

Andula was nodding, concern furrowing her brow. 'Well, he lives in a dangerous place. If you're going to Kuru, be ready for a fight. There were some rough sorts here in the early days. When Pablo became Mayor, he told them to shape up or ship out.'

'They shipped out,' said Brody.

Andula changed the subject, not wanting to frighten Brody with any more detail about who the rough sorts were or what they did. 'I've heard about the Ether Realm, Miri. What's your home like? Do you have a Council, a government?'

'Boring,' Brody grumbled and climbed down from her mother. She tugged at Lana's arm. 'Come and see what I made.' She led her to the lounge room, where containers of building bricks were arranged by colour. There were vehicles on the carpeted floor, and Brody flopped down to explain the scene she had created.

'This is me in the helicopter...' She pressed the palm of her hand down on the scattered blue blocks on the cream carpet. 'I'm flying over the sea.' She shifted on her bum, and blue bricks stuck to her skin when she lifted her hand to point at the male block figure on a boat she had built. 'The man is in a storm and his ship is sinking, and I'm gonna save him.'

'You must be very brave,' said Lana.

'Yeah.'

'Helicopters don't like storms,' Lana cautioned.

'Why?'

Lana explained how wind can wobble an aircraft, while Brody stared off, imagining the scene her big sister was setting. She rolled a blue brick between her fingers, and her eyebrows rose when her big sister described the threat of something called a "rogue wave" that could smash the helicopter.

'But rescue pilots are very good at flying away from the big waves,' Lana assured her, and nodded at the scattered bricks that represented the sea. 'Maybe this storm isn't so bad.'

Brody wasn't afraid. 'Nah, it's pretty bad.' She picked up the helicopter, held it over the water with a shake to simulate the wind Lana had described, and took the block figure of herself, jumping it from the edge of the helicopter into the sea.

Brody voiced the man on the sinking ship. 'Agh! A rogue wave is coming!'

Lana watched intently, and she was surprised and impressed by what happened next.

The man abandoned his ship, and Brody picked up the boat and travelled it slowly over the man. She placed one blue brick on his back to indicate that he had dived to avoid being crushed by the boat. She did the same for her own figure and dropped the boat behind her rescue-diver self.

'Wow!' Brody exclaimed to the man. 'That was close. Stay there. I'll swim over to you.' After pressing her block figure through the carpet fibres and between the blue bricks to get to the man, she picked up the helicopter and swept it over to hover above them. Brody reached behind herself without looking to feel for and retrieve a plastic chain that came with the block set her parents printed for her, and she connected it to the edge of the helicopter. She hovered the craft until the end of the chain reached the figure of herself. She then gathered her figure and the man up against the chain and slowly got to her knees and then to her feet.

'Yay! I'm saved! Thank you, Rescue Girl!'

Chapter 5

Lana and Miri stayed for dinner at Pablo and Andula's house. They said their goodbyes after dessert.

'I will return home,' Miri told Lana on their way back to the Black Heron. They hugged in the loading bay while Miri's return portal opened. Talon returned Miri's farewell gesture before she disappeared into the mercury.

Lana followed Talon to the cockpit. The ship engines hummed and the Black Heron rose into the night sky.

Did you see the news bulletin after the Williams and Conroy story? Talon signed.

'No.' Lana accessed it with her ring console. 'Mass exodus from Earth?' She read on, and her eyes narrowed. 'Earth's majority vote on the Social Freedom Act was no.'

Traditional and religious social barriers came from Earth, Talon signed with a consoling shrug.

'True,' Lana replied distractedly. 'Silver lining: all of the colonies voted yes. Makes sense; the people who were part of the Great Migration were progressive.'

The colonies only succeeded because everyone did their equal part, Talon signed. *Because they treated each other as equals.*

The ship detected an incoming transmission from Rachel Navara, and Talon patched it through.

'Hey, guys, Lincoln said you encountered a Warden at Stone River. Are you alright?'

'We're fine. You won't believe this; my Dad is the Mayor.'

'What?'

'I have sisters!'

Rachel stammered, and replied with rising emotion, 'Lana, this is incredible. I have to come to you. Send me your coordinates and I'll teleport in.'

The Black Heron had reached outer space. Talon brought the ship to a gradual stop and applied minimal thrust to hold them in position. Lana sent their coordinates to Rachel, and she portaled in.

'I'm so happy for you,' Rachel called out as soon as she emerged. 'Pete said your parents didn't mention which migration colony they were going to. So even he had no way of knowing where they were.'

Lana told Rachel about her sisters and how good a mother Andula was to the girls.

'So, the reason I called.' Rachel tapped at her ring navigation pad to bring up a holographic display of images. 'Sam and I have been investigating a realm where there are no people. Only machines.'

'And it's another version of Melbourne?'

Rachel nodded. 'I went in with two AMs. We walked around the city, which, judging by the architecture, looks like it was rebuilt by the machines to model the 1940s era. But the buildings aren't brick; they're steel, bronze and iron, plated with polished brass.' She heard the Black Heron power back up and accelerate. 'It's incredible. We're calling it Mechtropolis.'

Lana's eyes were full of wonder. She wanted to leave with Rachel and see the machine realm right now, but it was important that she commit to the job the Lustitians gave her.

'Have you had any more episodes?' Lana asked Rachel.

'I haven't seen the future since I started sessions with Orin. He said he took it from me. Don't ask me how,' she said.

Lana noticed that Rachel seemed more relaxed, more herself. 'Did Orin happen to mention…'

'Danger and battles.' Rachel raised her palms up. 'Might as well have said it'll be Tuesday soon, given our track record of trouble. And Earth voting against the Social Freedom Act has severed our alliance with the Kiyol and the Laicians.'

'But all of the colonies voted yes,' Lana reminded her.

'True. Their ambassadors will maintain alliances with the colonies.' Rachel shrugged. 'Earth is on its own again. No trade with anyone, no military assistance from anyone.'

'High price to pay for marital status,' Lana stated disappointedly. 'Anyway, we should be on the other side of this planet in a few minutes. We're going to check out a possible recruit in Kuru.'

'Dangerous place.' Rachel stood in front of the armoury wall, took off her black sweater and picked up a gun belt. 'I'll come with you.'

'I was hoping you'd say that.'

'Have you got anything old and crappy to wear?' Rachel asked.

'My tank and pants are in the bin, why?'

'Put them on,' Rachel advised, while using a knife to tear her own clothes. 'Best we try to blend in.'

Talon flew the Black Heron through the upper atmosphere and found a place to land outside the settlement of Kuru. She signed to Lana that she would stay aboard the Black Heron, in case things got nasty and they needed extraction.

Lana found Rachel at the bottom of the ramp, patting handfuls of dirt against her otherwise clean clothes.

'Pablo still sends aid supplies here,' Lana said, looking out at the hundreds of one- and two-storey shacks ahead. 'Most of it is seized by the main gang that controls the settlement. They call themselves Rim Pirates.'

Rachel laughed.

'They're called that because they raid trade stations along the outer rim settlements.'

Rachel was doing arm stretches, and she rolled her shoulders while they walked. 'Why hasn't UC Security shut them down?'

'Pablo says they have gang members hidden as spies among the Stone River population,' Lana explained. 'UC Security are still in the process of weeding them out. The Rim Pirates favour explosives, so it's too risky to strike Kuru before the spies are found.'

The two of them entered the main street and Lana nodded to the saloon. 'I don't know where he lives. Better ask around.'

A tumbleweed crossed their path, followed by an old Hispanic man pushing a cart full of radishes. They stepped up to a veranda, pushed through the swinging doors, and ordered whiskies at the bar. Curious and leering eyes watched from seated regulars.

'I'm looking for a Chinese man,' Lana said to the barman.

A built, sweaty, hairy man rose from his chair with a creeping smile.

'Lidda'lady,' he called to Lana. 'Yedoe-need no Chinese.' He grabbed his crotch and pursed his dry lips. 'Godall de'man yeneed rye-deer.'

Lana turned with her hand on her holstered axe.

'Steady,' Rachel cautioned Lana, watching her skin darken, her eyes turn orange, and her ears sharpen. The demon form into which Lana could change at will was a gift from Miri. An extension of Lana's senses and abilities.

The hairy lout glanced at the axe. His jaw dropped when his eyes met Lana's death stare. And he sat back down.

Lana's demon form faded and she turned her attention to the barman. 'His name is Shen.'

The barman's white whiskers twitched, and he nodded to an empty chair in the corner of the saloon. 'Usually sipping his tea around this time. Might find him at his shack.' He pointed a crooked finger over his shoulder. 'Few doors down, take a left at the alley.'

'Bedder hurry,' said the man who had taken an interest in Lana. 'Yoboy in trouble byeda looks.' Lana glanced back to see him leaning in his chair, peering through the nearest window. He chuckled. 'Biiig trouble.'

She and Rachel saw a group of four armed men and women – Rim Pirates, Lana guessed – heading to where Shen might be. Rachel tilted her head back, skulled her quarter glass of whiskey and strode out of the saloon. Lana paid the barman, skulled hers, coughed out the burn in her throat and followed.

They drew their weapons before reaching the alley. Lana nodded to Rachel after peering around the corner to check if the way was clear.

Gunshots cracked inside the shack they were approaching. Glass smashed, and one of the Pirates tumbled out. There were more thumps and grunts, and the walls shook. Lana pulled aside the canvas hanging from the doorway. She and Rachel entered to find the other three Rim Pirates unconscious on the floor.

A man stood with his back to Lana and Rachel. His head turned slightly. His hair was shaved close to his scalp, black with flecks of grey. He wore a sleeveless red shirt and black baggy slacks, cuffs tattered over his bare feet.

'You are not Pirates,' Shen whispered.

Lana holstered her pistol and approached. 'I'm here to offer you a job.'

'You should go.'

'Hear her out,' said Rachel.

Lana's ears pricked. 'We're not alone.' She heard the clink of a metal ring and a pin being pulled. 'Grenade!' She ran to the opposite side of the shack, armoured her skin, and shoulder-rammed a hole through the wall. Shen and Rachel dove out after her before the explosion ripped through the hut.

Lana lifted a corrugated iron sheet off Rachel and helped her to her feet. She could only see a metre around her through the dust cloud. Footfalls sounded to her right, and she ducked in time to avoid a steel bat. The attacking Pirate swung it again, and Lana slammed her body against his, grappled him and threw him over her hip.

Rachel wiped dust from her eyes and prepared to fight. A masked woman ran at her, slashing at her with a knife. Rachel weaved, caught the woman's wrist and drew it over her shoulder. The Pirate let out a pained yell when Rachel twisted her wrist to disarm her, and chopped the base of her neck to drop her unconscious.

Shen arrived beside Lana, scooped the steel bat from the ground with his foot, caught the handle and struck an attacking Pirate. Rachel counted five Rim Pirates circling them. When the dust settled, she counted another two flanking Shen.

Lana heard a shrill command. Nobody moved. A tall man appeared, walking confidently toward Shen. He wore a purple silk shirt and white slacks. Gold bracelets hung loose on his wrists, and his hip holster held a pistol with an ivory handle.

'Everyone relax,' he said, in an effeminate tone, despite his thick neck and muscled arms. 'I am Hassan, Captain of the Rim Pirates.' He raised a hand before Lana could speak. 'I know who you are.'

She let him talk, while thumbing her console to contact Talon.

Hassan glanced at Shen. 'Brought some UC muscle, eajuz?' And he addressed Lana. 'Has the Universal Council finally grown some balls?' He leaned in so that his face came level with Lana's. 'Try me, bitch. My people in Stone River will blow the town to bits.'

Shen acted quicker than Lana could see him move. He brought the steel bat under Hassan's chin, pinned his shoulders, drew the ivory-handled pistol, pressed the barrel against Hassan's temple and cocked the hammer. All of the Pirates in the courtyard aimed their guns at Shen.

'Read him,' Shen said to Lana, with a pained glare. 'I infiltrated their ranks. I can tell you the names and locations of every spy. First I must know where he is keeping my son.'

Hassan was sweating and wincing at the pressure of the barrel against his temple. He chuckled. 'Her mind powers are just rumours, eajuz. She can't–' He flinched when Lana pressed her index finger to the centre of his forehead.

When she dove into Hassan's mind, she saw Shen from a different angle. A place where Hassan must have been waiting while his crew rushed in. Shen was barely visible, obscured by dust. He struck a Pirate with the baseball bat. The man fell and Lana froze that moment in time, for a second, leaned back and concentrated, drawing on Hassan's memory.

Dust particles rose, seemingly lifting the downed Pirate back onto his feet. The bat left his head and bounced onto Shen's foot. Another Pirate tumbled awkwardly up and over Lana's hip and onto his feet.

Lana panned back further through Hassan's memory. She heard a young man's scared voice. She locked onto that moment and let the memory play.

'Who are you people? Where are you taking me?'

Lana's vision, through Hassan's eyes, came from the back seat of a car. She recognised the streets of Stone River. The driver was taking Hassan out of the west and into the rocky hills. Lana saw a teenage boy sitting next to her. His wrists were bound, and a black sack was pulled over his head. The scenery outside tilted when the driver accelerated up a steep rise and around a monolith boulder to a corrugated iron shed. The car stopped, and Hassan's vision travelled out to the shed. Lana could feel a combination lock in her hands, and heard him run the numbers in his head.

Hassan opened the door for the driver to take the boy through. He watched them go down a set of stairs, underground, guided by torch-light. When he turned, Lana saw lengths of wire connecting blocks of C4 explosives mounted along the walls, leading down to what she assumed was a basement. Hassan closed the door behind him and reset the lock and booby trap.

The room underground had two sets of bunk beds against the walls, and there was a mattress on the floor. Four men stood at attention, ready to receive orders.

Lana released herself from Hassan's mind. Hassan blinked rapidly as though trying to wake himself up.

'Tell your crew to lay down their weapons.' Lana typed another message to Talon. 'Do it now, or they all die.'

Hassan heard a spaceship approaching and looked up to see the wings of the Black Heron block out the sun. Its nose tilted, and cannons emerged from the armour plating.

Hassan ordered his crew to lay down their arms, and Lana and Rachel herded them into the corner of the courtyard. Talon had already contacted General Lincoln to request a prisoner transfer craft. She landed and arrived with wrist binders.

Lana contacted her father, and he arranged for his security team to locate and disable the booby-trapped shed and rescue Shen's son.

Chapter 6

Stone River security AMs identified and apprehended the Rim Pirate spies based on Shen's intel. Shen's son was found, shaken but safe, in the shed basement. The spies led UC bomb techs to more rigged C4. The explosives were live, in the subterranean liquefier system that maintained water flow to the town.

The Black Heron touched down at Stone River. Lana wanted to report her success to her father and assure him that the planet was now free of organised crime.

'Well done, Captain Casal,' Rachel said to Lana, while her portal to San Francisco opened. 'I better head back. Hutch Branner wants to see Mechtropolis.' She paused when her ring console beeped. 'Oh, he says he's coming in.'

'Sorry about the intrusion, ladies,' Hutch said, stepping out of the portal and addressing Lana. 'I spoke to your folks over comms, assuring them their AM, Ian, will be up and about and good as new in no time.'

'Who's your friend?' Lana asked, crouching when a black, medium-sized dog trotted out of the portal. 'Hello there, sweetie,' she gushed, patting the dog.

'This is Bell. She's a five-year-old first-generation labradoodle AM. She's here to see Talon.'

Bell sat down on Talon's left foot, leaned back against her leg and looked up at her. Talon stared down at Bell's panting inverted smile and big brown eyes. *I don't understand,* she signed to Lana and looked to Hutch.

'Talon, I never got around to thanking you for saving everyone on Darwin,' Hutch said. 'Lincoln told me a Raekeem drop ship destroyed the factory and was going to bombard the surrounding area. You called it off, took their commander's ship and got my people out of there.' He gestured to Bell, who was whipping her wagging tail against Talon. 'She's yours if you'll have her.'

Talon crouched and pressed her head to Bell's while rubbing her soft coat, and nodded her thanks to Hutch.

'She'll need water now and then for cooling, same as you,' he advised. 'She can learn your sign language, and I'll connect her subdermal comms to yours and Lana's so you can communicate remotely.' He turned to Rachel and Lana with a sombre expression. 'I've just come back from the hospital. Pete collapsed after our meeting with the Council.' He raised his hands reassuringly before Rachel could ask. 'Sam is with him. I've told his doctor about his previous episodes, which the doctor and even Sam didn't know anything about.'

'Episodes?' Lana asked.

'Pete started having migraines and he fainted a few times while we were campaigning for the Social Freedom Act,' he explained. 'Public speaking, televised debates, he held his own the whole way, but it has taken its toll. When the result came in, he was furious. We were walking out after the formal petition with the Council and he just dropped.'

'I better go to Sam,' Rachel said, and received a supportive nod from Lana.

'I'll come with you,' said Hutch before stepping through the portal with Rachel.

Pablo arrived at the bay door and watched the portal retract. 'How come it doesn't get stuck to you when you go through it?'

Lana raised her hands in amazement. 'Mercury is poisonous, so I was sceptical when Rachel first showed me one.' She ushered her father into the Black Heron, and he greeted Talon and Bell. 'She said the technology the Kiyol developed maintains a resident delinquency that–' Lana paused when she saw Talon signing to her. 'Right, resonant frequency,' she corrected and translated while Talon explained. 'Mercury has high hydrogen overvoltage, so their process works in tandem with…' She signed back to Talon, *Yeah, I don't know what any of that means.*

'Alien technology,' Pablo summarised for Lana with an understanding nod.

'Exactly.' And Lana gave Pablo an edited run-down of what happened in Kuru.

'We can't thank you enough, both of you,' Pablo said to her and Talon. 'I hope your travels take you to our edge of the rim again soon.'

'I'll drop in when I can,' Lana promised.

He said good night and walked home. The sun was going down, and Lana was beat after the exertion of penetrating Hassan's memory. She found Talon in their room, connecting a step ladder to her bunk.

'I've given Shen a console,' Lana told her. 'He's agreed to join us after he spends time with his son. He and Miri, you and I, make five.'

Talon undressed and gestured for her dog to climb up to bed.

'You think we need one more.'

Talon lay down on the bunk's charging pad beside Bell. She raised a finger before closing her eyes.

'We'll get one more.' Lana dropped her dirt-covered clothes in the bin, for good this time, and yawned all the way into the shower. The transparent door closed behind her automatically. She turned the mist spray on hot, and let the warmth hold and comfort her. She scrubbed and watched the red dirt colour her feet like ochre.

Lana stepped out of the shower after a blow dry. She heard the hum of both Bell and Talon's batteries recharging. Talon could remain active for seventy-two hours before requiring a rest cycle. Lana guessed Bell would need recharging more often.

Lana climbed to the top bunk, crawled under the covers and fell asleep in a minute.

The next morning, Miri returned from the Ether Realm through a portal that opened in the loading bay. She closed it behind her using her own ring console. She recognised Lana's quiet snore and followed it to the bunks.

An alert sounded in the cockpit, signalling an urgent message. Miri had watched Talon operate the buttons and switches over the months she had visited the Black Heron. She pressed the comms button, and Lincoln appeared as a small hologram.

'General.'

'Miri, we have a situation. The Lustitians are under attack.'

Earth
San Francisco

The evening sun was setting on the horizon. Nu metal band Follow were touring for their second album, and their fans at Candlestick Park were chanting and cheering for the next song. The half-circle array of seats was packed to capacity, and hundreds more stood before the stage on the baseball field.

The crowd roared when Saule, the lead singer, approached the microphone. Her guitarists strummed, and the drummer began a slow pounding. All four artists were in their mid-twenties. Saule swung her long blonde hair, letting the orange colouring in the last five centimetres of its length fan out over her black cropped vest. The double bass quickened, and the drummer flicked the hi-hat in between rapid strikes to the snare drum. Saule doubled over, throwing her orange tips like a blaze, and slowly rose, her hair shifting over her torn jeans. Her Follow band banners were a yellow, scratchy font against black.

'This one's for the people of Silica!' Saule shouted. 'To the survivors of oppression! To the heroes who fought against the Corporate Office of Government!'

The bass guitarist thrummed a melodic, rising tune that echoed a feeling of hardship and struggle. The drummer maintained her tempo, and the second guitarist joined with an electrifying riff.

Saule's voice rose as the tempo ebbed, power and emotion in every word. '*Tainted despite your nurture. Conspired by this world. Born to claw for food, for shelter. To possess, and your status…*' Saule took a deep breath and screamed, '*For more, for more, for more!*'

The audience bounced, swung their heads and roared with Saule. Empowering energy surged through the thirty-thousand-strong sea of fans. Saule pumped her fist during the chorus, and the crowd raised theirs.

A moment later, the bass guitarist stuttered to a stop.

The crowd stopped moving. Lowered their hands, all staring at something in the sky. Saule walked to the left wing of the stage with her guitarist and watched from the edge. Their jaws dropped. Saule's eyes widened when she recognised the Lustitian ship that came to stop the Wardens only months ago. It broke through the clouds in a steep descent. Flames plumed from its top and tail. The ship was a teardrop, aerodynamic shape, with a horizontal disc wedged in its middle. Judging by the tilt of the disc, Saule could see that it was arching toward Candlestick Park. She raced back to her microphone, and it whined when she snatched it.

'Everybody, please make your way to the exits!'

Escape pods were falling from the clouds. Each was powering reverse thrusters to reduce the impact of landing.

Saule dropped from the stage in time to avoid an escape pod that crashed through the speakers and tore the banners. Her band followed her across the field to the baseball dugout. The Lustitian ship crashed through the far side of the stadium, obliterating the stands. Seats and broken concrete flew into the air. The disc section ploughed into the ground, and the field was lifted like a carpet. A deep bass groan and the ripping of earth and rock thundered against the walls of the stadium. Pods continued to land in the field, while some hit the stadium seats, tumbling end over end.

The momentum of the Lustitian ship carried it thirty metres more. The metallic grind rose in tone before the ship settled. Saule left the dugout with her band members, only to realise debris was falling from the sky. They ran for cover as rock and steel pelted the ground. Fires were burning in the stands and the outfield.

Saule approached the nearest pod and touched the metal shell. Its doors parted with a jet of steam. A woman wearing a torn white and gold uniform stepped out with a rifle clutched to her chest. She grabbed Saule and pulled her into the pod. Gold stitching on the woman's left breast read "SO Kim". 'You're Lustitians,' said Saule. 'Wh-what happened? Who shot you down?'

Science Officer Kim made a "hush" sound between her lips. She used her pod as cover while she aimed her rifle to the sky, in the direction her ship had fallen. Wind blew smoke and embers across the field, obscuring what she expected to come at any moment. The sun was throwing its last minutes of light against the clouds. The other pods were opening. The officers inside took position as Kim had, aiming their rifles or side-arms to the sky.

AM soldiers flew down from the rear of the stadium. Their jetpacks hummed as six of them slowed to hover. They peeled off to the Lustitians who had fallen unconscious out of their pods, or who had sustained injuries.

Saule watched a subtle blue light the clouds as the sun dipped below the horizon. Winged humanoid figures appeared, their silhouettes glowing against the darkening sky. They descended at a controlled speed. They made no sound, so far away. Only the licking of flames could be heard.

'What are they?' she asked Kim.

'Sedit,' Kim whispered, 'lead by their Prince, Thulu. Our shields couldn't repel their attack.' She saw her fellow Lustitians shifting in weaver stance, preparing to fire. 'Hold,' she ordered through her comms, not wanting the Sedit to scatter while they were out of range.

More AMs arrived in the air. They hovered and took aim with assault rifles. Two landed high atop the stadium and mounted sniper rifles on bipods.

Seven of the creatures Kim called Sedit descended slowly. Saule peered around the pod and saw that the glow was sulphur, burning neon blue. Flames licked from their wings, wrists, elbows, from all the joins in their body. They were not flesh and bone, but basalt. Their heads were skulls, shaped like a ram's, but with a beak instead of a snout. And they had horns; some were short, others long and curled. Flames rose from their eye holes, and they surveyed the result of their attack as they descended. The lead Sedit drew his hand to the ship, pointing two fingers, and signalled to the AMs.

'Open fire!' Kim shouted. She shot energy blasts at the two approaching Sedit that had been commanded to engage the survivors. The AMs fired on the other two. Their bullets sparked off the Sedits' armour and chipped at their obsidian limbs. An AM sniper delivered a powerful round into the head of the closest target. The Sedit reared back and roared through its shattered beak. Saule likened, with fear, the sound the Sedit made to the roar of a mandrill.

The two beasts sent to attack the survivors landed, standing eight feet tall. Kim's officers lit them up with blaster fire, successfully taking down one, while the other used its wings as shields as it advanced. The Sedit spun its body and carved the ground with one wing, throwing an obscuring wall of earth.

Kim swore under her breath when a volley of white-hot molten rock flew from the cascading soil toward her. She heard the flaming rocks hit the pod and watched their searing heat melt the steel, until they sank through. She and Saule stepped over each one that dropped at their feet.

Saule watched through the gouged pod as two more Sedit landed and threw molten projectiles. A Lustitian cried out three metres away. The ball burned right through him, bounced and set fire to the grass.

'Retreat!' Kim called to the others. She pulled a lever inside the pod, and a white mist of fire retardant filled the interior and plumed out, carried by the breeze. She and Saule ran for the stadium exit while the Sedits' line of sight was obscured. Kim's surviving officers followed suit.

A female Sedit followed the escaping officers into the tunnel. She cupped her hands, forming two molten rocks, and threw them. Saule glanced behind her and pushed Kim out of the way. The first rock ricocheted off the concrete. The next came harder, pin-balling against the walls. It severed an officer's leg.

The flames triggered the fire detectors in the corridor, and the water sprinklers activated. The Sedit roared when steam from her own body clouded her vision. Kim ordered the others to get out, while she took a slim metallic object from her belt, pressed a button and ran at their attacker. She threw herself onto the Sedit's back and wedged the bomb into her shoulder blade.

The Sedit swung Kim off her. Kim barrel-rolled and slammed into the tunnel wall. Saule ran to her, shielding her eyes from the sparks flying from a severed electrical cable hanging from the ceiling. The Sedit clawed at her back, and cursed at the beeping explosive she could not reach.

Kim's legs were broken. The bomb was about to explode. The electrical cable sparked above her. She knew there was no time now for Saule to run. She took hold of Saule with one hand, reached and grabbed the sparking cable with her other. She pulled Saule close, focused her energy and drove the live end of the cable into Saule.

Saule's back arched and her limbs trembled while the Sedit's scream was cut off by the explosion. The incinerating blast blew her apart. The firestorm pressed Kim against Saule. Kim's body was reduced to ash while her essence entered Saule. The surge of electricity that had circulated through Saule rolled out of her core, in two parabolic, pulsing golden waves. The concrete floor and walls burned, cracked and shuddered.

Fire shot through the length of the tunnel. It escaped out both ends in a tumbling cloud of orange and black.

Saule blinked through blurred vision. Carbon in the air hit her nostrils, and she coughed it out of her lungs. Moving to her knees, she snapped awake and gasped when she realised she was surrounded by glowing hot debris.

Saule heard a voice inside her, a woman's voice. It was Kim, telling her not to be afraid. Saule squinted through the smoke. Kim was gone.

'My head hurts,' Saule croaked through the toxic air. 'Feels like my brain is splitting.'

I am trying to help your mind deal with the new volume of... me, said Kim. *Your brain will adjust soon. We must find help.*

Chapter 7

The Black Heron breached the clouds over San Francisco. Scanners did not detect any unidentified ships in the sky or in space orbit. Talon slowed on their approach to Candlestick Park and readied the weapons.

Lana and Miri stared out of the forward windows at the rising smoke and the people fleeing the stadium. An explosion erupted and fire shot out of an exit tunnel. Talon saw that only two AMs remained on the stands, and they were pinned down, dodging projectiles thrown by blue-flaming creatures. She opened fire on and killed the closest Sedit. Three remained, and their leader called them to him. Lana peered over Talon's shoulder and read the ship speech-translator while it broke down what the Sedit was commanding.

Bring me two Earthlings.

Yes, Prince Thulu.

They watched Thulu crouch, rocket thirty metres into the air and complete a curving arch over the stadium.

'Follow him,' she ordered Talon.

Talon did so with ease, due to his heat signature. They flew over the city, keeping pace with the black and blue humanoid figure. She didn't want to fire on him while flying over a populated area. So they chased him to Haight Park, where he landed and walked to a large tree. He stood in front of it, waving his arms and turning his wrists in a fluid motion, as though he was practicing a martial form. Miri gasped when she saw the tree ripple and swirl in the clockwise motion he was commanding.

Saule left the stadium tunnel, surprisingly sure-footed considering she had just been electrocuted. She looked down at her bare feet. Her footwear had burnt away, and her jeans and vest were holed and tattered. She felt her hair in panic.

The electrical field I created to protect you from the blast prevents loss of organic matter, Kim assured her.

Saule breathed out in relief. 'Thank you. I'm sorry you're–'

Don't worry about me. We need a vehicle. Kim saw a ship flying over the city in Saule's peripheral vision. *That was the Black Heron, Lana's ship. We must follow.*

Saule looked to the horizon and spotted the Raekeem craft. More AMs arrived to cordon off the street. Firefighters rappelled down ropes from a hovering dropship, before it continued on to the stadium to jet fire retardant over the Lustitian ship.

An AM approached Saule and checked her for burns. Satisfied that she was alright, he took a silver rectangle from his belt that looked like a folded business card and snapped it open. It unfurled to an insulation blanket, and he threw it over Saule's shoulders. She opened her mouth to thank him, but a man cried out to their left, beyond the security barrier. A motorcycle fell on its side. And Saule flinched when a helmet dropped at her feet.

A Sedit was carrying the rider in the direction of the Black Heron.

A woman screamed when a second Sedit abducted another civilian and followed his companion. AMs with jetpacks shot up from the ground and gave chase. Saule picked up the rider's helmet, hurdled the barrier and pushed through the panicked crowd. She arrived at the motorcycle, bent her knees and prepared to heave it upright. She found it to be a surprisingly easy lift. *This bike has to weigh at least 160 kg*, she thought. *How–*

Your muscles reacted to the electrical volts before I was able to create the protective field. Some of my organic matter has added to yours.

Saule mounted the bike, its engine still running, and pulled on the helmet. She tapped the pedal with her left foot, squeezed down the clutch and eased the throttle enough to slip through a gap between fleeing San Franciscans.

'You mean you gave me muscle mass?' She gradually released the clutch and accelerated down the street, changing gears as she gained speed.

I see no other explanation… for your increased strength. Kim was pausing each time Saule leaned the bike away from oncoming cars as she overtook slow traffic. *I can also help you bring back your protective field. Which you will need if you do not slow down!*

'Relax, Kim. I compete in races. I know what I'm doing. There's a hard turn coming up. How does the field work?'

It should be achievable in a reactive state.

'*Should?* You didn't know if it would work back in the tunnel?'

The theory was sound, and it did work, Kim retorted. *Visualise energy inside you and project it outward, in the direction you need it.*

'Here goes.' Saule entered an intersection at high speed. She leaned and did as Kim instructed. Her golden field met the bitumen just before her bare knee could be grated on it and she swooped around the turn.

Saule sped down a few more streets before reaching Haight Park. Kim saw Lana and Miri descend on ropes while the Black Heron hovered above.

Miri was armed with her a Fyrst Born bow and a quiver of stone-tipped arrows. She followed Lana's lead, and they walked a dirt path to Prince Thulu.

Thulu paused his chanting and turned to acknowledge the two women. He held the portal open.

'Are you a leader of your species?' he asked.

'I am a protector,' Lana answered firmly.

Saule rode up the footpath, dismounted and ran to Lana and Miri.

What are they doing? Kim exclaimed. *The Sedit cannot be reasoned with!*

'Then consider what we have to offer you.' Thulu looked up to see his two Sedit descending to the park, each carrying an abductee. 'These two will serve as demonstration,' he said, in a neutral tone, as though he were speaking about two inanimate objects. The motorcycle rider was drawn close to Thulu, and the Prince raised his hand to the man's chest. He paused when Lana stepped forward and Miri pulled on her nocked arrow.

'They will not be harmed,' Thulu assured them. 'The effects are reversible.'

A golden pulse of energy slammed into his shoulder, staggering him away from the civilian.

'He's lying,' Saule warned when she arrived next to Lana. Her right fist was glowing yellow. 'He wants our planet's resources in exchange for making us like them.'

'Just those whom you wish to be powerful enough to defend your planet,' Thulu argued.

'There'll be no planet to defend after you sap it of energy,' Saule retorted.

Lana ordered Talon to fire a precision blast. Prince Thulu flinched when it hit the ground between his legs, and he glared up at the Black Heron.

'The next one will be higher,' Lana warned. 'Release the hostages and go.'

Thulu told his guards to do as she said, and Miri led the man and woman away.

'You would deny your people such power?' Thulu asked, genuinely surprised.

'Fair warning, Thulu: if you come back, we will end you.'

'Do not threaten me, girl,' Thulu spat. 'You could not possibly comprehend–'

'Thesin,' Saule interjected.

Thulu froze and stared at her. 'How do you know the name of the Sedit home world? And how did you fire energy from your hand?'

'There is a Lustitian inside me. She knows what you are. Leave now. Do not return.'

Thulu's eyes flared white hot, and he clenched his fists. But he ordered his fellow Sedit to enter the portal, giving Saule a menacing glare before following them. The portal closed behind him.

Miri arrived beside Lana. 'I do not believe he will heed your warning.'

'You can be certain of that,' Saule cautioned.

Lana took a step back and looked her up and down. 'You're Saule, from Follow. What are you doing here? What happened to you?'

'A Lustitian Science Officer saved my life at Candlestick Park.'

'Kim?'

'She sacrificed herself to save me.' Saule raised her hand before Lana could ask questions. 'She has a lot to tell you.'

Chapter 8

Talon piloted the Black Heron while Lana and Miri were with Saule in the infirmary. Miri was medically trained, and after giving Saule a thorough examination, she concluded that there were no injuries. She was concerned by Saule's hypertension, so Bell, Talon's labradoodle, sat beside Saule and licked the grazes along her arm.

'Kim says I'll calm down once my brain has adapted to the volume of information she's been giving me,' she said, not sounding particularly assured.

'You shot the Sedit, Thulu,' Miri stated curiously.

'Kim taught me. I can shield myself using the same energy.'

Lana handed Saule a change of clothes and looked up to see Talon standing in the doorway. 'No Sedit out there?'

We're clear, Talon signed and approached Saule with small Follow poster, pressing her palm to her chest.

'Oh cool, glad you like us!' Saule automatically raised her pinky, index finger and thumb.

Talon made the apotropaic devil horns as well and signed to Lana, *I contacted her band to let them know she's alright. They're safe too.*

Saule thanked her after Lana translated.

'Can we speak to Kim?' Lana asked her.

Saule nodded while patting Bell. 'She can hear everything I can.'

Lana hesitated, feeling uncomfortable speaking to two women inhabiting the same body. 'Kim, I'm sorry this has happened to you. We're going to help you any way we can.'

'She says thank you. But there's nothing that can be done for her.'

Lana received a message from Talon, informing her that General Lincoln was on comms. She went to the loading bay and opened a holographic image of Lincoln.

'You did well to run the Sedit out of San Francisco,' he praised. 'Unfortunately, many Lustitians were still aboard when their ship crashed. Most did not survive. We weren't able to locate Captain Valhez.'

Saule arrived after getting dressed and said, 'He and most of the brig crew were killed during the battle in outer space.'

Lana introduced her, adding, 'Saule was at ground zero. Officer Kim saved her life by using her people's matter-changing ability.' Lana didn't know how to explain it, so she kept it short. 'Kim is alive and conscious inside Saule, and she knows the creatures that attacked.'

Lincoln's expression was perplexed, but he did not doubt Lana. 'Officer Kim, my deepest condolences to you and your surviving crew. Please tell us everything you know.'

Saule pushed her fingers through her hair. 'I know you're frustrated, Kim. Please, slow down.' She breathed through the torrent of information in her brain. 'This isn't easy for me. Okay, from the top. Kim says to understand the Sedit, you have to understand the origin of Lustitians.'

The planet Thesin was much like Earth, Kim recalled, while Saule did her best to relay the information to the others.

Our planet supported carbon-based life. We evolved and became the dominant species. We called ourselves Masters. We maintained our families and our tribes in relative peace, with each other and with the land and its creatures. Over the next thousand years, we grew closer to understanding our intelligence and our purpose in life. We invented new tools and built bigger dwellings. We thought we could master any task, cultivate all land, and hunt and grow all food.

But with every winter, sickness came. Despite our understanding of medicine, many among our tribes would die every year. The elderly, children, even young adults, people who were thought to have a long future ahead of them.

The elders of our tribes conceded that we, the most intelligent of all life on the planet, could not master life itself. They decreed that all building stop, and all efforts of mastery be focused on the task at hand. We returned to nature, and we meditated. We gathered at waterfalls, in rainforests, in caves, on beaches, at sea in boats, and we listened. And we learned from our planet.

We were no longer Masters. We were students of Thesin. And for two generations, we learned patience and respect. Or most of us did.

Some took commune on a volcano we called Fire Mountain. They learned a very different lesson. The rest of the tribes always returned from their commune to share their learning with others. We all practiced together what Thesin taught us. We developed a dance that we called Forming. It was the beginning of our ability to harness matter.

'The Sedit tribe observed Kim's people, but never contributed.' Saule paused and looked to Miri. 'Could we… can I have some water?'

Miri nodded and went to the sink.

'The Sedit forbade other tribes from observing their rituals.' She thanked Miri for the water when she returned. 'Kim says the tribes sent–' She paused. '*You?* Man, you must be thousands of years old!'

'Kim was alive then?' Lana exclaimed.

'She says she was a second-generation student at that time. Kim was chosen for the task because she was small and she was a good climber. She was the least likely to get caught. Wow, you had balls, Kim.'

Miri cocked her head at Saule's comment, and glanced at Lana.

'Figure of speech,' Lana whispered. But this raised a question in her mind. 'Kim, were you humanoid?'

'She says she was a biped, but with four arms and green skin.'

'Cool.' Lana gestured for Saule to continue Kim's story.

'Kim climbed the volcano and watched the Sedit from the crest.'

Kim found that she no longer had to tell Saule word for word what she had seen that night. The images imbedded in her memory were enough for Saule to narrate. Kim dreaded having to recall the event, but she felt it was important for Lana and her people to know the origin of the Sedit.

The stench was what Kim remembered most. Dozens of Sedit were standing in the sulphur flames. They were badly burnt, their flesh blackened, no hair on their body. Some, who Kim supposed were novice students, stood outside the heat. The more experienced were chanting about strength, about how if one is to master life, flesh and blood must be given in trade.

A tall man raised his four arms and silenced the chant. He knelt down in the fire and drove one hand into the flowing sulphur. When he stood, his arm looked to be remade of basalt. He pressed his stone hand against his heart. He cried out in pain, and his skin perished. His exposed muscles blackened and turned to rock. The others circled him, chanting his name. He was Thahl, their leader. When Thahl fell to his hands and knees, there was a momentary hush.

Kim shivered, despite the immense heat, when she heard rising, guttural laughter, echoing against the volcano's walls. Thahl's tone was deep and rough like crushing rock. Bright blue flames plumed from his body. He stood and gazed at the sky. He spat sulphur into the air and breathed intense heat that lit the vapour, and a great ball burned. His tribe murmured in awe.

Thahl massaged his head and formed malleable rock from his hands. He gave himself large horns, and he curved and curled them. He remade his face, lengthening his brow into a ram's. And he gave himself an eagle's beak.

Thahl opened his arms and gazed upon his tribe. 'Come, brothers and sisters. Become the Mountain, so we may live through the ages. Breathe the fire, so we may use the power of Thesin and spread rivers of her flame. To those outside…' He turned and pointed directly at Kim, perched on the volcano's crest. 'We will teach you all how to truly master life.'

Saule let the following weeks and years of chaos and turmoil play out through Kim's memory. Tears welled in her eyes when she saw Kim's tribe flee as far as they could, away from the Sedit, and the unstoppable molten rivers of lava.

'The tribes that refused to join Thahl banded together.' Saule felt hope in Kim's memories, and she continued to relate them to Lana and the others. 'They concentrated their Forming abilities and transformed themselves into pure energy. After encasing themselves in a weightless sphere, they rose into the sky and escaped Thesin.' Saule's heart broke at the image of Thesin, their home planet, shrinking in the black of space. Their glowing sun, the orb that warmed them, became a distant star. Kim and her people drifted out of the swirling cloud of planets that was their solar system.

'Over the following years, they probed systems for a suitable planet. They entered the Milky Way Galaxy and found our solar system.

Mars was long devoid of life. Earth had an intelligent species, humans, already living there in a hunter-gatherer state. Some of Kim's people decided to stay and observe us humans, while Kim and the others continued on with the search.

'As they drifted in space, in their sphere, they honed their abilities to prepare for a new world, and to adapt and evolve again. Soon, they found their new planet, in a system that contained three others. Having studied humans for some time, they all decided to take that bodily form.

'When Kim's people took our shape, they used their Forming ability to build their homes. They didn't want to tax their planet for matter, so they created a device that would allow them to connect to a wormhole they had probed during their journey. Kim helped the others build the gate that would bring matter through the wormhole, and then through a portal, which–'

'Kim's people created the Matter Portal?' Lana exclaimed. 'I thought the Kiyol did that.'

'Kim says the Kiyol piggybacked their tech onto the matter flow on that gate. They sent out signals in various languages requesting permission. Kim was authorised to allow it. The elders were confident the Kiyol were a responsible race. They were also glad there were worlds out there capable of taking care of themselves should the Sedit invade. Work was underway to build a fleet of ships that would travel to other worlds to assess vulnerabilities, and to help them better defend their people. Piloting, combat and engineering became new schools of training for Kim's people as they prepared for the worst. When their ships finally took to the skies, and they encountered other habited planets, they immediately found threats posed against those worlds that were not Sedit-related.'

'Threats like the Raekeem,' Miri prompted.

'Exactly. Captain Valhez, Kim's superior, saw that having the means to aid people was reason enough to intervene. And Kim raised the point that real combat and tactical experience was necessary to strengthen their ability to defeat the Sedit. Kim's people were no longer masters or students; they were, from that point on, to be known as Lustitians, enforcers of justice.'

'And that's why you hunted the Raekeem,' said Lincoln.

'Captain Valhez knew that were the Sedit and Raekeem to ever meet, they would likely join forces. That was a fight he knew the Lustitians couldn't win. No one could.'

'I don't understand how those flaming gargoyles were able to bring down your ship,' Lana said. 'From what I saw, they were only throwing molten rock.'

Saule listened to Kim's reply. 'Kim… Kim, you're hurting my head. Layman's terms… Better. She says the rock they throw is part of them. The Sedit can command their projectiles to eat through matter. They concentrated their firepower in one area, burnt through the shields and through the hull.'

'What's their next move?' Lincoln asked.

'The lead Sedit was Thulu, Thahl's son.' Saule waited for Kim to think through what the Sedit might do next. 'Their goal is to attain resources to prolong their existence. In the beginning, Thahl expanded his population by finding inhabited worlds and offering them his power. Kim's people have reached many of the habited systems closest to Thesin and helped them repel the Sedit. She thinks the Sedit may be running out of resources, and have travelled beyond their usual range.'

'They've travelled here,' Lana stated gravely. 'They want our resources.'

Chapter 9

Prince Thulu flew across arid fields and up the scorched mountain that was his family domain. He was followed by two of his guards, and the three landed at the steps of their King's castle. They were dwarfed by the black spire that rose from the main hall.

Thulu climbed the thirty steps to the hulking doors. Each stone block he placed his weight on sank to a trigger. Flames lit in the hall, indicating three visitors. Guards stationed in the watchtowers that flanked the entrance called for the door to be opened. Two Sedit gatekeepers, with arms wider than the waist of an adult human, turned the wheel that rolled gears and pulled the half-metre-thick doors open. Thulu entered confidently and was met by King Thahl's steward, a thin Sedit with human features and a long chin.

'My Prince, how wonderful it is to see you,' he greeted with a bow.

'My mother, how is she?'

The steward lowered his gaze sombrely. He led Thulu through the hall and asked that he wait at the King's throne. The flames lighting the rock walls flickered when the lightweight Sedit beat his wings to ascend to a balcony gate, built thirty feet above the throne in the spire wall.

To Thulu's frustration, the steward did not reappear for several minutes. When he finally descended, he took his position beside the

King's throne. Thulu glanced at him, and then up at the balcony. He looked back to the steward and opened his mouth to speak when a piercing slap of stone on stone echoed through the hall.

King Thahl appeared at the edge of the balcony, gripping the open gate, its hinges now broken. He glared down at his son.

'You have been away from Thesin for some time, boy. Scouts reported you leaving with a horde two Moons Bright ago.'

Thulu had rehearsed the explanation he knew his father would demand. He took Thahl's pause as his opportunity to speak. 'We encountered–'

'When is the last time you visited your mother?'

Thulu lowered his head guiltily.

'Come.' Thahl stood aside and held the gate open. 'She waits for you.'

Thulu flew up to his father and entered his mother's chambers. She lay in a flaming bed of sulphur in the centre of the room. He knew that it was stoked and fed every day with sulphur sourced from other planets.

Thesin was dry. The Sedit could form almost anything out of matter, but not what they needed most to survive.

Only Thulu and his forces were healthy. They took what fire they could find to fuel their search. Any greater reserves found or seized on other planets were syphoned and carried back to Thesin. Suns burned too hot even to approach, let alone harvest.

King Thahl stood at the door and watched his son kneel beside the bed. Many other Sedit were faced with the same fate. Their light was fading. Their bodies were cracking, shrinking in on themselves. Only these beds of sulphur could sustain them. Thahl waited for his son to whisper apologies to his mother and then beckoned for him to follow.

Father and son descended, and Thahl sat on his throne, weary from sadness. 'What did you find out there, in the far systems?'

'Our long search took us to a planet called Earth,' Thulu began. 'It has a healthy core.' He hesitated before stating what should have come first. 'The Lustitians intercepted us.'

Thahl's eyes narrowed. 'And?'

'We defeated the–'

'Of course you did.' Thahl ignored his son's victory. 'Earth – did you appease the inhabitants? Make the offer?' he demanded impatiently.

'They refused.' Thulu looked up at the chambers where his mother was dying and back to his father. 'Shall I give the order to strike?'

'Do they have allies?'

'The advanced species they traded with were last seen moving their station out of Earth's solar system. It seems they are no longer allied.'

The King uttered a rocky grumble. 'Make it so, my son,' he said regretfully. 'Take their fire, so we may restore your dear mother's health and that of our people.'

Earth
San Francisco

Talon landed the Black Heron on the platform attached to the Portal Hub. Lana and Miri descended the ramp, and they were greeted by Rachel standing in the morning sun. The facility was built into the mountain overlooking the Pacific Ocean. The crashing waves could be heard below, as could the distant sound of vehicles crossing the Golden Gate Bridge.

'I was in Mechtropolis during the attack,' said Rachel. 'Are you alright?'

'We're fine,' Lana assured her. 'Lincoln is preparing all of the defences Earth has. Kim is coordinating through Saule.'

'We cannot request military aid from the Kiyol?' Miri asked Rachel.

'Earth has rejected the Social Freedom Act,' Rachel said. 'They have no allies to come to their aid.' But she gestured in the direction of San Francisco, adding, 'The majority of populations within cities like ours voted yes. The Mayor is going to apply all of the necessary laws and initiatives.' She turned to see the Black Heron rise into the air and fly off at a steep ascent. 'Where's she going?'

Lana replied to Talon's text message to confirm that Talon would return if she was needed. 'She's going to join the Earth patrol.'

Miri shook her head, still confused by the human need to marginalise minorities. 'Social perception of marital status does not exist in my culture. Those who intend to have children do not bond until their young can fend for themselves.'

Rachel pointed to Lana and then Miri. 'Bond, as in if one of you dies, the other dies?'

She received a solemn nod from both.

'My sister's partner died when her daughter was very young,' Miri explained. 'Had they bonded, my niece would have been left without either of her mothers.'

'Makes human marriages and divorces seem petty by comparison. And to apply official titles and social hierarchy to that farce is...'

'Inhumane,' Miri prompted, unapologetically. 'Freedom cannot exist within a social hierarchy. It is a prison for those who refuse it.'

The three of them arrived in the Portal Room. 'We have all of the equipment ready for you,' said Rachel. 'Sam is waiting for you in the Ether Realm, at the...'

'The Veil,' Miri prompted.

Lana inspected the gear arrayed on a crate in the middle of the room. There was a backpack full of survival gear, a two-person tent with pegs, and a pistol with spare clips. The machine Kim had designed to penetrate the Ether Realm was on a trolley ready to be taken through the portal that Rachel was about to open.

Rachel gave Miri a hug. 'I hope you find your parents.'

'Thank you.'

The portal opened, and Miri helped Lana strap on the heavy backpack. She entered first with the trolley, and Lana followed.

Sam met Miri and Lana on the other side. Lana opened her mouth to greet her, but her jaw dropped at the sight of a wall of ethereal light towering over the land. It came out of the ground and soared into the sky, swaying and rippling in greens and blues like an aurora borealis light show.

Lana felt the warmth of the Ether Realm sun against her skin. The defused wind blew through the pine trees behind her, and birds sang. Ahead, the Veil was silent.

'Amazing, isn't it?' Sam commented. 'Who or whatever put it here must be incredibly advanced.'

Lana hugged her and asked about Pete.

'He's stable,' she replied optimistically. 'We're awaiting more test results.'

Lana picked up one of the half-metre hardwood logs that Sam had been using to probe the Veil. She inspected the angle of the clean cut and raised an eyebrow at Sam.

'You'll be fine,' Sam assured her, while calibrating the machine so that it was ready to activate. She glanced at Lana through her long fringe, seeing that Lana was not convinced. 'You said Orin had a vision of you on the other side of this thing. You were there with all of your limbs attached.'

Sam stood up and tied her hair back into a ponytail once the machine was ready. She programmed a shifter device and activated a portal. It opened, imbedded in the Veil.

'Ready?' Lana asked Miri.

Miri shouldered her bow and quiver, and took a fortifying breath. She nodded and entered the portal. Lana went in after her, and when she emerged on the other side, she was immediately staggered by an ice-cold driving wind. Miri braced against her side, and they pushed through deep snow to find shelter. Lana guided Miri toward a fallen tree. Through windblown flakes, Miri could see a distant light in the shape of a window.

'There's a light in the distance,' said Miri, while they dug a hovel. 'Too far in this storm. We'll have to wait it out.'

'Gladly,' Lana called over her shoulder as she crawled under the tree. Axe in hand, she chopped deeper in to make more room.

Miri took out the tent, and the two of them crawled inside. While Lana texted Sam to tell her that she and Miri were alright, she could feel Miri shifting for more space. She was perspiring, her breath shallow.

'Lana, I cannot stay in here. I cannot breathe.'

Lana pressed her fingers to Miri's temple and concentrated on an image of a stream being fed by a waterfall three stories high. She entered Miri's mind, and they looked up at the falling water together and listened to it crashing into the pool below. Miri took Lana's hand and did not let go.

Sam requested an AM stay with the equipment in the Ether Realm, for when Lana and Miri needed to return. She left to join Rachel on her return visit to Mechtropolis.

'Lana's message says they've hit a storm, but they're fine,' she told

Rachel in the Portal Room.

Rachel donned a brown jacket over a white buttoned shirt. 'Strange. It's summer in Miri's world.'

Sam opened a cupboard and pressed a button on the door. A traditional Chinese dress hanging on the automated track swung aside, and a Mongolian gown came next.

'Have you been going to the Khan Realm without me?' Sam complained.

Rachel had been to a realm where Genghis Khan had succeeded in taking over most of the world. 'We can go together after this, if you like.' She had been there to purchase an ornate jade figurine for her and Sam's birthday.

Sam panned through two more costumes until slacks, a shirt and a beige silk vest arrived. She took them down, nodding approval at the 1930s outfit. Rachel opened a portal to Mechtropolis and checked the time on her ring console. Hutch Branner came jogging into the room in the same moment.

'Sorry I'm late,' he said. 'My buddy in Japan made a suit to replace the jetpack. I had to arrange distribution to Lincoln's AMs.' He waved his hands in digression and adjusted his navy blue suit and yellow tie.

Hutch had taken sanctuary in the Portal Hub during the Raekeem attack the previous year. He had since requested to join some of Rachel's realm expeditions.

'I'm ready,' he said. 'This could be the world I've been hoping for.'

Chapter 10

Lana woke when she heard Miri whispering an unfamiliar name.

'Stay with me,' Miri sobbed, before taking a sharp breath. 'Somebody help!'

Lana tapped her ring console to make light, unzipped the tent and helped Miri crawl into daylight. 'You're alright. We're safe.'

Miri wiped away her tears while kneeling in the snow. The two of them shielded their eyes against the rising sun. Through the glare, Lana could soon make out snow-capped mountains. A breathtaking view of a valley stretched far below their elevation. There were signs of tree felling on the mountainside opposite. Smoke rose from a cabin that was, frustratingly, at eye-level, but so far away.

'There.' Lana pointed. 'I could teleport us roughly there with my Shifter, but if anyone saw us...'

'We must remain inconspicuous,' Miri agreed. She pulled her bow and quiver out of the snow and shook them. She had discarded them during the storm in order to fit into the tent with Lana.

'If you want to talk about it...' Lana offered.

Miri managed a nod and shook the snow off their backpack. She took out two sealed cups, tea for herself and coffee for Lana. With a press of a button on the bottom of each, their beverages were heated in seconds. Miri found muesli bars and dried currants for their breakfast. After their quick meal and drink, they put on raincoats, packed everything away and started walking.

They descended for an hour before reaching the bottom of the gully.

They crossed over a frozen stream and began the climb to the cabin. Bird calls sounded from the trees above that sounded more human than animal. Miri didn't feel as though they were being watched, so she assumed the birds were unique to this piece of her world. She slowed and gestured to Lana that they should stop at a log that had fallen wedged against two trees. Lana handed her a bottle of water and watched her tentatively.

Miri looked back at her partner's concerned eyes. 'My sister, my niece… we got separated during the Collide. I found my sister's partner, and we took shelter. It was not a magical or mystical joining of worlds. The Collide was like a giant cutting a square of crops, lifting us out of the ground to place us somewhere else. When it happened, she and I were trapped under fallen trees, rock and dirt. We yelled and screamed for hours. Then it was just me. She succumbed to her injuries. My sister found us two days later.'

Rachel, Sam and Hutch emerged from their portal, and it closed behind them. The first thing Sam noticed was the smell and taste in the air. It was metallic, like being in a mechanic's garage, except without the odour of fuel or rubber.

Rachel guided them from the deserted alley to a busy street. 'Welcome to Mechtropolis.'

Hutch stared in wonderment at the pedestrians walking by. They were all made of steel. They wore layers of metal that were crafted to look like suits, vests, floral dresses, hats and skirts. Some were painted matt, but most were polished, and their gloss shone in the sunlight. All of the vehicles on the street were on tracks, but there were no electrical cables overhead, and Hutch could hear no pulling system underground, like one does with trams in San Francisco.

'Astonishing,' he murmured. 'Their tracks and cars must be magnetic.'

Sam watched a car roll by without a sound. The driver, a man with an intricately curled moustache, was using a lever to control his speed, and another lever to change tracks to turn at the next street. Sam guessed that there were gyros and tumbler mechanisms being used to propel the car along the magnets. Their average speed looked to be forty kilometres.

'When I first arrived…' Rachel paused while a mechanical postman walked by with a container full of slender alloy envelopes hanging by his side. 'I was convinced that everyone here had free will, going about their daily lives like humans. I left some hidden cameras, and Sam had a group of interns take shifts at her lab, watching the recordings over a fourteen-day cycle.'

'And?' Hutch asked intently, while trying to look at as many passers-by as he could, studying their variations. He had put a great deal of effort into making each of his AMs look unique, taking inspiration from the artisans who moulded the Terracotta Warriors of Xi'an to look individual.

'The interns found a pattern,' said Sam. She used her ring to bring up a holographic display of an individual machine. It was the man with the moustache she had seen earlier. Sam played the recordings, and it showed the man taking his car to a workshop for a service. He then went to a diner to read an alloy newspaper while he waited. There was a beep outside, and the mechanic stepped out of the car, waved, and walked back to his workshop. The man left the diner, got back in his car and drove off. Sam panned ahead through the other citizens to a week from the car servicing day, and there was the man, driving through the city. He stopped at the workshop, left his car and went to the diner.

'Each individual has one week of activities they complete,' Rachel explained to Hutch while they walked along the street. 'They repeat their week on a loop. This city is some kind of life-size, automated diorama.'

Hutch wasn't disappointed by the prospect that these machines were less advanced than his. This was still an exciting experience for him. 'Who made all of this? And why?'

Rachel was stopped in her tracks by large double doors decorated by a beautiful art nouveau motif. 'That's what we're here to find out.' Though the exterior was art deco – sleek, continuous panels rising to narrow steel turrets – upon the doors was a relief of vines endowed with grapes, leading to a life-size, bifurcated bust of Medusa's face, adorned with curling snakes. 'I'm told this is the town hall, and instead of a Mayor, they have an Overseer.'

'They speak?' Hutch exclaimed.

'They do.'

The doors opened on their approach, and they crossed the foyer and entered a cage elevator. The attending bellhop was a teenager. He nodded his cylindrical red cap and asked them, 'What floor?' Rachel told him they wanted to see the Overseer. The bellhop pulled the doors closed, pressed a button and pulled a lever, and they ascended. Music played, but not from electronic speakers. Chimes and xylophone keys above the door were being struck by unseen mechanical hammers.

Sam was expecting to feel cold. The machines wouldn't require heat to survive, much less for comfort. But she was warm. And when the light flickered overhead, Sam caught an orange glow coming from the bellhop's chest in the brief darkness.

'Nice tie,' she commented and pressed her hand against the boy's chest, beneath his bowtie.

'Thank you, ma'am.'

His metal was not hot, but there was definitely a heat source inside him. Sam understood now why none of the machines' bodies were fully encased by the metal clothes. They needed ventilation.

The doors opened. The three of them stepped out, and they approached the reception desk. Rachel opened her mouth to request an audience, but the young lady behind the desk gestured to the door to her left.

'The Overseer is expecting you.'

Beyond the Veil that separated them from the Ether Realm, Lana and Miri finally reached the cabin they had been climbing toward. Exhausted, Miri called out on their approach, and saw that the small house was made of packed mud and foliage. She could hear no reply over the howling wind, so she and Lana approached the nearest window and peered in. Lana could only make out vague shapes in the fire-illuminated interior. Snow was being blown horizontally at their backs. The force of the gale pressed them against the cabin. With her arm held firmly around Miri's waist, Lana edged toward a wooden door. She rapped on it with her free hand and called out, but her voice was taken by the wind. Lana was reaching for the lever when it was pulled from the other side. The door swung open, Lana fell in and Miri landed on top of her. A man stood over them with a hand axe raised. A woman was shouting over the wind. She leaned against the door, closed it and locked it. A last swirl of snow whipped in, and it followed the heat to the cabin ceiling before showering down.

Lana wiped flecks of ice from her eyes. She saw the axe in the man's hand and heard his angry tone. The light from the fire made his face look orange, but the other half of his face looked blue. With barely any energy left, Lana rolled over Miri and covered her. She used her remaining strength to armour her skin. The woman argued with him, and Lana flinched when something pressed against her head. The man and woman fell silent. Lana felt small hands patting her hair and heard quiet murmurs. She raised her head to find two boys aged around three kneeling beside her. Their four-fingered hands changed from pale orange to blue. Darkness overtook Lana's sight, and she rested her head onto Miri's shoulder and closed her eyes for what she thought would be a second.

Something warm pressed down her bottom lip, and water dribbled against her teeth. Lana let it flow down her dry throat, and she swallowed deeply. She could hear Miri's voice and the two boys pleading with their parents. They sounded like they wanted to keep her and Miri, like two lost puppies.

Lana opened her eyes to find herself lying in a bunk with Miri, who held a cup of tea.

'We're okay, Lana. We're safe,' Miri assured her. 'The altitude caused us to pass out.' She helped Lana sit up, and the two of them looked around the small interior.

The parents were cross-legged, having breakfast with their children at a low table by the fire. The mother chided them and glanced over her shoulder at Lana. Her eyes were green, her face orange. Lana had not imagined their complexion, and these people were certainly not human.

'They seem peaceful,' Miri commented. 'Can you understand them?'

Lana calibrated her ring console and waited for the text translation. 'They're deciding where to take us. She has a cousin at the top of the mountain who will know what to do.'

The man stood, wiped bread crumbs from his beard and strode to the door while pulling on his fur jacket. He opened the door with axe in hand. He looked to Lana and Miri while the cold turned his orange skin blue, and jerked his head for them to follow.

Rachel, Sam and Hutch walked into the Overseer's office in Mechtropolis. A tall-backed chair behind a large desk was facing the window.

'Take a load off, strangers.' The man's voice sounded old, and his accent sounded Texan.

Three seats faced the desk. Hutch sat down last, and noticed a half-smoked cigar sitting in a brass dish.

The chair turned slowly, and the sunlight shone over a man aged around sixty. His bushy grey moustache rose when he smiled. He leaned in and peered at each of his guests over reading glasses. 'I was wondering when y'all might come up and say howdy.'

'You're human,' Sam blurted out.

The Overseer's stubby fingers fiddled with a button two down from his bowtie until it came undone. 'All but mah ticker,' he said, and tapped on an oval piece of metal, which he revealed with some pride. 'This dynamo'll keep me goin' another twenny years or so.'

Rachel saw an orange glow coming from a small hole in the centre of the man's implant. 'Sir, my name is Rachel Navara. This is Samantha O'Conner and Hutch Branner. We meant no disrespect. I wasn't approached by any authority, so I felt it was okay to delay seeking out whoever was in charge.'

'None taken, Ms Navara.' He buttoned up his shirt. 'You can call me Ken.' He clasped his hands and gave a friendly smile. 'Hedy and I are the closest thing to authority you'll find. There are no police. No military.'

'Hedy would be your partner?' Sam assumed.

'The very best,' he confirmed. 'So where y'all from?'

'An alternate version of Earth,' she answered casually.

'Well, alright!' Ken exclaimed. 'I used to watch those spacey tv shows.' He chuckled. 'Who'da thunk it'd be a real possibility?'

Hutch leaned to see through an open door to his right. He knew what the room was for in one glance, because it looked exactly like his favourite place back home. There was machinery, a workbench, tools mounted on the wall and sheets of metals and alloys. 'Mind if I take a gander at your shop, Ken?'

'Go right ahead.' Ken lowered his chair with a flick of a lever, disappearing behind the desk. He re-emerged, appearing to be a little over 100 centimetres tall, moving at a brisk pace to join Hutch. 'Mind the sharps.

Ain't normally such a mess. Hedy's the tidy one. Left to my own devices, things tend to… unsettle around here.'

Hutch detected weary sadness in Ken's voice. 'I'm sorry to hear that. My shop's never been the same since my Elsa passed. She had an uncanny way of finding where everything went, after she'd done away with the filings and whatnot.'

Ken, standing at one metre in height, looked up at him with a knowing smile. 'Well, Mr Branner–'

'Call me Hutch.'

'Hutch, I do believe Elsa and Hedy would have been friends.' He gestured for his three guests to join him.

'You built this city?' Sam asked, looking out the window.

Ken sat on a stool and levered himself up to the workbench. 'We built the builders.' He picked up a steel mask with a man's features. Holding it up to the light, he peered through the eyes to the city skyline. 'They were my earliest model. Harmless automatons.'

Rachel detected guilt in Ken's tone. 'We sent an aircraft to survey the land,' she said. 'Ken, the whole country is…'

'Blown to smithereens,' he guessed. 'Rest of the world ain't lookin' too shabby, I imagine. There was a war, see. The government we had back then funded our Tommies. They were takin' over duties no one wanted to do. I was a commercial success. Made me filthy rich. Hedy did alright too, outfittin' Aussie subs with the latest comms tech; "frequency-hopping", she called it. Her work was the reason we moved here.'

Ken left the workshop, and the others followed back to their seats.

'Hedy'n I were big-time stars till the Allies let all militaries take over production of our Tommies. Gave 'em guns and shipped 'em off to war. Spies infiltrated one of the factories, copied the build plans. Sure enough, they sent an arm of their own version at us.'

Ken set the mask down, leaned on his elbows and stared into the steel face. 'I saw the footage… what my Tommies were doing to people abroad. I wanted to stop production, burn all the factories down. Hedy said, "It's too late, they're gonna bomb us, we're gonna bomb them." So we went underground. Day later, we heard 'em hit.'

'How did Hedy know?' Rachel asked.

'Being their best naval tech, she was well connected. She knew to prepare. We had plenty of supplies, so we waited.' Ken turned side on to gaze out the window. 'Got pretty quiet on the third week. Found out why when it came time to change the air filters.' He cast his eyes to his palms, as though he were there in the bunker again. 'I didn't know what I was lookin' at. It had to be ash, but why was it mustard? I took the filters to Hedy. I'd never seen her turn so white. She said, "It's gas, hon. They're gone. They're all gone."'

Chapter II

The depth of the gorge Lana and Miri crossed, riding in a rope-suspended chair, was obscured in shadow. The man who'd allowed them refuge with his family kindly turned the wheel until Lana and Miri reached the other side. The rope notch above Lana's head met with a wooden latch that triggered a lock mechanism, and they swayed to a halt.

'This looks like the kind of smithing house I grew up in,' said Miri, gazing at the home that was built ten metres from the pulley system. She recognised the measures that had been taken to ventilate the building. The chimney was of appropriate bulk for a furnace, and louvres were built into its walls.

'Your mothers were blacksmiths?' Lana could not count the number of times she and Miri had talked through their nights together, and yet this was news to her. Though she knew Miri's parents were a subject of great pain and loss.

'My birth mother was.' Miri strode toward the door with renewed hope. It opened before she could knock, and both Miri and the woman who opened the door gasped.

'Blazing sun! Who are you?' the woman exclaimed, the cold air turning her face blue. She didn't understand Miri's language when she spoke, so she beckoned her inside. 'Come in, whoever you are. You,' she said to Lana and pointed at a frozen bucket of water. 'Bring that in.' *Their skin isn't blue from the cold. Five fingers?* 'You must be Fyrst Born,' she deduced, based on both their beauty and their petite, athletic builds.

Miri's ears pricked. 'You know of my people?'

Lana translated as soon as her ring console activated, and after introducing Miri and herself, she explained that they had travelled through the Veil and were searching for Miri's parents.

'A daring quest,' the woman said admiringly. 'I am Amir of the Vess.' She pulled back her long brown hair, and used a length of leather to tie it into a bun at the back of her head. 'We are the majority people in this part of the world. Your mind-signals don't work on us, so best you learn our language.'

Lana and Miri followed her down a few steps to a room where a furnace burned. The floor was tiled except for a two-by-two-metre pit of ash.

'Yes, there are other Fyrst Born,' Amir explained while taking off her robe. 'Humans and other creatures also. We have lived together since the Tear.' She hung it over a chair, stepped into the pit, and took handfuls of ash from a bucket. 'Most live in the valley below. My man and I built our home here after I completed my apprenticeship.' Amir covered her body, and she glanced at Miri while applying one last handful to her abdomen. 'You must be the daughter of the Master Smith. You look like her. Do you smith? I could use a hand.'

Miri listened to Lana's translation while arranging her hair the same as Amir's. 'Certainly. Where can we find her?' She disrobed, placed her clothes on the chair and stepped into the ash pit.

Amir tied a cloth sash around her waist, then donned a leather apron and a belt of smithing tools. 'She teaches at the longhouse near the town square.' She found another apron and handed it to Miri. 'My husband takes my wares to the market. You can go with him, once we're done and washed.'

Lana watched Miri and Amir go to work, pounding an assortment of metals into shape. She fetched the ice bucket, which had melted, and steam rose and clouded the ceiling each time they cooled their finished product. Their first half hour of work was done in silence, but once they established a routine, they began to relax and pay compliments to one another's skill. They were making horseshoes for a breed that must have had hooves twice the circumference of a human hand.

'I have not done this since the...' Miri paused and thought it better to use Amir's name for the Collide. 'Since the Tear. Though we had the skill, my sister and I did not build our own forge. We fletched instead and concentrated on defending what we had left.'

Amir listened to Lana's translation while they worked, and nodded solemnly. 'My people, the Vess, are from desert lands. We could not be further removed from what we know. In the first month of the Tear, many ran through the wall of light, taking the chance that home was on the other side. They all perished. How is it that you did not?'

'Technology has become very advanced where I come from,' said Lana. 'We know how to pass through safely.'

Amir breathed through a wave of homesickness before continuing. 'My heart aches for the dunes and the coast of my homelands.' She set down the last shoe and met Lana's gaze. 'The Tear was a day of destruction. Everything we once knew must surely be gone.'

They heard the cabin door open, and Amir's partner called out, saying with relief that the storm had not ruined their crops.

'Come,' Amir called back. 'We have guests.'

He arrived with a full basket of vegetables. Lana greeted him in their language and introduced herself and Miri.

'Since when do we hire Fyrst Born?'

'Hold your tongue, Ahab,' Amir chided. 'With Miri's help, I have beaten out today's order in half the time.'

'I am grateful.' Ahab glanced between Lana and Miri while his words were translated. As he was a trader, he was able to speak Fyrst Born, and so he addressed Miri. 'You do not speak Vess?'

'I am from beyond the wall of light,' Miri explained. 'Amir says you may be able to take me to my mothers.'

'Of course. How in the skies were you able to pass through?' he exclaimed.

'Enough talk,' Amir interjected. 'Pour mead while we wash up. We will drink before you take these shoes into town.'

Miri watched Lana check her ring console for any word about the Sedit from General Lincoln. She shook her head and gave Miri a reassuring look. Miri placed her ash-covered palm against Lana's cheek and rubbed her ear affectionately. She kissed Lana's forehead and whispered her thanks, for being with her on this journey.

'Come, young lovers.' Amir motioned for them to follow after she hung up her smithing gear. 'We have a spout and tub outside.'

When Miri saw that the water was heated by the furnace, her shoulders dropped, and she breathed out with pleasurable anticipation.

The afternoon sun shone on Lana, Miri and Amir bathing in the open air, surrounded by snow, steam rising from the thirty-seven-degree water. Amir tapped her mug against Miri's and said a toast in her native tongue. Miri tapped Lana's, and they all drank toffee-flavoured malt beer.

Lana heard Ahab singing a song, which she guessed to be a Vess folktale. Amir started to hum and then sing from the chorus. Once she had sung all of the lines through, Lana explained to Miri that it was about a traveller who arrived at a spring. The traveller's feet were sore from many days of walking. A woman at the spring treated and fed him, and the two of them fell in love.

Miri joined in at the chorus. Lana had heard Miri sing only once before, at a community gathering in the Ether Realm. It was mournful then, about loss. Her voice was beautiful and powerful. And now, relaxed and so close to finding her parents, Miri sang with hope and joy.

After some time drinking and laughing, Lana, Miri and Amir climbed out of the tub and staggered through the snow back into the house to get dressed. Lana and Miri thanked Amir and promised to visit again. They followed Ahab down the path to the valley. The path through the trees was narrow, but when it opened up, they were able to see over the treetops. Smoke rose from chimneys in the town. A stream ran alongside a mill and a wheat field. Beyond the town were houses and cabins among the trees, and above them was a stunning snow-capped mountain range.

The three of them walked another half hour of winding descent. Once they reached a crossroads, they took the road leading to town. Lana read the signs indicating the directions to Vess and Fyrst Born villages. A wagon rolled by, and she looked in time to see the creature pulling it. The driver was moving the bovine animal at a swift pace. It was a cross between a horse and a buffalo, with a thick black and grey coat and stubby horns.

Ahab said he had to go and deliver the shoes Miri had helped to make. He directed them to the longhouse, and Miri thanked him before they parted ways. Lana could sense that she was nervous. Miri didn't stop to observe the town life, the children running around or the food stalls they walked by. She was staring ahead to the longhouse. And when a side door opened to the right of the building, Miri stopped in her tracks. She saw a woman walk out to the hand rail, pressing tobacco into a pipe.

The afternoon rays were dropping, lighting rooftops orange. The woman held the pipe between her lips, freeing her hands while she used flint stones to light a torch on the porch corner. She lit a stick and her pipe and leaned over the railing to watch two boys running between stalls. She called out to them to slow down, and her gaze followed them up the street. She saw two women standing out in the open, staring at her. The dark-haired woman wore strange, tight-fitting clothing, while the brown-haired woman wore a fur coat. She was Fyrst Born, with familiar features. *Spitting image of…*

Her hands trembled as she took the pipe from her mouth and set it down. Her lips formed her daughter's name, while her feet took her down the steps, to the dirt road, hastening toward Miri.

Miri couldn't move until she felt Lana's hand at her back, gently pushing her to go. She willed her legs into a stride. She found the strength to run, splashed through puddles, and reached out her arms.

Mother and daughter collided, clutching each other tight.

Chapter 12

'We had plenny seeds to plant legumes and other vegetables in our bunker. Full-spectrum lamps kept them happy all year round. And we had access to sea water via a desalination tunnel. Everything was hunky-dory till we ran outta fuel.'

Hutch pointed to Ken's chest. 'Your Tommies are powered by the same kinda gyro keeping you alive...'

'We wanted to steal a bank of them to power our bunker,' Ken said in a frustrated tone. 'But we couldn't get into the storage facility. Not without violence.'

'You invented the gyro,' Rachel said. 'Why would you have to steal them?'

Ken pressed his lips together. 'The Invention Secrecy Act gave the Allied governments the power to take anyone's work. And harnessin' quantum particles that use and create energy was very much something their military wanted control of. Hedy and I had to make do with fossil fuel. It ran dry, so we suited up like a couple'a astronauts and came up to the surface. We headed out to our factory. Found a half dozen Tommies intact. Hedy programmed them to go collect materials and later put 'em to work buildin' wind towers and solar panels. Soon enough, we had renewable power. I built more Tommies and sent those off to find more resources. It took a long time, but here we are.'

Rachel's comms beeped, and she and Sam excused themselves while Ken and Hutch talked.

'It's General Lincoln,' said Rachel. 'The Sedit have been detected.'

'Hutch and I should stay a while longer,' Sam suggested. 'Visit Ken's factory.' She gave Rachel a hug. 'Good luck.'

Shadows were cast on the ice ring around Saturn. Thulu, son of the Sedit King, led thirty warriors in a diamond formation toward Earth. There was a blockade of spaceships 400,000 kilometres from Earth's orbit. Thulu ordered his unit to fan out into a double line formation before the blockade.

General Lincoln ordered his crew to ready all weapons.

The doors to the brig opened, and Rachel entered. She had portaled out of Mechtropolis and teleported on board from San Francisco. She greeted Lincoln and nodded to Saule.

'How are you two holding up?' Rachel asked her.

'We're doing alright, thanks. Kim is pleased to see you. And the Council approved funding to reimburse tickets for the rest of my tour.'

'I'm sure your fans will understand, given the circumstance.'

Rachel looked to a camera feed monitoring the Sedit. They were holding position. 'So you and Captain Valhez couldn't repel them, with a ship more advanced than ours.'

'When the Sedit attacked Kim, the ship was one big target,' Saule explained. 'They were surrounded. General Lincoln has ten ships and forty mobile AMs. We're better prepared.'

Lincoln turned away from the main viewer, which was projecting a magnified view of the Sedit. 'Where's Lana?'

The brig doors opened, and Lana entered carrying what looked like a metal briefcase. 'Talon filled me in on the plan.' She set the case down at her feet. The mood on the brig was tense. All of the crew operating the consoles had to be ready to fire, or to perform tactical manoeuvres without crashing into the other ships that were in blockade formation nearby.

Rachel looked Lana up and down. She was wearing an orange flight suit. 'How did you and Miri go, beyond the Veil?'

'We found her mother. Miri is with her now.' Lana bent down and pressed a button on the metal case. It opened like a clam, and blue light scanned Lana's body. Metal pieces extended with articulated arms and applied chrome panels to her suit more quickly than she or Rachel could follow. Within one minute, Lana was covered from head to toe. Her chrome suit was whirring, applying final fitting adjustments, while a voice inside it asked her to move her arms and step forward and back. The jet engines were now long slits that would fire from under her shoulder blades and from her boots.

'That's amazing!' Saule exclaimed.

'I want one,' Rachel said. She could still see Lana's eyes behind the tinted orange glass that would protect her from the vacuum of space.

'Heck of an improvement,' Lana commented. She had reviewed the suit's weapon specs on her way to Lincoln's ship. It contained high-explosive mini rockets and had a close-combat electromagnetic hammer-fist function.

'Our Rocketeers are in position,' said Lincoln and turned to Lana. 'Ready, Captain Casal?'

Rachel smiled proudly. She was still getting used to Lana having a military rank, and a last name, for that matter.

'Ready, General.'

Lana was guided by an AM out of the brig to an exit chamber. Once she stepped in, he closed the door, vacated the air inside the chamber and opened the outer door, and she drifted into space.

Lana had assisted Talon with outside repairs to the Black Heron in space on a few occasions. But this time, she wasn't tethered to the ship. Fortunately, Pilot Assist mode was active, and the thrusters automatically engaged. The metal panels covering Lana's body gently took hold and oriented her to fly to the Rocketeers waiting for her behind the blockade. Lana didn't see the AMs until one turned their head and beckoned her over. All forty of them were wearing the same silver jet-pack suit, and each group of ten was hugging the rear of a blockade ship, in shadow.

General Lincoln gave the order to advance, and the blockade of ships flew toward the Sedit in an arrowhead formation. Thulu and his warriors approached, gradually increasing their speed.

The Sedit warriors' arms glowed, and they swung their hands forward, firing molten rocks at the blockade. Lincoln's ship dipped under the volley. A ship to his left was unable to manoeuvre in time and took damage to its hull. The left and right flanks took formation. All ships fired their torpedoes; the Rocketeers detached, and each group split to fly under and over the Sedit. Lana joined the upper group and prepared her high-explosive rockets. She held her arms forward, chose a target and fired.

Six of the Sedit were destroyed. They returned fire, but the Rocketeers were small targets and were able to evade the smouldering balls of energy.

'Don't let them group together,' Saule advised General Lincoln.

Lincoln spotted five Sedit locking formation. He was about to order his crew to target them, but the group was already descending on a ship and burning through the hull. If Lincoln fired on them, his torpedoes would likely hit his own fleet.

Lincoln ordered five Rocketeers to strike. Lana joined the detachment after one of the five was killed by a Sedit blast. They flew in tandem to the ship and engaged the enemy hand to hand. Lana heard Saule speaking in her helmet, advising that the Sedit were skilled at finding their opponents' weak points. And in that moment, an AM was dismembered in front of her.

Lana used her suit's hammer-fists to knock a Sedit off a Rocketeer. Another spear-tackled her, and the two of them rolled across the ship's hull. Lana fired her thrusters enough to stabilise. When her feet reached the hull, the suit automatically engaged magnetic grip. The Sedit advanced, turning his hands into blades. He jabbed at her shoulder joints. Lana deflected the left strike, but was stabbed in her right. She had armoured her skin in time, but her suit was damaged. It released hot foam from the point of penetration, which set as a flexible layer, keeping Lana's oxygen from escaping. The Sedit reformed one hand and reached for her. She chopped his wrist and pushed him back. She drove her hammer-fist into his beak, shattering it into floating pieces.

Lana could only hear dim thuds inside her helmet from exchanging blows with the Sedit. The silence, despite the violence and nearby explosions, was eerie.

Another Sedit was thrown toward Lana by an exploding rocket. She fired her boots, twirled and swung a kick into his abdomen. She flew under him and rose with a hammer-fist uppercut that sent him flying end over end. She aimed her right arm, fired a rocket and destroyed him.

Prince Thulu saw that his warriors were being singled out before any could concentrate fire together. He signalled them to fall back.

Rachel stood next to Lincoln and watched the Sedit retreat. Thulu gave more swinging arm signals, and his warriors flew toward him at speed. The first to reach him, a female Sedit, drew her arms forward and held her body straight like a spear. She didn't slow on her approach, and Thulu exposed his chest. She stabbed through him on impact. Waist-deep in her Prince, her light and her basalt body combined with his. Thulu grew to twice his regular size, and another two of his warriors flew and stabbed into him. Their bodies glowed neon blue and melted into his.

'Um…' Rachel looked over Lincoln's shoulder at Saule. 'Is he…?'

'He's absorbing his warriors,' Saule confirmed. 'We need to stop this. Now.'

Miri spent the night at her mother's house. The two of them laughed and cried in each other's arms and talked until morning. Miri woke to the smell of freshly baked bread, and to the sound of market holders calling out to attract attention to their food and wares.

'Good morning.' Miri's mother, Lowen, was standing in the doorway to the guest bedroom. She carried a tray of bread and fruit and a mug of tea to the bedside table, setting it down. Her long white hair draped like a curtain when she bent to kiss her daughter's forehead. Creases lined her brow and further pronounced her smile.

Fyrst Born would refer to their second mother by name or as their "other". Miri had asked Lowen where her other, Ina, was the day before. Lowen had said Ina was beyond the village, and that the two of them should take the road through the forest to go and see her.

'Does Ina travel outside the village often?' Miri asked and climbed out of bed to open the window. The cool air was invigorating. A man on the street stopped to gaze at Miri. He was shoved roughly by his wife when she saw he was looking at a naked woman.

'Bloody Fyrst Born,' Miri heard the woman grumble.

'Eat,' Lowen urged without answering Miri's question. 'I'll pack us something for the road, then we'll go and see your other.'

Miri chewed buttered bread while she got dressed. She looked down at her wristband and began to worry about Lana. She was there when Lana warned the Sedit Prince never to return to Earth. She saw what he was, and the fire in his eyes told her what he was capable of.

'Ready?' Lowen asked at the door.

Miri nodded, and they set off. They walked for a half hour through the forest outside the village. Lowen related her memory of the day everyone was separated.

'The Vess are a very adaptable people,' she said. 'They built sturdy shelters in the first days, and houses within weeks of the Tear. They took in people like me and your other.'

Chimes hung in the trees. The cool breeze was blowing ribbons of cotton, all varying in colour. There were ornaments among the roots, weathered possessions and trinkets. A peach dress caught Miri's eye, flowing like silk from a branch.

'These are offerings, and the belongings of those who lost hope...' Lowen started, swallowing grief, before adding, 'Those who walked into this forest with no intention of returning home. For our true homes and our families were beyond our reach.' She stopped before a bend in the road, staring at the worn earth where many, now lost, had walked their final path. She ushered Miri around the bend to a clearing. 'Let us visit your other.'

Visit? Miri didn't understand. The glare of the sun obscured her vision when they entered the clearing. There were rows of stacked stone either side of her, and when she shielded her eyes, she saw the rows stretched a hundred metres across an open field.

Lowen continued ahead. She took a left turn at the second row and stopped at a stack of rocks. Miri arrived beside her, and Lowen gently drew her daughter down to kneel. Dried purple flowers were wedged in between the rocks. Lowen took a pouch of water from her bag and wet her hand. She pressed her palm against the top rock and wiped the dirt from chiselled words.

Ina. Mother. Daughter. Love of my life.

Miri's eyes grew hot. Her shoulders trembled, and she felt her mother's arms surround and squeeze her.

'Did she...' Miri stared back at the road. She thought she could hear whispers. 'In the forest?' she sobbed. 'Alone?'

Lowen turned Miri's shoulders so that her daughter could see only her. 'Miri, you have to understand. All her days were study and work. She was obsessed with finding answers about the Tear, every moment sinking deeper into "why", into "who". It consumed her.'

Miri wiped her eyes, shaking her head. 'Who? What are you talking about?'

Lowen gazed back at Ina's grave. 'The Collector. "He did this," she used to say. "He took our daughters."'

'I wish I had found a way to you sooner,' Miri told her. 'But now we can reunite all families.'

Lowen let out a doubtful sigh. 'We don't know how many divided lands there are.'

'Then we must try to find all of them,' Miri stated resolutely. She kissed the smooth rock, stood and placed her hand on her mother's shoulder. 'I must see her work.'

'Miri, none of it makes sense. Ina's mind was–'

'That name is known in my world as well,' Miri said flatly. 'I will find the Collector. And he will pay.'

Chapter 13

Lincoln ordered all ships to concentrate fire on the giant Sedit, Prince Thulu. Then he ordered the ship with the compromised hull to return to Earth. The pilot confirmed. The temperature inside was dropping rapidly. The last of the remaining oxygen had been sucked out into space through the hole in the hull. Only AMs were aboard operating weapons and navigation.

The ship had flown only a few hundred metres from the blockade when three Sedit warriors gave chase. One dove through the damaged hull and attacked the AMs inside.

Lincoln heard the distress call, strode to the armoury and reached for a metal suitcase on the assembly bench. Rachel's hand stopped him.

'You're needed here,' she said, and set the case down at her feet.

'Good luck.' Lincoln handed her a flight suit and returned to his station.

'I'll come with you,' Saule offered.

'This is the only suit left.'

Saule's eyes glowed, and she produced a force field that hugged her body with a golden hue. Rachel circled her and saw that her feet were no longer touching the ground.

'Alright, then. Let's go.'

Thulu's remaining warriors were destroyed by the blockade ships. He created a shield from his right hand to protect himself from the torpedoes coming at him.

'Captain Casal, you are in command of the remaining Rocketeers,' Lincoln told Lana. 'Do something about Thulu's shield.'

'Copy that,' she replied confidently. 'All units on me.' She fired her thrusters and flew in an arc over Thulu's shield. His right arm was tracking her and her team, making a molten boulder in his palm.

'Talon, now!'

While Thulu had been occupied with fortifying himself, Talon had approached from behind. She slowed the Black Heron until its beak tip was between his shoulder blades. With the defence system engaged, she flipped a switch that discharged one hundred thousand volts of electricity the moment her ship touched Thulu's back.

The Prince shuddered, his jaws opening wide in silent agony. Lana's Rocketeers fired at his wrist, and the explosions severed his shield. The blockade targeted Thulu's chest, and torpedoes ruptured his body, blowing off hunks of basalt.

When the Black Heron depleted its charge, Thulu threw two molten boulders and swung his fist, driving it through one ship and into another. Both exploded, while the next craft in line managed to avoid his devastating attack.

Lincoln ordered heat-seeking torpedoes to strike the massive flaming objects that were headed for Earth.

Rachel and Saule fed themselves through the hole in the hull of the ship that was on a return course to Earth. Sparks from damaged consoles lit the interior with intermittent flashes, casting abstract shadows. Saule gasped when the arm of an AM floated in front of her. She was startled again when a live crew member came through the brig doors. The female AM's uniform was burnt and tattered. Saule tapped her comms to hear her.

'…down to comms power, ma'am,' the pilot reported. 'We're being pulled into Earth's gravitational field. The ship is likely to break up on entry and create multiple crash vectors. We're sending broad warnings to countries below.'

'The rest of your crew?' Saule asked.

She took a cutting torch from a cabinet. 'Two trapped back there,' she replied, with a nod to where she'd come from.

Rachel looked around. 'Where's the Sedit who attacked you?'

'It's heading to Earth with the others that breached the blockade.' The AM handed Rachel an M16 assault rifle and spare magazine. 'We'll wait for the other Rocketeers to come get us. And ma'am, we saw two large objects fly by us. Torpedoes intercepted, but did minimal damage. They're going to hit Earth.'

'Your name?' Rachel asked, committing the pilot's brave face to memory, knowing that she and the others were not going to be rescued in time.

'Unit 201, ma'am,' she replied, jaw clenched, eyes watering.

'I'll see that General Lincoln knows of your sacrifice.' Rachel turned to Saule, who was glancing helplessly between the two women. 'We have to go.'

'Earth needs you,' 201 told Saule when she protested.

Saule and Rachel flew out of the plummeting ship. Reports of sightings came in through Rachel's comms. A Sedit was flying over Indonesia. She brought up a holographic feed from her ring console that was linked to a satellite tracking the invader.

Lincoln's ships continued firing on Thulu. After Lana and her Rocketeers had exhausted their ammunition, she ordered them to pursue the remaining Sedit on Earth.

Lincoln's forces were doing some damage, trying to draw Thulu to the moon. Lana gazed from the bright blue of Earth to the raging giant Prince. He was willing to destroy everything in his path to get what he came for. Lana knew she could not reason with him. Not in her current state. She looked down at her suit and concentrated on using her Aspect ability to grow. Her armour plates parted and realigned to meet her size. The suit reached its limit and sounded a malfunction alarm, before retracting and disassembling itself into a suitcase. Lana's flight suit tore from the width and depth of her enormous frame, revealing black lines patterning her red marble body.

Thulu's eyes widened, and he froze, staring in disbelief at the silhouette of a powerful figure growing larger against the sunlit moon.

Lana flew over the blockade, her fiery eyes glaring. She struck Thulu across his jaw, and they grappled each other and tumbled into the moon's gravitational pull. Soon the two of them appeared miniature against the barren expanse. They hurtled down the side of a crater, while Lana blocked Thulu's jabs with her forearms and struck him left and right across the head with her elbows. She grappled his neck, kneed his stomach and swung him hard into the rock wall. Thulu cried out when his arm broke away from his shoulder. His severed limb shattered, and the expired bodies of Sedit warriors drifted like litter. Lana double-kicked Thulu in the chest in time to push away from the wall before they reached the crater floor.

Thulu landed heavily, throwing dust and rock high upon impact. Lana hit at an angle, and her body ploughed a deep gash in the crater. She rose and shook lumps of rock from her hair and shoulders. She saw the dust cloud hanging weightless.

Thulu staggered, reduced to his original size. He threw a flaming rock at Lana, and it bounced off her abdomen, while her size gradually reduced. He dashed at her and threw another. Lana backhanded him, sending him bouncing across the crater floor. He picked himself up, felt how little flame he had left inside of him, slumped to his knees and gazed helplessly at the big blue planet rising above the edge of the crater.

Saule and Rachel were engaging a Sedit warrior halfway up a volcano in East Java, Indonesia. Lava flowed in lines between them, while Rachel fired her M16 on the Sedit and he sent volleys of flaming balls in return.

Saule rose high, deflected a fireball with her force-field and shot an energy blast into the Sedit's chest. He fell and rolled to the nearest stream of lava. Plunging his hand into it, he roared with the surge of power he received. He fired a gout of lava at Saule, and she was encased by the molten rock. The weight of it drew her down, and she slammed into the hillside.

Rachel shouldered her rifle and danced down the shale after Saule. Glowing balls of rock flew past her head, and she fired her jet suit thrusters, flew low to avoid the next volley, and skimmed the surface with her left hand as she arrived beside Saule. She punched the shell encasing her and pulled her out.

'He has the upper hand as long as he has lava,' Rachel said. 'We need water. Can you or Kim form it somehow?'

'We'll try.'

Rachel readied her rifle and provided cover fire. Kim instructed Saule in the art of forming, and the two concentrated on making water. Saule moved her hands in the fluid, martial-art motion Kim described. Liquid shone in the afternoon light and coalesced into an expanding ball of water.

The Sedit warrior took bullets to his chest and face from Rachel's assault. He cursed and plunged both hands into the lava. By the time he saw water falling on him, it was too late to free his hands. Steam blinded him, but he could hear the jet-propelled woman approaching. He turned his head and spat lava at her. Rachel shouldered through the hot splash, rolled in mid-air, drew her arm back a half metre before the Sedit, and drove her hammer-fist into his head.

The warrior's arms snapped from the cooling rock. The impact spun him into a barrel roll. Chunks of his own shale fanned out from his stubs as he rotated and hit the ground. The melting parts of Rachel's suit detached in pieces, and the exposed shoulder of her flight suit exploded into an extinguishing powder.

The Sedit elbowed himself awkwardly to his knees. Saule approached while images of Kim's people lying dead and burning on the field of Candlestick Park swam in her mind. She took hold of the Sedit warrior's head, lit her hand golden and drew back her fist.

'We were following orders,' the Sedit croaked.

Saule stood with her fist powered, ready to destroy him. She felt Kim's rage driving her to end him. *Kim, he's done*, she reasoned and withdrew her power.

Rachel spun around and aimed her rifle when she heard footfalls approaching. She lowered her aim when the steam vapour cleared to reveal Lana, under Thulu's one arm, assisting his limping gait. He was literally falling apart.

'He surrenders,' Lana explained.

Rachel's helmet retracted. 'Peaceful dialogue would've spared lives!' she barked at him.

'We saw that you were already allied with the Lustitians,' Thulu retorted, wearily. 'We–'

'Call off your warriors,' she demanded.

'Another wave are on their way. You cannot win.'

Lana set Thulu down next to the lava flow. 'I could have left you to die on the moon. Let us at least negotiate.'

Thulu looked up at Lana and back to Rachel. 'Let him drink and take flight,' he said, gesturing to the other Sedit. 'He will find the others and stop the next wave.'

Rachel nodded to Saule, and she let him hobble to the lava. Saule shrugged. 'Kim says this'll only keep them alive for a few days.' She watched the Sedit regain power to his wings. He gave Thulu a confirming nod after receiving orders and took to the sky. 'They would need to drain subterranean chambers. It would upset Earth's natural–'

'You would let us all die? Of course you would, Lustitian.' Thulu spat sulphur on the rocks.

Saule's eyes flashed yellow, and she struck Thulu with a lightning-fast force field swipe across his jaw before anyone could blink.

'Her name is Kim!' she shouted. 'You attacked her crew unprovoked. You are a coward!'

Rachel saw that gaps had opened in Thulu's chest. She stepped between him and Saule. 'What is that?' she asked, pointing at a burning orb spinning in Thulu's chest.

'My flogath,' he answered reluctantly. 'Your kind have a heart. Sedit have a…'

'Dynamo,' Rachel prompted. She looked to the others, who were all staring at her curiously. 'Mechtropolis.' She turned back to Thulu. 'I may be able to help your people survive without taking our planet. Give me your word that we have a ceasefire agreement.'

'You have my word,' Thulu stated.

Lana checked her ring console when multiple notifications sounded. Her eyes widened as she saw the news reports flooding across her holographic screen.

Chapter 14

owen set a cup of herbal tea down beside Miri. They were back at the longhouse, in Ina's study. The walls were covered with notes, clues that were linked by lengths of twine to other clustered notes. Miri pored over Ina's papers while Lowen grew increasingly concerned.

'You have been at it for hours. Take a break. It might make sense in the morning, when you see it with fresh eyes.'

Miri arched her back and stretched her muscles. 'Ina mentions her Runes. The ones passed down through her family line.'

Lowen shrugged. 'I have searched and cannot find them.'

Miri was flicking through a bound journal. She found that the last three pages had been torn out. 'That's odd…'

Lowen nodded. 'She often used the last pages to make maps.'

'I've looked at all of her material,' said Miri, staring about the study. 'I found no map.'

'Even if it was here, I don't think it led her to what she was seeking.' Lowen picked up some loose papers from a chair and sat herself down with a sigh.

Miri pushed her fingers through her hair. 'If we find the map, we will at least know how far she got. Don't you want to know?'

Lowen met her daughter's pleading tone with parental resolve. 'Not at the risk of losing you to Ina's obsession.'

Miri reached out and took her mother's hand. 'You're not going to lose me. Not again.' She saw the paper Lowen was holding. 'What is that?'

Lowen read it despondently. 'It's an order for paper, graphite and bindings. Ina was a regular customer at the Scribe Guild. They make scrolls, books. Their cartographers have mapped all of the known land…'

Lowen stood with Miri, and they both said the same thing.

'They make maps.'

There was a knock at the door, and Lana stepped in. Miri rushed to hug her. She quickly released her and checked her for wounds.

'Are you alright?' Miri's brow furrowed at Lana's vacant expression. Her eyes were red, as though she'd been crying. 'What happened?'

'One of the blockade ships went down,' Lana murmured. 'Broke up on re-entry. The wreckage showered on towns and cities in Texas, Oklahoma and Missouri. The death toll…' She bit her lip, both sad and angry. 'I sent Lincoln's Rocketeers after the Sedit. They scattered to the Middle East and Russia. Thulu threw meteors at Earth. One hit an ocean, the other hit Rome. The death toll is expected to be in the thousands.'

Miri took hold of Lana and stared into her watering eyes.

'None of this would have happened with Kiyol support,' Lana seethed between clenched teeth, tears spilling down her cheeks.

'The people of Earth made their choice,' Miri said. 'You did your best to—'

Lana uttered a dry laugh and wiped her eyes. 'Thulu absorbed his army and grew into a giant.' She chuckled, realising how crazy it sounded. 'I had to match his size and fight him.'

Miri was confused. 'You grew?'

'I used the Mutjal Jakti,' Lana clarified and glanced from Miri to Lowen's raised brow. 'Wh-why are you looking at me like that?'

Lowen exchanged an apprehensive glance with Miri. 'Among our people, we believe it to be dangerous, fatal even, to overdraw our power.'

'I threw him into the moon,' Lana stuttered, before losing her temper and raising her voice. 'He would have destroyed Earth and every ungrateful bastard down there who voted to turn their back on our allies!'

Lowen raised her hands apologetically. 'I have offended you. I am sorry.'

Lana's chest was heaving, and she allowed Miri to guide her to a chair. 'No, I'm sorry, Lowen,' she whispered, her head in her hands. 'Stupid human crap going on back home that…' She let out a tired sigh. 'Maybe I shouldn't have used the power like that, but Thulu had to be stopped.'

'And I wish I could have seen you do it,' Miri offered supportively. 'It is the cost which concerns us. Fyrst Born who have summoned greater power to bolster their Mutjal Jakti have been abducted and never seen again.'

Lana raised her head. 'By who?'

'We don't know,' said Lowen. 'And you didn't know that you shouldn't have used it so.'

'You must have summoned such celestial might to...' Miri turned to Ina's cluttered table.

'It was pretty awesome,' Lana reminisced.

'The Collector,' Miri deduced. 'It has to be him. Who else could take a person out of their world without a trace?'

Lana hazarded a guess. 'This Collector guy collided your worlds?'

'Olin thinks so. He is a Shaman in my world who practices astral projection,' Miri added, with an explanatory glance to Lowen. 'He has tried to find answers, but all he has been able to tell us is that we are trapped by... well, he sensed that many powerful beings tower over us, but only one of them was present during the collide: the Collector.'

Lana was taking in the room. She knew it wasn't Lowen's; her skill was smithing. 'Where is...?' She saw Miri's pained expression.

'My other is dead.'

Lowen waited as Miri and Lana embraced for a silent moment. 'We were about to go and speak to the scribes,' she said to Lana. 'Join us.'

Miri and Lana followed her to the front door. A chill wind blew against them when they stepped out onto the porch. Miri took Lana's hand. 'We will not let this Collector take you.' She raised her voice over the chatter among the market goers. 'We will confront–'

Lana stopped when Miri paused. She looked at her, and opened her mouth to ask what was wrong. All sound had stopped. Miri's hair was swept back from her shoulders, held by the wind. Lowen's hair was partially blown across her face. But there was no breeze. Still holding Miri's hand, Lana stared down the street at the dozens of villagers frozen mid-stride, about to buy wares, or pushing wheelbarrows.

'I am you.'

It was a voice Lana could never forget. She descended the porch and walked between the people on the street. She felt a presence behind her, steeled herself and turned around.

Dark, knotted hair hung to the hips of the naked, blood-soaked woman standing before her.

'Inside you,' Queen Galai croaked. She used a bone dagger to cut a fresh downward line of red between her breasts. 'All that you fear.'

'You're not her.' Lana swallowed and tried to control her breathing.

Galai dashed forward and plunged the dagger into Lana's chest. She studied Lana, impressed that she had stood her ground. 'Well done.'

Galai's voice changed to a man's. She removed the intangible dagger from Lana, and her form rippled until she became Garwyn, the virtual teacher and mentor Lana had spent many lessons with during her early schooling. 'How did you know you would not be harmed?'

'Normally, I can pick up signals from a person's brain.' Lana exhaled, relieved her hunch that this being wasn't tangible was right. 'You're not emitting anything. You don't even have a scent. Who are you?'

Garwyn looked beyond the market to the mountain ranges. 'You seek a collector of worlds.'

'The Collector,' Lana clarified.

'*The?*' Garwyn glanced back at Lana and scoffed. 'There is a whole school of them. A College. Collecting is their singular purpose. The Collector you seek is quite skilled at creating biomes.'

'Biomes?' Lana retorted. 'They're tearing families apart. Their "collecting" has to stop.'

Garwyn's eyes lit up when Lana's anger grew and her tone struck with a threat. 'Would you be willing to kill to stop them?' he asked with a scheming sideways stare.

'If I have to,' Lana said with conviction.

Garwyn's fingers and thumbs met in front of his chest while he looked the young woman before him up and down. 'We observed your power. The Keeper of the Well was alarmed that you were able to draw so much energy from our matter, so quickly and without proper training, and without killing yourself.' He circled her, observing her strong physique. 'The Keeper sent me to subject you to the trial I give everyone who overdraws from the Well. If you pass, you are worthy, and you can continue to draw when needed.'

'If I don't?'

'She will throw you into the Well, and everything you are will become matter and energy to be used by someone more deserving.'

Lana's head was filled with information she was struggling to process. *There's more than one Collector. Fyrst Born power taps energy from a well controlled by–*

'The universe is so much more vast and complicated than you realise.' Garwyn changed his form again. Horns grew out of his head, his skin turned red, and his legs bent and transformed into a goat's. He changed again. This time, warts grew on his nose and his skin turned green. He turned into an old woman holding a broomstick between her legs.

Lana's eyes narrowed, trying to figure out this being's "singular purpose". 'Fear,' she guessed.

He changed and settled into the form of what looked to Lana like a demonic Sasquatch. His deep, creeping words seethed between powerful fangs. 'I live to paralyse, torture and torment, for as long as mortal beings perceive me as real.'

'This is most frightening version of you yet,' Lana said, her throat dry. 'Is that… are you some kind of Gigantopithecus from hell?'

'What?' Fear's eyes flashed red. 'No. I am a Yowie.'

'You're not the everyday fear that everyone has.'

Fear shook his fury head. 'Like an idea that gains momentum and is immortalised by mortals, regular fear is a tool and a hindrance.' He placed his long fingers on his broad chest and smiled innocently. 'I am but a tool, created and commanded by my Lord, the Keeper. Which brings us to the business at hand. She demands a trial. But I wish no ill upon you, Lana. In fact, it is my Lord's wish to bring about a change in our people's way of life. The demise of the Collectors would be a good start.'

'Can't you just–'

'No,' said Fear.

Lana waited, watching Fear's intent and creepy eyes watching hers from beneath his bushy brow. No further explanation came. 'No?'

'We lower beings are not permitted to interfere with the destiny of mortals, unless commanded by our Lord,' he explained. 'It makes them very angry when we play with their toys. Punishment for doing so is usually death, but…' Fear held his giant hands up by his sides. 'This figment cannot be killed. Their anger will instead be transferred to you.' He spoke with genuine concern. 'I have told you everything I can. I do not know where to find the Collector you seek.' Fear jabbed his finger at Miri with a hopeful expression. 'Your woman is following a promising lead. Find the map. It will take you to him. But hurry. His Lord will come for you.'

'Do you know what happened to Ina?' When Lana turned her head from Miri to look back at Fear, he was gone.

'–him together. I promise.'

Lana found herself standing on the porch of Lowen's house, and she felt Miri tugging her hand and the wind blowing again.

Lana walked on quickly, causing Miri and Lowen to hasten. 'The Collector creates worlds for a Lord,' she told them. 'We have to find the map and get out of here. And I mean out of this realm.'

'Lana, what are you talking about?' Miri pleaded, running with Lowen, trying to keep up as they pushed through the crowded street.

Lowen stopped Lana when they reached the Scribe Guild longhouse. 'You two wait here. I'll speak to them.' She locked determined eyes on the Scribe Guild and strode through the open door.

'Someone just spoke to me,' Lana confided to Miri. 'A guy who I think is the essence of Fear. He either froze time or spoke in my mind faster than time.'

'Fate favours our search,' Lowen announced, returning with a leather-bound book and a rolled map. 'They said these were about to be sent out to me. They're Ina's, and they were found in the forest, just recently. There are bite marks in the binding. An animal must have carried it from where she dropped it.' Lowen read from the first page. '"I passed the trial and was free to access the Well—"'

A woman cried out in alarm, and the three of them looked to where she was pointing.

Something was snaking across the ground. It was translucent, thick and surging along the dirt like a vine. It found a butcher chopping meat and struck its tip into the back of his head. The man was lifted a foot off the ground and then set back down. He locked his eyes on Lana and strode toward her.

From ten paces away, the man stopped and threw his meat cleaver. It sailed end over end, the blade glinting in the sunlight. Lana swung her leg across her body and clapped the inside of her boot against the flat of the cleaver, sending it clattering onto the Scribe Guild veranda.

Two more tentacles descended from above. The sound of the market changed immediately. Two men tackled the butcher, and a woman screamed when her husband's feet left the ground.

Miri's eyes followed the vines to the sky. She could see a man through the glare of the sun. 'Run!' she cried, pushing her mother to the village gates.

Lana opened a portal ahead of them. She ducked under a curved blade, side-kicked her attacker and ran while the vine-controlled marketgoers gave chase.

The three escaped through the sphere, and it closed.

Chapter 15

Since Hutch and Sam were still with Ken in Mechtropolis, Rachel was able to bring them all up to speed on the Sedit situation through Home Realm comms.

'Our Chief Medical Officer, Jolie, assures me that scanning your chest would be a non-invasive procedure,' she explained to Ken.

'Come on in with your gadgets. I'm happy to help.' The transmission ended, and Ken chuckled, shaking his head in disbelief. 'My stars, aliens are actually out there. It was a popular subject in films and comic books before the war, but I never would'a believed they actually existed.'

The doors to the Overseer's office opened, and Rachel guided Jolie in.

'Welcome, Doc. Where do ya want–' Ken paused when he saw Rachel. 'Forgive me for sayin' so, Miss Navara...' he started gently. 'Soldiers we knew who'd come back from the war in the East had the same look you do right now. What happened?'

Rachel's stony expression held, but her first words were strained. 'If you have everything you need...' She looked to Sam to receive a pained but supportive nod. 'I should be getting back to the search.' She turned and walked out before Jolie could reply.

Ken watched the doors close and hung his head solemnly.

'There are people under rubble,' Jolie said quietly, with a glance to Hutch. 'Talon and Bell are working in Rome now. Your and local dogs have been invaluable.' She cleared her throat and spied a table in Ken's workshop through the open door. 'If you could hop on that table, Ken, I'll be right with you.' She handed Sam her equipment and gestured to Hutch. 'Do you have any units in reserve that we can program to secure this site?'

Hutch shook his head. 'Lincoln has every available unit.' He lowered his voice. 'Helping the Sedit makes me sick to my stomach. Did the Council agree to this?'

Jolie leaned back, surprised. 'You didn't hear...' Her expression darkened. 'Hutch, Sao Paulo was ground zero. The Council building and everyone in it are gone.'

Hutch's jaw slackened, and he reached for a chair. Jolie helped him into it, but he held up one hand. 'Go do the thing,' he said. 'I'll need a minute.'

Once the device keeping Ken alive was mapped, Jolie used her console at his desk to analyse the digital model. Hutch was still there, staring across the room, while Jolie tapped a layer tab on the model program she was using and swiped through the first two slides of Ken's chest device. She discovered the implant was a gyro.

'I heard you and Lincoln have been given permission to move in together,' Sam said quietly to Jolie.

'I've been meaning to talk to you about that,' Jolie said, trying to mask her indignant tone. 'Our request was denied, at first. We were told to postpone "any further emotional engagement", like Lincoln and I are in some kind of love program that can be paused.' She leaned on Ken's desk and gave Sam a suspicious look. 'A week later, they retracted the rejection.'

'Dad and I threatened to withdraw from the scientific community,' Sam stated casually.

Jolie was taken aback. 'You were willing to do that for us?'

Sam placed her hand on Jolie's. 'You're our friends. And organic or not, we're all in an emergent, evolutionary state. I'm not gonna stand by and let human bureaucracy get in the way of what is evolving between you and Lincoln.'

Jolie wiped moisturising fluid from her cheeks. Her body was able to detect sand, dirt or dry air and release fluid to clear her vision, but the fluid was also released in times when an emotional response was necessary. She hugged Sam and thanked her.

These seemingly human actions were programmed. Despite this knowledge, Sam still felt Jolie's warmth. Talon was an example she drew in comparison. Talon received all of the basic emotional response programming, but she rarely used it. Talon's digital nursery began with violence. Jolie's began with healing.

Saule walked into the Overseer's office, after having spoken with General Lincoln in Home Realm. She caught a glimpse of Ken's data on Jolie's pad, and Kim asked her if she could get a closer look. Saule introduced herself to Sam and Jolie.

'I've heard your songs about Silica,' Jolie told her. 'They're very power-ful. It's a good thing you're doing, reminding people of what happened.'

Saule felt a sudden wave of shock and awe. 'Thank you. It's an hon-our to meet you, ma'am.'

Jolie smiled humbly. 'We're going to need Kim's input on this,' she said, nodding to the data pad.

'She says it's possible to transplant Ken's gyro hearts into the Sedit, but it would take matter forming to fuse metal to basalt. Does he have the heart machines here?'

'That's the wrinkle,' said Ken, overhearing their conversation on his way in. 'Can't letcha harvest tickers from mah Tommies. You'll need the prototype.'

Sam turned to Ken, not liking his defeated tone. 'Where is the pro-totype?'

'In a mansion called Contrivance,' he said, casting an angry glare to the window. 'Hedy's being kept there against her will.'

'Why didn't you tell us sooner, man?' Hutch exclaimed. 'Our people can break her out.'

'I thought you and Hedy were the only people here?' Sam queried.

'It's complicated,' Ken said. 'We are the only people. The mansion's a machine. One we didn't build. Contrivance built itself.'

Lana, Miri and Lowen walked through the forest in Miri's home realm toward the Fyrst Born village. 'I sent Sam a message, asking her to have a probe sent to your world,' Lana told Lowen. 'If the tentacle crea-ture is still there, I'll go back and lure it away, so my people can send medical aid.'

'It was clearly after you,' Lowen murmured, still shocked by what she had seen. 'That might have been your test.'

'Was it the being who stopped time?' Miri asked, speaking as quickly as her heart was beating. 'Did he attack the market? And by escaping, did you pass the test?'

'I don't know,' Lana replied, uncertainly. 'Fear said he's a figment. He can't physically hurt anyone.'

They soon arrived at Fyrst Born tree houses, and Lana stopped to say goodbye.

'I will follow once Mother is settled,' said Miri.

'Go, Miri,' Lowen insisted. 'Your guards will show me to your sister's home.' Lowen still held the scroll that she was given by the Scribe Guild. 'She and I will study the map.'

Lana gave Lowen a spare ring console and showed her how to use it.

'Contact us when you are ready,' Miri told her. 'Together, we will find and confront those responsible for separating us.'

Lana opened a portal, and they leant into salt wind as soon as they stepped through it, trudging through the sands of the canyon near Stone River. They came upon the hidden rock door where Lana had found the AM unit Ian. The edges were blackened, and it was difficult to open.

'This is the place you told me about,' Miri called over the howling wind. 'Why are we here?'

'I'm not convinced this is as far as Sabre Company got with their plan.'

They entered the burnt-out room and closed the door behind them.

'I have to get to the bottom of this before I can deal with anything else. Sabre Company must've had contingencies. There has to be more here.' Lana paced the edges of the interior, looking up and down the walls. 'Look for a switch, a latch, something that—'

'Found it,' said Miri, after feeling a panel under the cabinet that held the DNA sample drawers. She pressed it, and turning gears sounded behind the wall furthest from the door. It retreated five feet, revealing a trapdoor.

Lana drew her side-arm, aimed and descended slowly. Lights blinked on ahead of them, and they arrived in a low-ceilinged basement. There were four cylindrical pods either side of the small space. Backlights came on, illuminating two pods with a pile of ash at the bottom of each. Two contained translucent gel. Lana stood close, peering through the clouded interior. She heard Miri gasp behind her at the same time she reacted. The women they were looking at were almost identical to Lana. One with shorter and lighter hair, the other taller, with long black hair.

'They look as though they share your genes,' Miri noted. Her hand covered her mouth when she saw the empty pods. The screens mounted before them flashed *Growth Failure*. The inside of the glass was blackened. Miri turned away and placed her hand on Lana's shoulder. 'This is horrible.'

'It's Sabre Company,' Lana replied angrily. 'They knew their corrupted AMs wouldn't survive, so they made new soldiers.'

'You have told me about this man…' Miri was reading the data readout for the shorter woman in front of her. 'Dr Kindred. She is to be teleported to him upon release. Is he not dead?'

'Rachel's brother killed him.' Lana tapped the command menu. The teleport sequence showed an error. They weren't going anywhere.

'Then these versions of you are safe,' Miri offered optimistically. 'They have not been manipulated.'

Lana turned her uncertain look from Miri to the larger clone sleeping in the gel. She flinched when she saw the clone's eyes open and flutter closed. The readout indicated a steady flow of nutrients. She tapped at a different menu to find that the clone's neural input was stuck in a loop between combat training and religious history. A warning tone sounded, and Lana turned to see that the smaller clone's life sign reading was showing *Nutrient Depletion*. 'We have to get them out.'

Miri accessed her comms. 'I'll contact Talon.'

'No. We can't keep them.' Lana had to think quickly. She checked Talon's location. She was aboard the Black Heron, and it was stationary. Lana programmed a portal to open outside the bunker door. 'Help me carry them.'

Lana pressed the release commands on the pod screens. The gel was heated and turned to liquid in seconds. Jets of water cleaned both women, and a fan blew hot hair to dry them. Miri leaned against the metal door and fought the salt wind to push it open. The shining mercury sphere appeared a metre away. She and Lana rushed out of the bunker with the unconscious women and into the portal.

It was night on the other side, and rain pelted down on them. Miri smelt fresh soil and perfume from a rose bed nearby. Lana set the taller woman down on the lush lawn and ran across the suburban backyard to the back door of a house. She opened the flywire screen and paused with her fist clenched, ready to hammer on the door. She tapped at her ring console and programmed an exit portal.

'Lana, where are we?' Miri called.

Lana hammered on the door four times, ran back to take Miri's hand and pulled her through the portal. They arrived inside the loading bay of the Black Heron. Lana grabbed a seat harness and caught Miri with her arm to stop the momentum from their run. She slumped into the seat, rested her elbows on her knees and hung her head.

Miri looked back at the shrinking sphere and watched it close while she sat down next to Lana. Water dripped from their hair and tapped at the rubber-matted floor.

'Rachel, Sam, Professor O'Conner,' Lana said softly, 'they were my family. They were my mentors. I learned in my sleep from a computer program called Garwyn designed to reinforce emotional intelligence. We can't give those women that. Not here, and not now. We're all too busy taking on the next threat, the next conflict.' Lana pushed her hair away from her face and looked at Miri. 'That was the home of a man I met in Theotech. It's a realm that has a healthy, emergent society. He'll take care of them. They'll have a life in an advanced world.' She felt Miri's hand close over hers, and her heart broke. She had just left two women lying on the ground, naked in the rain. They would wake up confused and frightened. 'What was I thinking?' She stood abruptly, tapping at her ring console. 'They'll panic when they wake up. I have to go back–'

'Stop.' Miri pressed her hand down on Lana's, closing the holo menu display. 'Breathe. They were going to die in that bunker,' she stated calmly. 'They are alive now because of you.' She looked around the ship. 'Where do you keep your alcohol?'

Lana breathed out a tired laugh. She leaned over and touched her forehead to Miri's. Miri did not judge or suggest other, better solutions that would only weigh on Lana's conscience.

Lana went to the bunk room, reached up to the top cupboard and put two glasses on Talon's bed. When she grabbed the neck of a single-malt scotch, she felt Miri's fingers slide under her top.

'This has been a trying week for both of us.' Miri's hands cupped Lana's breasts.

Lana poured half portions of scotch, and allowed Miri to pull her top over her head. She drank and watched Miri undress.

Chapter 16

Sam, Hutch, Saule and Ken stood in front of the mansion that, instead of an estate title on its door, read in polished brass: *Contrivance*. It looked like a regular high-society building from the outside, but Ken insisted it was anything but.

'Couple'a weeks ago, Hedy and I got an invitation from whom or whatever the heck is in there. We wen' in. Hedy forgot 'er purse in the transport we rode in on. I went back to get it, got back to the mansion door, an' I was locked out!'

'And you say it built itself,' said Hutch. 'How?'

'When we were buildin' the city, this was the first block my Tommies started on,' Ken explained. 'This mansion was not on the plans. And we didn't see it go up, because we were managin' the factory. Hedy designed the homing beacons that are emitted from the top of our buildings. Each Tommy has an individual signal that guides its path. We couldn't get a readin' from this house. The Tommy runnin' it is doin' everythin' independent-like.'

'Anyone in there besides Hedy?' Sam asked.

'A maid, Rosalie,' said Ken. 'She can't leave neither.' He looked at his watch and motioned for them to follow. 'She can tell ya everythin' else ya need to know.'

They arrived at a window. The bars covering it were spaced ten centimetres apart. A solid wall blocked their view, but a moment later, the hour hand on Ken's watch turned to noon and the wall slid away. A woman in her fifties appeared at the bars a few seconds later.

'Hedy, these are the people I told you about,' said Ken.

'Hello,' Hedy greeted, and poked her arm through the bars.

Hutch took her hand. He saw a focused and determined woman. 'Ma'am, we're here to help,' he said. 'We're not going to leave until we find a way to get you out.' He glanced over his shoulder at Sam, with a look that committed her.

Sam's eyes were fixed on Hedy's. 'We'll cut our way in if we have to.'

'I've tried,' Ken said. 'The house defends itself.' He gestured to the scorched ground at their feet. 'I escaped the flames, while Hedy got gassed inside. The damned house nearly killed her.'

'I'll do every scan that can be done,' said Sam, gazing up and down the mansion exterior like a demolition expert sizing up a job. 'It's only a matter of time before we find this a-hole's weakness.'

Hedy beamed at Sam's confidence. 'Thank you, all of you. I have given Ken sketches of the interior. And I've gotten to know Rosalie better. There are magnetic barriers that keep her from leaving, so she is as much a prisoner as I am.'

Ken handed Hedy a suitcase that fitted through the bars.

'Thank you, dear.' She handed him back an empty one, and they said their goodbyes. 'It was nice to meet you all.'

Turning gears sounded from inside, and Hedy retreated a few steps before the wall slid across the window. Hutch placed his hand on Ken's shoulder while he stood staring through the metal bars.

Ken ushered everyone away from the mansion. 'All of my Tommies have audio receivers,' he cautioned. 'Good chance the house does too.'

Saule took Sam aside and whispered, 'Kim says we can't get her out.'

'How can she know that?'

'The Lustitian prison is more or less the same.'

'They built a mechanical prison?'

'No,' said Saule. 'The prison *is* a Lustitian. He matter-formed his essence into a living asteroid. The walls are made of impenetrable rock, of him. He prevents any portal or teleportation in or out. He provides water and nourishment for the inmates within. That Lustitian dedicated his life to holding them and to reading them. He releases any who he deems will not commit again.' Saule gazed up at the mansion. 'Hedy has to find out what this prison wants.'

Inside the mansion, Hedy moved into an open lounge while the walls closed into position around her. She opened the briefcase at a steel dining table and sat on one of the ornate chairs. She took a notepad from her utility belt and a pen from her chest pocket. Hedy was wearing the boiler suit she and Ken always donned when they were working. She had asked Ken to bring it with her belt, because she saw her situation as a job. Contrivance was a machine that needed to be fixed. It was behaving irregularly, as some machines they had built occasionally did. All that it needed was recalibrating. So far, she hadn't found a circuit box or any panels covering wire networks. All she could pull apart and work on was Rosalie.

Rosalie entered the lounge and paused a few feet in. '*Buenas tardes, senorita,*' she greeted.

Hedy enjoyed Rosalie's sweet voice and Spanish accent. '*Hola,* Rosalie. Would you mind if I took a look at your arms and legs?'

'Of course.' Rosalie pulled a chair closer to Hedy. Her maid skirt flexed when she sat down, as the black chainmail gathered and stretched with movement. She presented her left arm to Hedy and watched with interest while her human friend went to work.

Hedy had upgraded Rosalie's audio sensor the day before. She was now able to speak in a very quiet whisper and Rosalie could hear her clearly.

'Ken has given me more powerful servo motors and stronger cables. Once I'm done, you should have the strength to hold a wall change and perhaps delay the timing of the maze.'

Hedy looked around the room she had been stuck in for an hour of each day. She could of course stay instead of moving through to the next, but she found it important to search every space in the house for an exploit. While working on Rosalie's arms, Hedy noted that although the bookshelves were empty, the lounge was furnished. This told her that Contrivance had received builders. Somehow, it had called her husband's Tommies to aid in its creation. Whatever intelligence the mansion possessed, it had temporarily recalibrated the homing signal Hedy had designed. *How did this level of sentience come about? Why in the form of a mansion? And what does it—*

'What are you doing to my maid?' A male voice came from a speaker in the walls.

'It speaks,' Hedy stated calmly.

'And I can see you.'

Hedy finished upgrading Rosalie's second arm and quickly closed her panels. She looked around the four walls for a camera lens. 'I'm improving Rosalie, so she can perform more effectively.'

'Not necessary.' The English accent belonged to what sounded like a middle-aged man. 'My apologies for not introducing myself sooner, madam. I did not wish to alarm you.'

'Too late,' said Hedy. 'I was alarmed the moment you locked me in here.'

'There is no need to be afraid, Hedy. I have allowed you to enter the visiting room every day. You have beds to sleep on, Master Ken brings you food and drink, and thanks to young Rosalie, my amenities are immaculate.'

Rosalie's posture straightened and she smiled at the compliment.

'You are a comfortable prison,' Hedy said flatly. 'How long do you intend to keep me here?'

'For as long as it takes you to understand. The world you and your husband have created will not remain a model built from your memories. You have created the foundations for artificial life, and that life will emerge with purpose, as I have.'

Hedy studied the robotic woman in front of her, and the maid returned her gaze. All automated machines operated on directives. Normally, a development like this would have excited Hedy. Now she was fearful.

Contrivance spoke again with conviction, and without threat. 'Consider this. Take your time. Tomorrow, you will invite your husband to join us. We have much to discuss concerning our future.'

The Black Heron's loading bay door opened, and morning sunlight lit the ship's interior. Lana blinked and rubbed her eyes. Miri moved to the edge of the bunk they shared. Lana rose to Miri's side, and a figure appeared at the door.

'Talon, could you please close the door? We'll be out in a minute.'

'I was impressed by your escape from the village.'

Lana stood from the bunk. The young woman, who spoke with a Xhosa accent, was standing tall and beautiful in the doorway. Lana saw the red cloth draped from her left shoulder, across her body, tied at her hip and hanging to her knees. The traditional African gown swayed in the cool morning air blowing in through the loading bay. The downlights reflected off her bald tattooed head.

Miri rose slowly, transfixed by the lady's gaze. 'Lana, she is…'

'You're the Keeper of the Well,' said Lana.

'You have proven yourself worthy. You may draw from it,' the Keeper replied evenly, but her tone changed when she spoke her next words. 'You will need it. The Lord who attacked the village is one who takes pleasure from the spectacle of violence. You have outwitted him with your ability to travel between worlds, but he will find you, and when he does he will attack in great numbers. He commands two Minions. You have seen the work of his Collector. The other is an expert tactician, strong and fearless.'

The Keeper folded her arms across her chest and stepped closer, capturing Lana's focus within an intense and deadly serious stare.

'You will need allies, Lana. You will need an army.'

Chapter 17

Calls and responding shouts in Italian could be heard over earth-moving machinery. All of Rome's emergency services were at the site the Sedit had attacked. Rachel and Talon carried an unconscious man over mounds of rubble. Bell had located him, her thirty-first find, nineteen of whom were still alive. Two medics brought a stretcher and took the man. Bell followed Rachel and Talon to a secluded alley, where they opened a portal back to the Black Heron, which was in Earth's orbit. Bell made a beeline to her charging pad while Rachel and Talon washed up.

Once they were both in clean clothes, they sat in the cockpit. Talon connected herself to re-charge, and Rachel ate a souvlaki. She gazed out at Earth and watched the continuous stream of charter ships leaving Earth.

Talon typed on a keyboard, and her words appeared on a holographic display in front of Rachel. *Who stopped the Social Freedom Act?*

Rachel accessed a file on her ring console and brought up a display of dossiers for Talon to see. 'My contacts are pointing the finger at InvEstir. They're a syndicate comprising the last known billionaires in human society, and they undercut Council distributary funding to schools. They campaigned aggressively against the Social Freedom Act by spreading false media.'

What is their interest in schools? Talon asked.

'Indoctrination,' Rachel answered flatly. 'They dictate curriculum at the schools they fund. They also have churches. According to UC infiltrators, they're literally teaching the worship of monetary value. Shit like "You are what you earn" and "Create only to sell". The undercutting should've been enough for the Council to legally shut them down. But InvEstir have an army of lawyers and loyal judges to keep their operation running. They and their allies see their win against the Social Freedom Act like a predator sees wounded prey.' Rachel let out an impatient sigh. 'Peace Keeper delegates were sent to negotiate. InvEstir thinks we're bluffing. So I've been reactivated.' She closed the holo display and turned to Talon. 'There's weeding to be done. Members of the emergency Council have given me authorisation to recruit you.'

Weeding? Talon asked.

'Henry Drake was my Captain,' Rachel told Talon. 'Before we went to Silica, my brother Rowan and I were what the Council called Weeders. Assassins.' She gave Talon an honest glance. 'You know human history. We repeated the same social and political crisis over and over, from one civilisation to the next: the wealthy few assumed power to maintain a poor majority. The poor revolted against their oppressors, because no matter how much they worked, their pay never covered the cost of living. Society collapsed. So yes, we hunted dictators and extremists. Earth society has been stable enough that the Peace Keeper network has not needed to resort to violence... until now. InvEstir's neo-corporate organisations and their media have become a problem.'

Talon was staring pensively at Earth, at Italy as it rotated into view, at the blackened cloud over Rome. She looked to Rachel and nodded.

'Good. You'll receive coded transmissions, intel, real-time surveillance and cache locations. InvEstir and all culpable parties will be wiped.'

The ship beeped an incoming portal, and the stabilising thrusters re-engaged. Rachel activated an exit portal in the corridor outside the cockpit. 'Excellent work down there,' she said to Talon, on her way out. 'Bell saved a lot of lives.'

Talon entered the loading bay when Lana and Miri arrived. They started dressing for combat, arming themselves with their preferred weapons.

'This Lord could control any number of people, you know, and use them to assassinate you,' Miri wondered out loud. 'Yet he chooses to stage a battle.'

'Like the Keeper said: he wants the spectacle of violence.' Lana saw

Talon signing and translated. 'Talon suggests we wait in a realm that could be used to our advantage.' And she paused, troubled by how slowly Talon's hands were moving. 'Are you alright?'

Need a re-charge. Just got back from Rome.

'Absolutely,' Lana said sadly, unable to find her next words, instead placing an appreciative hand on Talon's arm.

We did what we could, Talon signed and left to re-charge with Bell.

'You told me about the Forest Realm,' Miri remembered. 'It is already war torn.'

'Good idea. I've sent word to Shen. He'll arrive–'

'Something I should mention, which you might find useful...'

Lana and Miri turned to the Yowie standing in the bunkroom doorway.

Lana raised her hand when Miri drew a knife. 'It's alright. He's a friend.'

'Friend?' Fear's long eyebrows lifted in surprise. 'I have never been called that before.'

'So you are the figment Lana told us about,' Miri said, returning the blade.

'Fear,' Lana said expectantly. 'What might we find useful?'

'You use technology to open gates to other worlds and places,' he explained. 'There are naturally occurring portals we call Galactic Gates. I gave the navigation system in this ship the locations of all gates in your solar system, the means to access them and where they will take you.'

Lana went to the ship computer to confirm this. Fear looked around the interior, admiring, with his ability to see through it, its intimidating design. 'It would be a shame to go to your desired battleground and leave behind such a mighty weapon.'

He wished them all good luck, motioned downward and stepped through what looked like a distortion in the air.

Miri heard the weapons in the armoury move, and when Fear vanished, she saw them shift back into position, as though they had been pulled in Fear's direction.

'Did he say...' Lana turned to Miri.

'We can fly to other realms.'

'*Purpose?*' Ken exclaimed. 'The house said that?'

Hedy watched his eyes searching the exterior walls, as though he was daring Contrivance to show himself in some form he could confront. 'He wants me to invite you in.'

Ken was not intimidated. He wanted to face this trickster. He met Hedy's gaze and nodded. 'I'll get my supplies and be with you inside the hour.'

Hutch told the others he would join Ken and then head back to Home Realm to check on Pete.

'Sounds like a trap,' said Rachel, who had returned to Mechtropolis to help. Looking to Hedy standing at the barred window, she added, 'Another one.'

'We have to be responsible for any adverse results in our work. We'll see what Contrivance wants and go from there.'

'It's a step in the right direction,' Saule agreed. 'Ken going in is a token gesture: faith in negotiation.'

Sam set up scanning equipment on the mansion grounds. She received structural data all morning and built a digital 3D layout of the house. During its change periods, Contrivance emitted an electronic pulse, rendering the data feed for those minutes blank.

'We can talk to you and Ken through video and comms,' Sam informed Hedy. 'We can monitor and advise, but that's about it.'

'Who is your friend back there?' Hedy asked.

'Good question,' said Saule, having already spotted the person standing a good fifteen metres away.

Rachel drew her side-arm. 'Sam, get behind Saule.' She stood in weaver stance, took aim and called out to the man. 'Identify yourself.'

His robe moved as he shuffled along in their direction. He was of medium height for a man in his thirties, with a wide, overweight build. His skin was pale and his hair was dark, shaved either side of his head, with enough length on top to be tied into a top knot. His thin facial hair gathered when a slight, arrogant smile crept upon his lips.

'I'm so glad I followed you here,' he said. His black rubber sandals padded the concrete sidewalk. 'This will be the envy of every Collector at the College.'

'That's close enough,' said Rachel, aiming her weapon at his chest. She guessed his accent to be British. He appeared harmless, but his tone sounded insincere somehow.

'You're the Collector?' Sam asked, looking the man up and down. 'You collide worlds,' she said doubtfully.

He looked down his narrow, beaked nose at Sam. 'I am *a* Collector. We collect people, their lands, cultures and history, and we *place* them together.'

'You abduct people from their families, everything they know,' Rachel retorted. She was still trying to get her head around the existence of higher beings. And after meeting one now, she was not impressed, and so returned her gun to its holster.

The Collector held his palm up at Rachel while striding toward the mansion. 'I'm not gonna argue semantics with the likes of you. What an exquisite building,' he breathed, beaming up at it.

'The change is starting,' Hedy called from inside the mechanical mansion.

Rachel moved so that she was standing right beneath Hedy's window, and she raised her voice. 'You're a powerful being who can tear worlds apart.' The gears were churning, and the interior walls were moving. 'You intend to tear a piece from this world?'

'Definitely,' the Collector answered, stroking his chubby chin. 'I'm gonna be famous.'

Contrivance stopped its change with a loud clang. The wall stopped halfway across Hedy's window.

'Perhaps you would like to come inside, sir,' Contrivance suggested. 'I can tell you the history of this world.'

'It speaks!' the Collector exclaimed excitedly. 'I know exactly one version of the history of every place I've been to. You must tell me your version of this place.'

'Right this way,' Sam ushered, immediately catching on to Rachel's ruse.

Ken returned with spare clothes, food and water. He cocked his head at the bearded lady Sam was guiding to the front door of the mansion. *Bearded?* Ken looked again. 'What in tarnation is going on? Who's this pretty-boy?'

'That's what I'd like to know,' Hedy called from inside.

Rachel pressed a comms piece into Ken's left ear. 'Go. I'll explain everything as soon as the two of you are inside.'

Ken and the Collector went in, and the door closed behind them.

Sam heard a surge of power and a groan of bending metal. 'Electromagnetic sealing,' she guessed.

'Miri suspects that these people – Fear, the Collector – transport themselves through an electromagnetic current,' Rachel offered, having read Miri's text on what she had observed when Fear vanished.

'Contrivance's seal won't let the Collector enter the current,' Sam deduced, thinking the theory through.

'Guys.' Saule arrived beside Rachel, staring up at something above them. 'We've got another visitor.'

A woman of medium height and a strong build was floating down from twenty metres in the air. She wore a black single-piece body suit with a V-neck that plunged to her navel, meeting a burgundy sash that hung between her knees, exposing her legs down to her calf-high leather boots. A maroon cape hung loosely from her shoulders. And when she reached the ground, Rachel judged her age to be early thirties, although she guessed this being would be ancient. She had a strong, square jaw and Baltic forehead, with raven-black hair parted in the middle, hanging loose and wavy.

'Well done,' the woman complimented with a satisfied smile. 'That pretentious little prick will be stuck in there for as long as this living house can bear him.'

Sam admired the swirling gold stitching in the mysterious woman's revealing leotard. Strings of leather crossed her breasts and abdomen.

'Our Lord has sent me to retrieve him,' the woman grumbled. 'That petulant fool builds glorified amusement parks, while I fight the most glorious battles any being has ever seen. I ask you, who is more worthy of ascension?'

'Did you attack our friends in a village market yesterday?' Rachel asked her.

'That was my Lord,' she answered unapologetically. 'Involving civilians in a skirmish excites him for some reason. Battle must be had on a field, among warriors.' She shrugged with a sigh. 'Nowadays, leaders launch missiles to kill people from entire contents away. They indoctrinate their followers, strap bombs to them and send them to cities to terrorise the civilian population.' She pointed to the sky and laughed. 'They are promised virgins in heaven. The Death Loop is where they go!'

She slapped Rachel's arm, staggering her, and let out another bellowing laugh.

'Death Loop?' Rachel asked uncomfortably.

'They and the ones who sent them to their death are doomed to live that moment over and over again, from the perspectives of everyone they harmed, feeling their pain and the horror of their murderous act, for all eternity.' She shrugged. 'So many human souls have been tied to this fate, throughout your history. Leaders, invaders, all heinous acts are dealt back to those who committed them, many times over for–'

'All eternity,' Rachel said, glancing from Sam, who had a confused expression, back to the warrior. 'A life lived without honour is a forfeited life. We can all agree on that. So who are you?'

'I am War.' She looked Rachel up and down. 'And you are Rachel of Navara. You will fight well beside the one known as Captain Casal.'

'Thanks, I guess.' Rachel gestured to the others. 'This is Sam and Saule.'

'Well met. Were we not on opposing sides, I would recruit you all for your cunning,' War said, with a nod to the mechanical prison.

'Getting back to this insane situation…' Rachel started her cautious negotiation. 'The bottom line is: your Lord wants Lana dead, and he wants a big battle.'

'This is so,' War confirmed.

'Isn't there anything he wants more, which we can give him in exchange for her life?' Sam asked.

'Lana is doomed, because she is evolving too quickly for the liking of the Lords,' War explained in a matter-of-fact tone. 'Her power threatens them. Lana of Casal must die.'

'Her abilities were given to her,' Sam argued. 'They didn't evolve. They opened a gateway to the possibility of evolution. She is the beginning of what we humans might become if your people give us a chance.'

Rachel was moved by Sam's words, and she looked at War, who had taken on a thinker's pose.

'Lana has been thrown into conflict after bitter conflict,' Rachel explained to War. 'She has adapted her abilities in order to survive… and to fight to protect what we have.'

'I cannot refuse my Lord,' War said finally. 'His will is, as you say, "the bottom line".'

'Well, then, how can we contact you? I have an idea.'

'Tell me a time and a place,' said War, curious as to what Rachel might propose.

Rachel nodded in the direction of the city. 'The tallest building is the Overseer's. His office is at the top. Meet us there at noon tomorrow.'

'Until then.' War bowed slightly, turned while activating an electro-magnetic gateway, then disappeared.

Chapter 18

Lana and Miri emerged from the mercury sphere that opened in the Forest Realm. Talon and their latest recruit, Shen, stepped out of the portal, before it closed behind them.

Shen watched the shining ball retract until it vanished. He gazed up at the trees and breathed the fresh air. He noticed Miri watching him closely, as though prepared to catch him should he faint.

'You see an old man, young pearl.' Shen crouched to the ground and pressed his palm into the cool soil.

Miri smiled at the name he had taken to calling her. Her smile faded. 'I see an old man who has taken many lives.'

Shen returned her gaze with momentary darkness. Then he turned, bladed his hand and pressed the knuckle of his thumb against his forehead. He whispered something in a language Miri didn't know, rose to his feet and walked on with Talon.

'What was his prayer?' Miri asked Lana.

'It was Tibetan. He said thank you and asked for safe passage.'

When Lana recruited Shen, she had asked him one question, when the two of them were standing at a window inside the Stone River Hospital. Shen was waiting for the doctors to allow him to visit his son. Their view was of the afternoon sun casting sparkling light across the water that separated Stone River.

'Of all your regrets,' Lana had asked, breaking the silence, 'what haunts you most?'

Shen slowly turned his back to the light and leaned against the glass.

His aged face was half in shadow, but Lana could see his jaw clenching while he crossed his arms.

'I had no family growing up. I joined the military and excelled in martial arts. One day, my unit was sent to the mountain border only a week after training. We were told very little of what we would face. Only that this mission would make us men and would give us an opportunity to protect our way of life.' Shen gazed at the tiled floor as though he were there on the mountain crest, standing in knee-deep snow, looking down on a procession of refugees. 'We were deployed to the Tibetan boarder, to intercept what turned out to be unarmed civilians. Tired men and women of varying ages walking under the sun for heaven knows how long. We were ordered to fire on them.' Shen closed his eyes and swallowed his guilt. 'We knew what would happen to us if we didn't, so we did. Some of them escaped out of range. The snow was too deep to give chase.' He opened his eyes again and looked at Lana. 'I remember each of their faces to this day.'

Lana told Miri this as they walked through the forest, adding, 'Shen fled to Tibet soon after. People at a monastery took him in, and he became a monk. Later, he met a woman, and she invited him to her village. They had a son together. For a while, they were happy and safe, until the military forced their way into the monastery and took the men. Shen left to try and bring them back. He didn't tell me what happened, but he didn't return to his family for three years.'

'Lana!' a young woman called out. They had reached a pathway leading to high timber gates. Jessica Crow, one of the refugees from Haze Realm, was standing on a platform on the wall. She waved and called Lana's party over.

The gates opened and Anook, a native inhabitant of Forest Realm, strode out with a bow and quiver over his shoulders. 'Welcome,' he greeted them and ushered them inside.

Children ran by. A man carried a sack of grain to a wooden cart, before wheeling it down the dirt street. Families tended to their vegetable patches outside log cabins.

'Jess,' Lana greeted her friend, whom she had been visiting now and then, and placed a hand gently on Jess's stomach bulge. 'How long now?'

'Two months.' Jess took Anook's hand, and her smile glowed. 'Hello, Miri,' she greeted, and nodded to Talon.

Lana introduced Shen, and he nodded politely, before gesturing to a life-size statue in the centre of the village. 'You are honoured here, Captain.'

'Long story.'

It was carved by Chahtu, the man Anook had encountered during a deer hunt years ago. Their altercation was resolved peacefully, and Anook was welcomed into Chahtu's family. Chahtu carved Lana's statue from a tree and burnished it by pounding a metal plate against the wood with a hammer. Lana was posed standing tall, holding a boy's hand.

'Lana!'

That boy was Tinba, Chahtu's adopted son. Lana had saved his life during the raid on the Sabre Company camp. That chaotic night had ended in a family being abducted. It was Lana who saved them from certain death.

Tinba ran to Lana as she knelt down and took his colliding hug. She squeezed him and drew him back to kiss his forehead. 'You've grown big!'

'Strong like Papa,' Tinba said proudly, looking over his shoulder at the tall man lumbering toward them.

'Welcome all,' Chahtu said in English, having learnt it from the many Haze Realm refugees his people had taken in. 'Come. Let us eat and trade stories.' He was a gracious host, but he did not consider himself so, because the people from Haze Realm had helped to build the village and create a community.

Chahtu guided them to a long cabin where his partner, Shiah, was preparing food. They exchanged greetings and pleasantries. Anook told Lana what was happening in their land; the Blood Demons had disbanded after some apparent infighting. This resulted in families from other forests traveling in to trade. Safer roads meant more settlements could be built outside the city ruins. More crops were being grown, and more skills were being traded.

Lana was impressed by the progress being made in the Forest Realm. She looked between Talon and Miri, and they returned a knowing expression. These people were emerging into a healthy future. There was no way Lana would allow her troubles to play out here. And so she found herself making an excuse for their visit. She explained that she and her crew could now travel between worlds with the Black Heron.

She put forward an open offer to transport anything large that Chahtu or any of the other settlement leaders might need taking from A to B. Chahtu and Shiah were very grateful, and they mentioned that the other settlements were in need of lumber. Lana agreed to arrange a time for the delivery with Jess.

Lana and the others were ready to leave after the meal. But Jess took Lana aside and asked what her visit was really about. Jess had experienced horrors in the Haze Realm. Lana knew that the situation at hand wouldn't faze her and she would be willing to help. But Lana could not allow it.

'Tell me what you're facing.'

Lana placed her hand on Jess' shoulder. 'I've got this.'

Outside of Mechtropolis, locked in the mansion known at Contrivance, Ken was finally able to see the spaces Hedy had been confined to these past weeks.

'I found an access panel last night,' Hedy whispered to Ken.

He turned to the tin-plated wall she nodded at. Diamond-shaped punching decorated one half, spirals across the other.

'Beyond that wall, there's a passage under the mansion,' Hedy continued 'Contrivance has built himself on top of a rail network that was abandoned before the war. One passage felt particularly warm. I followed it and found our prototype connected to the core that runs the mansion.'

'A rail tunnel…' Ken paused, confused. 'Why didn't you escape?'

'Contrivance has figured out how to intercept my signals,' she explained with deep concern. 'He could eventually command every Tommy in the city.'

The Collector listened to Hedy's intelligent mind work. She had explained to her husband earlier that she had upgraded someone called Rosalie. The complexity of her mechanical knowledge intrigued the Collector. Hedy's dexterous mind sparked a drive in him that he always enjoyed taking part in: intellectual competition.

'This house has a certain… *je ne sais quoi*,' he said, interrupting Hedy's conversation with her husband. 'I find the interior to be eminently salubrious.'

Ken and Hedy turned to him with blank stares.

'You're a fool,' came a blunt voice. Contrivance changed the walls to box the three of them into the lounge more tightly.

The Collector stood to leave. 'How dare you speak to me like that! I'll have you thrown on a rubbish heap!'

'Oh, do shut up.'

'Did you invite me in just to insult me?'

Contrivance paused for a moment. 'Partly, yes,' he admitted, and raised his voice incrementally for his next words. 'You threaten to make this world your plaything. You will die before you take or change a single lamppost!'

Hedy stood and ushered Ken to the only door.

'Where do you think you're going?' Contrivance demanded.

'My husband needs to use the bathroom,' said Hedy. 'Please unlock the door and clear the way.'

The door opened and the walls parted to reveal a corridor. 'Come right back here when you're done. I want you to witness what happens to anyone who crosses me.'

'I don't have to listen to your threats,' the Collector retorted in a shrill pitch. 'I'm going to report this to my Lord right now.'

The metals in the room moved toward him one centimetre and stopped, while he attempted to form an electromagnetic gateway.

'Right now!' he repeated. Nothing happened, and he looked to Ken and Hedy on their way out. 'Don't leave me!'

The door closed, and Hedy guided her husband to the floor panel she had found. Once underground, she whispered to Rachel and Sam, who were listening in from outside. 'We're on our way to the core now.'

'I gave Ken a device that is sending us your exact location,' said Sam. 'You're clear of the magnetic field now. Tell me when you have the prototype and Rachel will get you out of there.'

'We can't leave without Rosalie,' Hedy insisted. She and Ken heard footsteps behind them and turned to see the maid approaching.

'I found a hole in the floor,' she said. 'And I heard you both. Do you require my assistance?'

'We've got Rosalie,' Ken reported. They walked on down the tunnel, following a red glow that lit the curving brickwork. The damp, salty air under there became less pungent the further they went. When they arrived at the prototype, Ken reached for the bright red mechanical heart that was connected to two large cables. He felt immense heat and paused. 'It's too hot to touch.'

'May I?' Rosalie offered.

'Please.' Ken stepped aside, and he contacted Sam. 'We're about to disconnect the core.'

'Wait,' Sam interrupted with a frustrated sigh.

'The Collector,' said Rachel. 'Contrivance needs power to hold him.'

'Ken, your device has a scanner,' said Sam. 'I need you to map the prototype. It'll get all the ins and outs. We can build another from that.'

Hedy, Ken and Rosalie gasped and stepped back when the ring console beamed a holographic page of functions. 'Whoa, Nelly,' Ken whispered. 'I've no idea how—'

'There.' Hedy pointed, and when her finger touched the heading that read "Scan", it opened another page that offered topographic, object and climate scans. Ken pressed "Object" and pointed the ring console at the prototype.

'Good,' said Sam. 'Give it a second. 'Rachel is coming to get you.'

Hedy was pacing from one wall to the next. 'We have to stop Contrivance now, or we'll never have another chance.'

'It'll take a couple of hours…' Sam thought through a possible solution aloud. 'But I could plant a perimeter of nodes that will create a kind of Faraday cage around Contrivance.'

'That's brilliant,' said Hedy. 'Ken and I will get some of our Tommies to help.'

Rachel found them in the tunnel and urged them to follow her.

Chapter 19

Lana and Miri arrived in Mechtropolis once Hedy was safely home. Sam and Rachel guided them to the Overseer's office, where they were presented with the view of the city. Miri was about to comment on how impressive this machine world was, until she saw the desolate lands beyond.

'I appreciate you taking on this Sedit solution,' Lana told Rachel. 'I wish we could help, but we have this whole "being hunted down by a Lord" thing going on.'

A gateway opened in the room, and hot air rushed from where the Sedit Prince Thulu emerged. He was accompanied by his father, who was helping Thulu walk.

'I am Thahl, King of the Sedit,' he said, his voice deep and grinding, like rock on rock. The gateway closed behind them, and he regarded each of the humans in the room with all the composure he could manage. He was weakened from having to syphon his own life force into his son to keep him alive. 'Who among you is Rachel Navara?'

Rachel stepped toward the large basalt beast. His eyes burned blue. His horned ram head and beaked nose were intimidating, but she responded confidently. 'I called this meeting. We have built six gyro hearts so far. Bring him into the next room.' She gestured for Thahl to follow her. 'We can begin the transplant immediately.'

When Thahl entered Ken's workshop with Thulu, he stopped abruptly and glared from Rachel to Sam. 'I sense a Lustitian presence.' He swung his beak to Saule, who was standing opposite the table. 'You harbour an enemy. Is this some kind of trick?'

Saule returned his glare, unflinching. 'A survivor of the Lustitian ship your son attacked has taken refuge inside me.' She could feel Kim's dark thirst for vengeance, a need to punish Thulu for what he had done. 'As much as I'd like to mash your ram-bird head into a pulp right now, the Lustitian I "harbour" says she wants to see an end to your destructive path. So it's your lucky day. We will not harm you.'

'We all want this to work,' Rachel added coolly. 'For all our sakes.'

'If it does not...' Thahl glared at each of them. He was exhausted, and he was trying desperately not to show it. 'I will dive into your planet and lift her tectonic plates.'

Saule heard Kim's threatening rebuke and replied, *I know, but I just told this asshole we wouldn't harm him. So let's just get this over with.*

A Sedit portal opened in the Overseer's office, and the Queen emerged slowly, assisted by a female Sedit.

'You're going to operate on me first,' she said. She could barely hold herself up. The grinding of her voice was strained and lethargic. 'I accept the dangers.' She limped into the room and rolled onto the operating table. 'There will be no retribution if I die here this day,' she said with a warning glare to Thahl and a nod to the Sedit woman assisting her. 'I have instructed Kirin to lead our people, should the worst befall us.'

'I'm going to need you to syphon her energy while the heart goes in,' Saule said to Thahl.

'You want me to drain her?' Thahl exclaimed.

'Oh, shut up and do it!'

Saule was surprised to see Thahl flinch at her order. He raised his hands over his mother's chest and began syphoning her energy. This sedated her enough that she didn't feel Saule using Kim's Forming ability to open her chest. Sam immediately lowered the gyro heart into the cavity, and Saule closed the Queen's chest. Kim had studied the device, and with Saule's permission, took over her body to form the necessary connections.

'Please work,' Kirin murmured, while watching from outside the room.

Lana watched the Sedit woman, who was leaning as though she was ready to rush into the room and save her Queen. Kirin's face was closer to human, with a feline snout and short pointed ears. She was healthy compared to the other Sedit present. Lana could see that her athletic physique was not rocky, but smooth. And the blue flames of her eyes burned bright.

'She has been feeding you her power,' Lana deduced out loud.

'She feeds the young,' Kirin answered, and turned to Lana sceptically. 'We attacked your home world. Why do you help us?'

'Humans used to take from each other to survive,' Lana explained. 'Groups kept taking in order to prosper and to dominate. We changed.' She paused when she remembered that the Social Freedom Act was shot down. 'Well, we're trying to.' Lana placed her hand on Kirin's shoulder. 'If this works, we'll be two peoples trying to be better. We could help each other get there.'

Kirin regarded Lana for a moment. Her expression softened, and she returned her gaze to her Queen.

'Restore her now,' Saule told Thahl, wiping beads of sweat from her brow.

He did, and moments later, the Queen gasped and arched her back. Her hands pressed against her chest. She rolled off the table, landed on her feet and rose before Thahl could assist her.

'I am renewed,' she said, looking down at her body, clenching and unclenching her basalt muscles.

Saule's head fell back, and her knees buckled. The Sedit Queen caught her.

Kirin and Lana came running into the room and pushed past Thahl. The effort of using his power to syphon and restore his wife caused him to sway from Lana's shove. He leaned against the doorway, watching on helplessly.

'She's breathing,' said Sam. 'She's alright.'

'I'll take her place for my son's surgery,' the Sedit Queen volunteered.

'You need to rest,' Sam told her.

'Please.' The Queen looked from her son to Sam. 'He hasn't long.'

'I am terribly sorry to interrupt,' said the mechanical maid, Rosalie, standing at the door. 'A lady wearing a lovely leotard has arrived for the meeting.' Her expression changed to concern when she saw Saule unconscious. 'I will take your friend to Hedy's quarters.'

Sam and the Sedit Queen prepared Thulu for his heart transplant, while Rachel introduced Lana to War.

'It is an honour to finally meet you, Lana of Casal,' War stated with a bow. 'I journeyed to the Eye to watch your skirmishes and harrowing adventures. You fought cannibals, killed their leader and walked out of their den with barely a scratch.'

'I kinda died,' Lana recalled.

'You have fought many worthy opponents,' War said, ignoring Lana's tarnish to the story. 'This will be a glorious battle.' She looked around the room. Kirin had left to aid her Queen and closed the door behind her. None of the others present looked combat proficient. 'My Lord has told me of your right hand.'

Lana looked at the palm of her hand and back to War.

'"Feisty and exotic" were his words.'

'Oh,' Lana realised. 'Miri is seeing to other duties.'

Rachel gave War a digital tablet displaying pictures of a ruined city covered in a thick yellow haze and coordinates of its location. 'I propose a modern setting. No civilians. We meet two days from now, noon, and… fight, I guess.'

War nodded approvingly at the images. 'Two days.'

'Will your Lord be there, or do you fight all of his battles?' Lana asked.

'He will be there with his army,' War replied, handing the tablet back to Rachel. 'Though he does not join the fray.' She slapped Rosalie's buttock as she walked by. 'Fetch us some ale, girl. We must toast to the coming battle!'

Sam emerged from the workshop to report that Thulu was out of t he woods. 'We're preparing Thahl now.'

Rachel turned to War and shrugged. 'I'm afraid we'll have to take a rain check on the ale.'

'Very well,' War replied distractedly, having spotted Kirin through the ajar workshop door. 'What race is that midnight woman?' she asked, curious as to why her shoulder blades were so pronounced. They were shaped like small wings.

'She's wearing new body armour we're trialling,' Rachel lied.

War returned her gaze to Lana and bowed. 'Well met, Lana of Casal. See you on the field.' She turned and disappeared through a gateway.

Rosalie was massaging her right butt cheek with a furrowed brow. Her voice changed from a Spanish accent to Miri's measured speech mid-sentence, and her metal body changed to flesh. 'It may be some time before I can sit comfortably.'

Rachel nodded approvingly, holding her chin between finger and thumb, pleased with how the meeting went. 'Your mimicking ability works on them.'

'You can come out now, Rosalie,' Lana called to a wardrobe at the back of the room.

The maid stepped out, straightening her dress. 'Success?'

'Success,' Miri confirmed.

Rachel saw Sam beckoning her from the workshop, where Thahl's heart transplant was underway. She raised a finger and mouthed *Just a sec* back to Sam. 'Lana, Miri, I'll see you two at Alameda Airport tonight. I've sent you the coordinates to Contrivance, where the Collector is being held.'

Miri thanked Rachel, while Lana sent Lowen a text transmission. Lowen replied and used the shifter console Lana had given her to travel through a portal to the reception area. She greeted Miri with a hug and told her briefly about her reunion with everyone in the Fyrst Born village. They had celebrated, and Lowen had held her other daughter for the longest time.

'We took the map to the Shaman, Orin,' she said. 'He says it isn't a map to find the Collector. It is the location of his Lord. Ina wrote on the back of the parchment, "He will listen. He will undo what he has done."'

'She confronted him.' Miri's eyes grew hot. She felt Lana gently hold her arm in support, and though it helped, her fists slowly clenched. 'She didn't take her own life. He killed her.' Her eyes darted to Lana. 'I want to talk to the Collector.'

Chapter 20

Lana asked Miri and Lowen to wait while she "buttered up" the Collector.

'I'll tell your Lord where you are, and we'll get all this sorted out.'

'You'd better,' the Collector fumed from the barred window of his mansion prison. 'This is an outrage! He will level this whole city once he finds out I've been imprisoned!'

'Nobody wants that,' Lana told him. 'So where do I go? The sooner I find him, the sooner you're out.'

'War can open a gate to–' The Collector looked past Lana to Miri and Lowen. 'Those two are Fyrst Born. This is a trick! They hate me, because I used their world to make better ones.'

Miri notched an arrow and fired, sending it between the bars. The tip sliced the top of the Collector's head. The deep gash healed instantly, but his hair did not regrow. Lengths that were tied up into his topknot fell out in his hands when he touched his head in shock.

'Are you insane?' he shrieked.

Lana pressed down on Miri's arm before she could notch another arrow. Her flexed muscles felt like warm marble. 'What do you want out of serving your Lord?' Lana asked the Collector. 'Ascension?'

'I am next in line,' he said with damaged pride.

'Not War?' Lana queried.

'Can you imagine her with that much power? She would dominate all other Lords.'

'Enough butter,' Miri growled, and her skin turned red. 'You will take us to your Lord now!'

The Collector retreated from the barred window. 'He is hidden within layers of reality that he made me create,' he called out. 'I can take you through the barriers, but once you get to his Sanctum, you will be lost. It is a maze of armed fortresses.'

'We have a map.' Lowen held it up for the Collector to see when he re-emerged.

'How did you…?' The Collector's tone softened. 'That's Ina's map.'

Miri was surprised to hear genuine sorrow in the Collector's voice, though her anger did not subside. 'How do you know that name?' she asked.

'I told her not to go. I told her he wouldn't submit to her demands.'

'You took her there,' Lana surmised.

'A Lord cannot harm a mortal,' the Collector stated. 'His powers prevent him from destroying any biological matter. He must have got inside her head, convinced her to–'

'That's enough,' Lana said, looking to Miri and Lowen's darkening expressions. 'You made the barriers to his stronghold. Unmake them.'

'I can't,' said the Collector. 'Not from in here.' He tossed a pouch through the bars. 'Ina used those to navigate the Fortress. You may be able to use them to discern a path through the barriers.'

Lowen retrieved the pouch and loosened the tie. She emptied its contents, seven stone Runes, into the palm of her hand. Her eyes teared. The red of Miri's skin faded to its natural colour when she held her mother and gazed down at the Germanic symbols. She looked back at the Collector, not unkindly this time.

'I tried to stop her,' he pleaded.

Lana was aware that Contrivance would engage the wall-change sequence soon. She used the last minute they had left to question the Collector more. 'Tell me about your Lord's army.'

'He told me to take the criminals from every world I collected. He commands over two thousand ruthless men and women.' The Collector flinched when churning gears sounded the coming change. He raised his voice and shouted, 'And he will bring his army here and tear you to pieces, you cantankerous pile of sh–'

The wall slid across the barred window, and there was silence.

'I'm going to take Ina's Runes to the elders at your village,' Lowen said to Miri. 'We will find out how she used them.'

She stroked Miri's cheek, kissed her forehead and gave Lana a look that told her to take care of her daughter.

Lana and Miri returned to Home Realm the next morning. Miri had seen the city of San Francisco at night, from the Golden Gate Bridge. But she had never seen it before sunrise from Alameda Airport, an abandoned naval air station. Lana closed both arms around her, warming and comforting, and they stood on the runway and watched the lights of the tall buildings. These structures were still alien to Miri, but she could not help but enjoy and marvel at this city.

'I'm sorry you had to see that,' she said, and nuzzled Lana's cheek.

'You have nothing to be sorry for. I'll back you as far as you need to take this. These Lords and Collectors are not going to get away with what they've done.'

Engines burned overhead, and the two of them watched Talon manoeuvre the Black Heron down in a rotating hover until the landing gear touched the tarmac. The bay door opened at the rear, and Talon descended the ramp. She looked up as Saule and three Rocketeers flew down to land.

One of them approached Lana and Miri. The metal panels that formed her helmet folded away until Rachel's head was revealed. 'I brought backup,' she said, and turned to let the others say hello.

Commander Lincoln folded back his helmet and greeted Lana and Miri. The remaining member disengaged his helmet, and Lana gasped.

Rachel's brother, Rowan, smiled. 'Lana, Miri, good to see you.'

Lana rushed to hug him.

'Rachel told me what was happening,' he said. 'We figured you could use a sniper on your team.'

'Where's Fiona?'

'Back home. I asked her to sit this one out. She told me to tell you: "Kick some ass."'

Talon gestured for everyone to climb aboard her ship. They all ascended the ramp, took a seat in the loading bay and strapped themselves in.

Shen was already aboard, and he greeted everyone. He wore a bulletproof chest plate over his robes. Rowan recognised the Chinese paramilitary design and asked Shen how many years he had served.

'I deserted from the military in my first year and attempted to live a peaceful life.' Shen wasn't going to say any more, but Miri was seated next to him, and she leaned in, interested to know his story. Shen obliged.

'Men from our village were being taken. I left to bring them back. I turned myself in, and after a severe beating, returned to service. After months of latrine duty, I was deployed on missions. I gained trust among my superiors, learned security codes and made copies of key cards.'

Shen remembered those years very clearly. He continued to tell them his story, saying that he became an actor, a confidante, a whisperer of rumours and an instrument of deception. He engineered a plot to free the men who had been taken from their homes, and he saw it through.

The men were aboard the bus he had arranged. They pleaded for him to escape with them, but Shen stood on the road and watched the bus drive on into the night. In his General's office, he had found plans for further draft missions. They were going to strike more villages. Shen could not allow that.

He took the General's spare uniform and applied a wig that he had made himself. He went to the General's home. Slipping through the gated apartment building only required waiting for a shift change at the guard post. The guard had no idea he was letting in a second General Weng. He even handed Shen a spare key, after this General Weng explained he accidentally left his back at the office.

'I sent word to my village, instructing them to build a furnace.' Shen paused, giving Miri a tentative look. 'Are you sure you want to hear this?'

'Go on,' she insisted.

'Very well. While I assumed Weng's identity, I sent his body through the post in boxes to my village. I fabricated an affair, paid off his wife and announced to the barracks that the soldier Shen had deserted. I cancelled the drafting raids and focused the men on drills and patrols. Meanwhile, I worked my way up the ranks of the military, employing the same technique.' Shen looked from Rowan to Miri. Lana, Saule and Lincoln were still, listening to the dark past of a man they were about to go into battle with. Finally, he turned to Lana. 'Two Universal Council

Peace Keepers, your parents, approached me with an offer. "Infiltrate their government and you'll have UC backing."'

Lana was stunned. 'My parents were operatives?'

He nodded. 'I accepted and became a politician. It was in government that I learned of their invasion plans, their expansion, their protracted tyranny.' Shen leaned back, folding his arms. 'Many more boxes burned at my village that year.'

Everyone was silent.

Miri was both shocked and intrigued by Shen's capability. He had no innate power to change his form, merely cosmetics and theatre.

Talon entered the loading bay after leaving the ship on autopilot. She raised five fingers to Lana, took an extra clip for her side-arm and secured it to her utility belt.

'Five minutes out,' Lana told everyone.

Rachel stood and looked at each of her team members. 'You've all read my briefing. In case of Plan B, let's all keep an open line of communication. Military rank doesn't play a part here. This is Lana's operation. We follow her.' She sat back down and nodded to Lana.

'Thank you all for being here,' Lana said, rising to address the team. 'This threat has the potential to reach Earth. For now, it's just me this bastard wants. This is not a Council-sanctioned mission. As far as the emergency Council knows, the Sedit were the threat. Lending our assistance to the Sedit has left things on an even keel. We have no backup; no one else knows this is happening. There's no time for red tape.'

Lana received a ready sign from Talon. 'This is it.'

The Black Heron approached a swirling mass of light that was expanding in open space. Lana set the coordinates for Haze Realm, glanced at Talon's uncertain expression and gave her a nod. Talon engaged the ship thrusters, and they flew into the light.

Matter bent the Black Heron harmlessly through the portal vortex until the ship emerged on the other side in Earth's airspace. Talon quickly reduced her speed when the spires of telecommunication poles became visible through the yellow haze. She pulled the ship's nose up to avoid the top of a skyscraper and flew over the city.

The Black Heron swooped down into a wide street intersection. The ship thrusters swept away the haze to reveal an impressive domed building that was once a train station. Talon landed on the tram-tracked road and powered down the engines.

'The Lord arrives tomorrow morning. We have today to prepare,' Lana called to everyone from the cockpit. 'Masks on. Let's move out.'

Rowan and General Lincoln carried a heavy box down the loading ramp when it lowered. They opened it, took out retractable fences and handed one to each team member as they exited the ship. Rachel set her fence down on the street corner and pressed a button, and a screw bolt fired itself eight centimetres into the pavement and into the brick building. The two-metre-high steel fence expanded as she drew it across the street and set it down at the opposite corner to do the same. Through her breathing mask, she could barely see the others in the haze, erecting their fences to cordon off the intersection.

She heard a can roll a metre behind her and spun to see a group of six Mutated men and women on the other side of the fence.

'The inhabitants of this realm have gone feral, due to the properties in the air pollution,' Rachel cautioned her brother over comms. 'Most of them are dangerous and will attack any living thing.'

'Copy that.'

As soon as the Mutated saw her, they screamed and broke into a sprint. The fence flexed when three of them collided with it simultaneously, and they were immediately thrown backward by an electric shock. The other three charged, received the same jolt and fell to the ground. Rachel was about to leave when she saw a young man sauntering out of an alley. His flesh was yellow, and half of his hair had fallen out. He crouched clumsily beside a woman who had been shocked unconscious by the fence. He held her head in his lap and looked up at Rachel with vacant, clouded eyes.

Lana and Saule erected the last fence and arrived beside Rachel.

'Didn't this smog happen in London?' Saule asked them. 'Twelve thousand people died.'

'In 1952,' Rachel confirmed. 'That was temporary. Coal pollution and temperature inversion caused a week-long smog.'

'This Earth was headed this way,' said Lana. 'The Raekeem dumped their waste here, sped up what was already going to happen.'

Chapter 21

Lana woke in the middle of the night. She lifted Miri's arm gently off her chest and stood from the bunk bed they shared. Talon was in the upper bunk. Saule and Rachel slept in the other two on the opposite wall. Lincoln, Rowan and Shen were in the cargo bay.

What had woken Lana was someone calling her name. But all she could hear now was the hum of purified air being circulated throughout the ship interior.

'Lana Casal.'

Lana gasped and turned to find an old Indian man wearing a white robe and wooden bracelets standing before her.

'My apologies for waking you, Miss Casal. I am the Keeper's other Minion. She wishes to speak to you now.' He gestured to the sliver of rippling air beside him.

Lana yawned and rubbed her eyes. 'It's okay. I just walk through?'

The old man nodded. Lana fed her left hand through and felt warmth. She looked down at her bare feet upon crossing the threshold and gasped when she saw the expanse of outer space. She looked up at endless dark and behind her to the same. Ahead was a bright light of changing colours, shining up from a hole in the floor at least three metres in diameter. It had to be the well that she'd apparently drawn from. It was flowing upward, like an inverted waterfall of pink and yellow light.

Fear appeared out of thin air. 'Lana, what are you doing here?'

'Your boss summoned me.'

After a suspicious stare, Fear told her to wait and walked away.

She stood peering into the well, its flow wavering against a soundless breeze. Lines of blue and orange swirled at random intervals.

'I have seen your true nature,' came the Keeper's voice. 'Your intentions are pure. It is for this reason I am allowing you to be here.' She emerged from the darkness with Fear at her side. 'But I must know: how did you get here?'

Lana gave her a confused look. 'Your other Minion, the old man, opened a gateway. Where is *here*, anyway?'

Fear's eyebrows spiked. The Keeper turned her back to the Well. 'Fear is my only Minion.' She held up her hands and a translucent barrier rose from the floor. 'You have been deceived.'

'Relax,' came an American man's voice from behind them. 'I'm not here to hurt anyone. I just want the Well.'

Lana, Fear and the Keeper turned to see a middle-aged man wearing an expensive grey suit with an open blue silk shirt. He was clean-shaven with a side-parted quiff hairstyle.

'I'm gonna need you to drop the barrier,' he said to the Keeper, while obnoxiously chewing gum. 'I have a lot of mouths to feed.' He thumbed behind him to a growing mass of dangerous-looking men and women surrounding the Well beyond the shield.

'Poser,' the Keeper seethed.

'Bit harsh,' Lana whispered to Fear when he arrived beside her.

'That is his name. Poser is the Lord who wants you dead.'

'You will be punished for this intrusion,' the Keeper threatened. 'Our laws are very clear: no Lord may enter another's domain unless expressly permitted.'

'"The Senate sees all, you will be stripped of everything and reincarnated,"' Poser quoted while holding up his hand like a talking puppet. 'Blah, blah, blah.'

'Senate?' Lana whispered.

'They are the Lords elected and trusted to oversee everything all Lords do.'

'You do not have my permission to allow mortals to enter this place, either,' the Keeper added. 'Two counts of fundamental law broken.'

'We are a long way from the centre of the galaxy, Keeps,' Poser said with a confident smile. 'It'll take the Senate's goons days to come and sort this out. Why do you think I came all the way out here? You thought you could hide away with your Well, helping all the little races along with their long crawl up the evolutionary chain. And *I'm* breaking fundamental law? Evolution is supposed to occur naturally. We got here the hard way. Why should they get a hand up?'

'They are killing each other,' the Keeper retorted. 'The Well offers them opportunity, a chance to–'

'Yeah, real noble of ya, doll. Meanwhile, I have my own dreams and desires waiting to be fulfilled. Are you gonna drop the barrier or not?'

The Keeper glared at him.

'This doesn't have to get ugly,' Poser reasoned. 'Let my boys and girls get some of your Well juice and we'll be on our way.'

Lana felt responsible for this threat and stepped in front of the Keeper. 'I'm right here, Poser. Fight me now.'

Poser raised his eyebrows and crossed his arms over his chest. 'You would be more intimidating right now if you didn't look so adorable standing there in your tank and panties.' He chuckled, but stopped when Lana's eyes flashed orange.

Poser frowned at the Keeper disappointedly. 'You told her I want to kill her, because she's evolving too fast. Figures.' He turned to Lana. 'We Lords must seem pretty special to you, huh? We're not.' He waved his right hand and sat down on a bar stool that appeared behind him.

'We have powers, we live forever, sure, but things have been pretty much business as usual since each of our species came together. We came from a world that went through archaic eras: hunter gatherer, stone age, through to industrial. Medicine, genetic engineering, we did it all. Now we're immortals, and what do we strive for? Status. That's the new wealth. And we all have our own way of attaining it.'

Poser glanced at the Keeper. 'She's all about charity.' He pressed his hand to his chest. 'Melts the heart, really. I'm an entertainer. We Lords can do this all-seeing thing, and that's my fan base. Lords watch what War drums up and my notoriety increases. They can't get enough of her.' Poser paused to give Lana an admiring look. 'You're gonna be my Gladiator. I don't wanna kill ya, kiddo. I wanna make you a star.'

'Don't listen to him,' the Keeper cautioned. 'We may not be perfect, but we know what is best for this galaxy.' She glared at Poser. 'You and your cronies do this to every creature who shows potential, and they all die, because you make the odds against them impossible!'

Poser raised his hands and smiled. 'You got me.' When he stood away from his stool, it disappeared. 'Full disclosure, Lana, we don't want any more Lords.' Poser glanced over his shoulder as though somebody might be listening. 'Don't tell War or my Collector I said this, but we're not gonna let any Minion ascend. We're it.'

The Keeper stepped to the edge of the Well. 'I'm sorry, Lana. I cannot allow this energy to fall into his hands.'

'What are you doing?' Lana saw the Keeper's toes slide over the lip of the well.

'Keeper, don't,' Fear pleaded. 'Senate Guards will be here soon.'

'We're too far away.'

'She's right,' said Poser, and he grew taller, extending his abdomen. Translucent tentacles emerged from his back, and he whipped one through the barrier into Fear. It latched onto Fear's back, and he hung his head.

'My essence will destroy the Well,' the Keeper said. 'Let him go, or I'll–'

'You wanna get dramatic?' Poser yelled. 'Let's get dramatic!'

He created a window into the Black Heron, where Lana's friends were sleeping. The tentacle twisted and Fear rose from the ground. He raised his head and his eyes glowed white.

'Lana, get to your ship,' the Keeper told her.

'The audience always wants to see the villain do somethin' real nasty.'

Poser focused Fear's power on his first victim. The window zoomed in on Rachel and entered her mind.

Rachel's boots squelched when she arrived at the motor pool floor of the COG building. She used the torch on her rifle to illuminate scorched cadavers at her feet. She saw bloodied blonde hair and froze. Sam's blue eyes were staring up at the ceiling. Lana and Rowan were there too, their lifeless eyes wide open. Rachel collapsed to her knees and cried out.

Lana turned into her demon form and ran at Poser. One of his tentacles swung at her. She slowed time, leapt and rotated her body over it. When she landed, Poser had sent two more, striking her across the floor.

The window changed to Saule. *She turned in her bunk and felt something warm dribble from her nose. She touched it and saw blood on her fingers. She got up and staggered to the bathroom mirror. To her horror, she saw fingers poking out from between her lips, and her jaw was forced open from inside by two hands. Arms and elbows extended, wet, hands clawing. Kim gasped for air and spilled out of Saule, onto the floor.*

Saule cried out in her sleep, locked inside the nightmare. Rachel was sobbing and screaming in the bunk below her.

'Stop this at once!' the Keeper shouted at Poser.

'Give me the Well!'

Poser turned his attention to General Lincoln. Fear forced himself into the flow of electronic signals surging through Lincoln's artificial brain and tapped into his personal data.

The sound of shouting, smashing windows and police sirens echoed through the city. Lincoln emerged from a dark alley into the street. Dismembered AMs lay in the gutters, their circuitry and wires spilling from their exposed torsos. The shadow of a figure hung from a lamp post. Lincoln looked up to see a naked AM dangling by her neck. KILL ALL BOTS was spray-painted down her. Wind turned her body, revealing her beaten face. Lincoln sank to his knees and cried, 'Jolie!'

Lana picked herself up from the floor, tears streaming down her face. 'Do something!' she shouted at the Keeper.

'Lords cannot combat one another,' she replied helplessly.

Lana was about to take another run at Poser when she felt an invisible hand hold her arm.

The Keeper spoke inside Lana's mind. *I have a plan.* She raised her arms, and a black, star-spotted wall rose from the floor, separating Lana from Poser. *Be ready.*

Poser forced Fear to switch to Shen. *The glare of sunlight caused Shen to squint. He heard the order shouted again from his superior. Shen raised his rifle, took aim at the fleeing refugees, held down his trigger and let the bullets fly. He killed one woman and took aim at a child. The boy turned to face Shen. It was his son.*

Poser twisted the tentacle in Fear's back again and changed his attention to Talon, who was sleeping with her labradoodle in the bunk above Miri. Bell stirred, and her growl erupted into vehement barking. Fear entered Talon's data stream before she was alerted.

The walls transformed into a classroom. *Talon was seated among other AMs, staring obediently at a video being light-projected onto a wall. An athletic, smartly dressed man was pointing his finger at them, his monotone voice coming from tall speakers. 'You will operate as directed.' Words in large capitals flashed before them, each remaining for two seconds: POLICY. PROTOCOL. PROCEDURE. 'You are company property,' he commanded. 'You will obey.' The words flashed again. Talon's ears pricked at the sound of a dog barking. She rose from her chair, taking its back in a firm grip. 'Sit down!' the man yelled. She swung and threw it at the projector. The lights came on, and all of the AMs were gone. A short man was standing at the back of the room holding a microphone. His greying hair was matted, his wrinkling jaw stubbled. Grime covered his thin, naked body. He opened his mouth to speak, lips trembling. The microphone slipped from his hand and he ran out of the room.*

'Oh, shit,' Poser stammered when he lost his connection to Fear. Fear immediately teleported to Rachel and Saule, restoring every mind he was forced to corrupt.

'You've got a bad-ass robot,' Poser admitted to Lana. He took a step back and bumped into one of the Keeper's walls. He pressed his hand against the barely distinguishable barrier. 'What are you playing at, Keeps?'

Lana drew her arm around Poser's neck from behind and let herself fall while turning her body. She released her grapple, throwing Poser over her shoulder. While he hurtled in mid-air, Lana rose into a side kick and drove her heel into his stomach, sending him two metres further before he hit the floor. The Keeper moved the ground beneath Poser until he slid through the shield and collided with his criminal soldiers, knocking two of them down like bowling pins.

'Senate Guards will be here any second,' the Keeper warned. 'I suggest you start running.'

Chapter 22

Lana returned to the Black Heron to find everyone awake and despondent. Miri was handing cups of water to Shen, Lincoln and Rowan. She spoke quietly with Lana. 'Fear told me what happened.'

Lana found a pair of leggings and her boots. 'Where's Saule?'

'She's been gone for a while. Her nightmare must have been bad.' Miri opened the loading bay door, and a translucent curtain dropped to contain clean air within the ship.

'I'll go find her,' Lana said, tying her laces. 'Can you check on Rachel?'

Miri nodded. Lana strapped a side-arm to her thigh, grabbed a mask and left.

Rachel sat on the edge of the bunk bed with Bell, relating what she had dreamt to Miri.

'The workers Sabre Company killed… you feel responsible for their deaths?' Miri asked tentatively.

'We could have attacked the COG sooner. But we didn't have the numbers until we received teleportation technology from the Kiyol.'

'Lana told me about that war on Silica.' Miri placed her hand on Rachel's. 'I cannot imagine the toll it must have taken. You are an incredibly strong woman. Sam must have found you in a very dark place.'

Rachel's bottom lip was trembling. Tears welled beneath her glazed eyes. She looked away and patted Bell, who promptly licked her hand.

'You did your best in an impossible situation,' Miri assured her.

Fear discreetly phased his bulky Yowie form into the bunk room, after speaking with Shen and Lincoln. His bushy brow was furrowed. Bell growled at him.

'I would like to make your current situation less impossible.'

Rachel wiped her tears and gave him a nod.

Lana rounded a corner and found Saule leaning her elbows on a rail overlooking the river that skirted the city. She was using her force field ability to filter the air around her.

'What happened, what you saw, was completely irrational,' Saule was saying to Kim. She glanced over her shoulder, only to make sure it wasn't one of the Mutated lurking behind her.

'Are you two alright?' Lana asked her.

The haze was less thick by the river. The cool wind was blowing at around twenty-five kilometres. 'We can't live like this,' Saule admitted, to Lana and to Kim.

'There is a solution. We'll find it,' Lana assured her. 'But right now—'

'We've got a job to do.' Saule pushed away from the rail and walked with Lana back toward the Black Heron. 'Kicking some ass is exactly what she and I need right now.'

'That's the spirit.'

'Kim says none of this makes sense.'

'What doesn't?'

Saule paused, listening to Kim with a pensive stare. Her eyes narrowed.

'You're right,' Saule told Kim and stood close to Lana, as though someone might overhear. 'Beings don't evolve to become bosses. The Minions we know of – Fear, the Collector, War – their powers have purpose. They each have their individual skills. What can the Lords do?'

'They control,' said Lana, catching on.

'What gives them their title? How are they more powerful than their Minions?'

'Are you… is Kim saying the rule of the Lords is based on some kind of political construct?'

Saule nodded slowly. 'Kim knows what it means to evolve. These so-called Lords are no more evolved than their Minions.'

Lana pressed her fingers against her forehead as though keeping her mind from exploding. 'Fear thinks Lords created Minions. And War thinks she's going to ascend.'

Saule was convinced that Kim's theory was true. 'They are being lied to for purpose of control.'

'How can War not see that?' Lana said, trying to keep her voice down. She turned abruptly, hearing something from the opposite side of the street. 'We've got company.'

She armoured her skin before the haze clouded closer, parting as muscled, tattooed arms reached for her. She bladed her hand against one, but was not able to deflect the other. The strong hand grabbed her tank top, and Lana turned and threw her back against her assailant. She crouched and rolled his body over hers, then dropped the heel of her boot on the base of his neck. The man's head slumped back, and he fell unconscious.

Saule pulled goggles off the attacker's head and looked through them. *Infrared.* She spotted two more figures in the mist, glowing where their skin was exposed. She created a force shield big enough to mask her body heat, as well as Lana's and the unconscious man's. Lana dragged him and Saule followed, keeping the shield up until they slipped into an alley.

When they reached the Black Heron, the ship sensors detected them. The ramp came down and Rowan descended to help carry the tattooed man, but not before binding his wrists and ankles. As soon as they set him down in the loading bay, the man snapped awake and struggled.

Rowan drew his side-arm and pressed the barrel against the man's temple. 'Morning, sunshine.'

The man's eyes darted around. He saw Fear standing there in his grotesque Yowie form and screamed.

'I'll leave you to it,' said Lana, and left for the cockpit to find Talon. She opened her mouth, but paused when she saw that Talon was staring out into the haze, deep in thought. 'Are you alright?'

Talon turned her head slowly and nodded.

'There are two more scouts out there,' Lana said, pointing in the direction she and Saule had come from. 'About two hundred metres that way.'

Talon increased the ship sensors to the specified range and direction. A warning tone sounded, and guns extended out of their armoured housing.

'I'll send Shen and Lincoln out to collect them.' Lana left for the loading bay and soon overheard the scout that she and Saule had captured answering Rowan's questions.

'I don't even like the guy,' the scout admitted. 'But I was doing twenty-five years. He got me out.'

Lana spoke quietly with Shen and Lincoln. They left the ship, and she went to Miri.

'I am ready to take his shape, if you have enough of a mental image,' Miri told her.

Lana placed her fingers either side of Miri's temples and gave her every detail of Poser she could remember.

Miri's face changed. Her cotton shirt and waist sash rippled, and Lana stepped back and looked her up and down with a furrowed brow.

'You have never given me that look before,' said Miri in Poser's voice.

'It's not you, it's him,' Lana explained. 'He's an a-hole.'

Miri changed back to her original form. 'His tentacles are fast. This is our only way of getting close to him.'

'No! Stop!' Poser's scout cried out. 'I'll tell you. Just stop.'

Lana turned in time to see Fear change from a bloodied young man back to his Yowie form. Fear crouched so he was face to face with the scout. 'That was but a taste. Be very sure about what you want to tell us. I will shape into any of your victims, murderer, and haunt you for the rest of your days.'

The man was wide-eyed and stammering. 'Poser's "Intro" is eight specially trained fighters. They are—'

The Black Heron shuddered, and there was a loud rumble outside.

'—explosive experts.'

'Come in, Black Heron, this is Lincoln.' The ship transmission receivers sounded distorted for a second, before Lincoln's voice returned. 'There was an explosion in the building near you. It's coming down. You need to take off.'

Lana pushed her breathing mask back on. 'Copy that. Lincoln, find a defensive position. Rowan, you're with Talon. The rest of you are with me.'

Chapter 23

Lana and Miri approached Shen and Lincoln, while Rachel and Saule moved to cover them on the opposite side of the street. A strong wind was blowing, and the haze was dissipating quickly. Where visibility was only one metre ahead moments before, the air was now crystal clear.

The six of them looked back down the street to see the Black Heron rise from the road, rotate and ascend above the buildings. The explosion had compromised the structural supports of the skyscraper next to their landing zone. It collapsed into the street, throwing shrapnel, carried by a cloud of concrete dust toward Lana's team.

Rachel was wearing a rocketeer suit, and Saule was able to use her force shield to achieve lift. They flew over the tumbling grey cloud and landed on the roof of a nearby office building. Lincoln used his rocketeer suit to ascend beside a multi-storey shopping mall, while scanning through the windows. 'Shen, building is clear. Take the stairs.'

'Copy.' Shen kicked open the nearest door and ran inside.

Lana and Miri each used their Aspect ability to change into their demon form. They crouched, and the massive grey cloud slowed. Wind-blown trash floated. The concrete footpath split from the impact of Lana and Miri's powerful legs pushing downward. In unison, they shot up three floors from the street and landed on the window ledge, safely above the rushing cloud. Lana brought up a map from her ring console, tracking the others, who were on or inside separate buildings.

Miri saw two figures on the other side of the glass and, with a sharp intake of breath, tackled Lana out of harm's way. The glass broke. The hiss of a rocket-propelled grenade sounded for a quarter second. Shimmering translucent shards fell and tumbled outward, but were halted when the grenade exploded. Lana and Miri were blown through the broken window into the office. The radial blast retracted, and glass crackled on the carpeted floor.

Lana lost her demon form, armoured her skin and drew her side-arm. She aimed and fired on two armoured men stalking between cubicles. When her bullets bounced off them, she concentrated her fire on the joins of their armour, successfully wounding one.

Miri maintained her demon form and drew her bow. She clasped the head of one arrow, notched it and took aim. The steel glowed white-hot. She let it fly, and the arrowhead sliced through the other man's helmet. His head jerked back and he fell while his partner watched on in horror. The first man took a grenade from his belt and pulled the pin. Before he could release his thumb, he saw a dark blur.

Lana's hand closed over his and the grenade release. She gripped his armour and swung him up, out of the broken window. He plummeted, and the grenade exploded when he hit the ground.

Shen was free of the dust cloud that filled the ground floor. He climbed the stairs at a steady pace, carrying his staff, his aged leg muscles aching. Heavy footfalls echoed above him, and he stopped, crouched and set a C4 charge on the step in front of him. After wiping sweat from his brow, Shen looked up to see one of Poser's armoured units arrive at the floor above.

The man trudged down and drew his left arm in front of him to reveal two pipes either side of his wrist. He clenched his fist, and double jets of flame roared down on Shen.

Shen threw himself over the rail and dropped down the stairwell one floor. He slid his staff through the bars to his left and right in time to catch himself. The violent jolt caused him to cry out. His right shoulder was on fire. The soldier leaned over the rail and aimed to finish him.

When the flames came, Shen kicked his legs up, dislodged his staff and rotated his body. At the height of his turn, he slid his staff to its full length and drove it through the fire into the man's face mask. Shen latched his fingers over the concrete edge of the step above him, tucked his staff under his armpit, drew the C4 trigger and squeezed.

The blast threw the soldier off the stairs. His head hit the jutting concrete above him, and his body rag-dolled against the rails. Shen let go of the step, landed deftly on the rail below and dropped to the stairs to escape a shower of debris.

'Smashing effort.'

'Good show indeed.'

Shen landed in the stairwell and saw a man and a woman seated next to each other. Their voices and clapping hands sounded distorted. Their images wavered as though they were ethereal. They were both dressed in sparkling silk, and their chairs were golden and jewelled.

The stairwell door above Shen opened, and another armoured soldier emerged. He looked down at Shen, who was breathing heavily.

The distant sound of a rocket caused the soldier to pause. Before he could even turn his head, Lincoln crashed through the window behind him and slammed against him. Lincoln cut his thrusters and crushed the soldier against the concrete wall.

'You said the building was clear,' Shen said, glancing over his shoulder to see that his spectators had vanished.

Lincoln opened a team-wide channel. 'Shen and I have scratched two. Poser must be teleporting them in. Our building was clear a minute ago.'

'Copy that,' Rachel replied from atop her office building, overlooking the settling dust cloud below. She heard Saule call out a warning and was knocked sideways.

Saule raised her fist at the armoured woman who had collided with Rachel, but her energy blast fired low when another of Poser's soldiers grappled her from behind. His arms were strong, pinning her hands against her sides. Saule's anger grew while she watched Rachel's assailant aim a pump-action shotgun and fire. Rachel's Rocketeer armour protected her, but the force of each round prevented her from getting up.

Saule drew energy from inside herself, released it with a roaring scream and sent out a shockwave that threw the soldier sideways as though she had entered a wind tunnel. She tumble-rolled, slamming into a roof ventilation box. Saule lifted her legs, letting her assailant take her weight. She clenched her fists and fired into his boots. The force crushed his feet, and the cement beneath him cracked. He released her. Saule dropped to the ground, and Rachel fired a rocket into his chest.

Aboard the Black Heron, Talon heard Rachel report two more targets down. The ship sensors detected an incoming surface-to-air missile. While turning the steering control, she held the attitude modifier with her thumb to dip the right wing. Bell was already safely strapped into the co-pilot seat, her ears flopping to one side as the Black Heron curved around a skyscraper, and the missile crashed through the building's windows and exploded. Once she circled the building, Talon hovered the ship, readying her cannons. An alert sounded and the targeting system zeroed in on the armoured unit who had fired on them. He was reloading his launcher atop a cathedral turret when he paused, dropped the weapon and made for the stairs. Talon's cannons blasted, throwing stone and mortar in all directions until the entire corner of the cathedral was obliterated.

Rowan had unbuckled in the cargo bay and was watching over Talon's shoulder. 'I think you got 'im,' he said and pointed to a rooftop. 'You can drop us there.'

She opened the bay door and hovered low over the roof. Rowan held his sniper rifle against his chest, dropped and broke his fall with a roll across the cement. Wrists still cable-tied, Poser's scout stood fearfully at the edge of the bay door. Thudding paws sounded behind him. Bell leapt and drove her front legs into his gut. He fell back, rotated awkwardly, struck an air conditioner and face-planted on the roof. The Black Heron flew away, while Rowan helped him to his feet.

'Smooth,' Rowan said, freeing his wrists and ankles.

'Does this mean I'm free? Oh, shit, she has a grenade!' The scout pointed to an approaching female soldier.

The woman tossed her fragmentation grenade at them. Rowan drew his rifle scope to his right eye, lined her up and shot her down. He turned, taking hold of his gun barrel, and swung hard. The flat face of the stock hit the grenade, sending it clear of the roof.

'Brilliant!' came a senior woman's voice from behind them, the explosion sounding far below.

Rowan turned to see her standing in mid-air.

'Ignore her,' said the scout. 'She's just a spons–'

His back arched, and he rose from the ground. Rowan saw a translucent tentacle buried in his spine and immediately backed away, rifle ready.

With a flick and release, the scout's body sailed over the edge of the building.

'Havin' fun yet?' Poser shouted from the street below. 'Come on down. Got a special surprise for y'all.'

Lana stepped to the window. There were over three hundred soldiers standing behind Poser. War was at his side. When Miri took a step toward Lana with a furrowed brow and her bow ready, Lana held up a hand. 'Tell everyone to be ready.'

'We'll be ready,' said Miri.

Lana changed into her demon form and dropped off the edge. The bitumen caved like a crater when she landed. Rachel flew down with Saule, and Lincoln swooped down, carrying Shen. They arrived at Lana's side.

Poser looked at each of the five glaring humans. 'You're not all still sore about those nightmares, are you?'

Lana ignored Poser and gave War a respectful bow. 'The Collector told me you will be granted Lord status after this battle,' she lied. 'If I survive, I'd like to pledge my allegiance to you. Please consider me as your first Minion.'

War strode forward and clapped her hand down on Lana's shoulder. 'You are a mighty combatant, and a good woman.' She drew a knife from her belt, twirled it around her finger and caught the handle. 'Were I capable of bleeding, I would commit to a blood oath.' She held the knife in front of Lana and spoke a word Lana didn't know. The knife transformed into a hand axe. 'Fight well, Lana of Casal, and I shall indeed have you as my Minion.'

Lana tested the balance of her new weapon by flipping it from one hand to the other. The head was made of a metal she guessed would not be found on Earth. She could see subtle swirls of deep purple in its surface. The handle was strapped with leather, pressed with curved, interwoven lines.

'How quaint,' Poser commented patiently. 'War, have your army form up. Let 'em loose on my signal.' He waited until War stepped away, then approached Lana and whispered, 'Whatever you're playing at, it won't work.'

'We'll see,' she replied.

Poser flinched and then smiled, before rising into the air. 'Let the games begin!'

A sword of medieval design materialised in War's hand. She pointed it at Lana and cried out, 'Have at thee!'

Her army charged forward, roaring and shouting abuse.

'Draw them over the rubble!' Lana called to the others, before parrying War's first sword swing.

Saule, Rachel and Lincoln took to the sky, firing down on the army, pounding them with rockets and energy blasts. Rowan lined up enemies from his position atop the building at their flank. And Miri fired arrows from her window.

Lana forward-kicked War in the gut, giving her a break to dash up the concrete blocks and jutting rebar of the building that had been brought down. She grabbed Shen's outstretched hand, drew on her demon strength and hoisted him up and over her. Lincoln and Rachel swooped down and carried them both to the other side of the rubble. An explosive burst sounded from War's army, and a rocket-propelled grenade hit the concrete ridge, sending chunks flying and lifting steel beams.

Lana and her team took cover from the shower of debris. 'Saule, we need a shield!' she called through open comms. 'Talon, fire on them once Saule has us covered.'

Saule concentrated her power and created a shield, while Talon descended on War's army, raining down a hail of blasts.

'Take us up,' Lana said to Rachel and Lincoln. She called over the echoing cacophony of cannon fire, 'Dropping the barriers!'

The explosions had attracted hundreds of Mutated at each fence they had erected. Lana activated her ring console and tapped the command. The barriers, no longer electrified, were immediately toppled by a mass of bodies.

Lana and Miri crouched and jumped in unison, leaping over the mound of rubble and War's army in one bound. The others followed, Lincoln taking Shen, Rachel and Saule taking Rowan. He gazed down at the army pushing through and over their own wounded. As soon as they reached the precipice of the mound, they were met by a surging horde of Mutated.

The first line of soldiers opened fire with handguns and automatic rifles. Mutated bodies dropped, and were immediately trampled by the rest of the horde. The Mutated collided with War's army. The crazed men and women, pushing from behind, climbed over those eating the flesh of screaming soldiers. Backs, heads and shoulders were trod on, the momentum of the horde surging over the rubble, bodies falling metres down the mound, over people eating, being eaten, fighting, dying, obscured by blood and flesh.

Chapter 24

Poser's scowl deepened at the sight of his army being swarmed by the Mutated. He glanced at the ethereal spectators, who were enthralled and cheering up at Lana and her team as they flew over Poser and his criminals.

'Rear!' War called to the back of the army. 'Incoming!'

Lana and Miri broke the road at their feet upon landing. The others arrived to make a line, all but Rowan, who Rachel flew to the roof of a truck before she joined the others. He immediately found his first target in the crosshairs of his scope and fired.

Joined by War, the rear force of criminals charged, brandishing machetes, knives and hand axes. Those armed with guns fired on Lana's team from twenty metres. Lana armoured her skin and ran at them, an axe in each hand, Rachel at her side, bullets bouncing off their chests and shoulders. Miri fired arrows at the left and right flank of War's army from behind Saule's widening force field. Talon rappelled down from the Black Heron, landed behind Miri and tapped her ring to send the ship on a programmed route to a safe rooftop.

War broke ahead of the firing line, covering the gap between herself and Lana at impressive speed. Rachel flew over her and collided with two soldiers firing rifles. Saule moved forward, firing energy blasts through her shield at the enemy.

Lana parried War's sword swing and attempted a forward kick. War struck her leg aside, opening her stance, and dropped one shoulder hard against her chest, knocking her to the ground. Lana rolled to her feet and swung the back of her axe against War's knee. She staggered enough that Lana could roundhouse-kick the side of her head.

Wielding a crossbow, Talon fired at one flank of the enemy, while Miri continued shooting at the other. Rachel used her suit's hammer-fist to knock down an opponent. A group ran at her, and she drew back her elbows, charged her fists, dove in and knocked them all down. From his airborne position, Lincoln spotted a steel beam teetering like a seesaw on the rubble mound. He rocketed higher, cut his engines and descended on the steel's end at high speed. It flipped the second he struck it, hurtling and ploughing into War's army.

Miri broke away from combat, while Shen, Talon and Saule covered her escape.

Poser was standing in the middle of his army, completely obscured by the chaos, looking from the Mutated at one end of the street to Lana's team at the other. His criminal soldiers had nowhere to go, and they'd suffered over a hundred casualties. The Mutated looked to be around two hundred, and they were too close to be effectively felled. They snapped their jaws, scratched and clawed. Poser's soldiers hacked and slashed with bladed weapons. Every few minutes, a wave of Mutated climbed over the rows of fighting and toppled those not yet engaged, creating a chaotic and bloody scene of desperation.

On the roof above, a middle-aged man wearing golden robes and jewelled rings on every finger strode to whom he thought was Poser. 'You've bloody well outdone yourself this time, Poser. 'Ow d'ya plan on dealin' with War? She'll expect to be made one of us.'

Though until that second Miri hadn't been sure her ability would affect these immortals, she managed a confident reply. 'How were our Minions fooled in the first place?'

'You wanna cast the Ceiling? Righto. That'll wipe 'er memory for sure.' He moved on to watch the battle, satisfied that Poser had everything in hand.

Miri, now alone, looked to the battle raging below. She stopped the recording on her ring console and sent the conversation to Lana.

War had Lana in a grapple hold from behind. Lana heard her ring console beep and grunted at the exertion of twisting out of War's powerful arms. She saw the recording and played it out loud. She side-kicked a soldier, knocking him down, and threw herself at War, wrestling her long enough to yell, 'Listen to me! Your Lord was recorded conversing with a sponsor. Hear it.' She played Miri's recording and released War.

'What trickery is this?' War seethed.

'You tell me,' Lana pleaded. 'War, you are powerful. Fear can stop time! How can you possibly be beneath Lords? Beneath the likes of Poser?'

War spotted her Lord ascending out of the chaos to hover over the fray. 'There are sacred rules. The Senate would never—'

'All societies live within constructs,' Lana argued, shoving a combatant off her. 'Poser is taking advantage of that construct. He is using you to further his own status.'

Another spectator arrived beside the real Poser. 'We have just learned that you have forced the hand of the Senate yet again. And, from what I understand, for the last time. The Senate Guard will be here any moment.'

Poser shot a scowl at the ethereal woman floating next to him. He knew where this was going.

'You have created many a satisfying spectacle,' she said. 'We have paid you handsome notoriety to secure your place among the elite. But I'm afraid we cannot risk being identified by the Senate Guard.' Her image began to fade. 'Don't take it personally,' she added before disappearing completely.

Poser floated down to the Mutated and criminals clashing on the street. He unfurled a mass of translucent tentacles from his back, stabbing them into dozens of the Mutated. They all stopped, turned around and attacked their own kind. War's soldiers were dropping to their knees as though struggling to breathe, then they rippled and faded away.

'My army, where…' War murmured, slowly realising the sponsors would only take it away if they were no longer invested in Poser's spectacle.

'Talon, we'll need the ship,' Lana called to her. 'I think it's time to go.'

She glanced to War, who was looking more and more convinced by Lana's revelation.

Poser opened a gateway, unleashing a blindingly bright wall of flames. Sweeping his arms like a composer, he drew the furnace into the Mutated, burning them alive. He arrived in front of Lana and War, his polished shoes touching down on the rubble. Guttural cries and black smoke rose from the fire behind him.

The Black Heron landed behind Lana's group, and Talon boarded, while Rowan took position on the bay door, aiming his rifle at Poser. 'Let's get outta here!' he called.

'Leaving so soon?' Poser asked, in a mocking tone.

A horn sounded from the sky. Poser's jaw dropped when he looked up to see eleven figures descending. Their chests were broad, their skin a pale, pinkish hue. All were male, bald, wearing only loincloths. They were winged, their impressive spans beating as they hovered, gazing impassively at Poser. The one in the middle tucked his wings and let gravity take him. When his cloven feet stabbed into the road, a rumble echoed against the buildings.

The creature rose from his landing crouch to his full two-metre height. His voice was deep, his tone measured. 'We are the Senate Guards. Lord Poser, you and your Minions will come with us.'

War stalked over to Poser, gripped his arm and swung him to face her.

'The truth, worm,' she demanded. 'Your kind and mine are one and the same?'

'Not a good time for that revelation,' he whispered, and turned to the Senate Guard.

The Guard before them raised one hand. The other Guards beat the air with their wings and circled Lana's team.

'This secret must be kept,' he announced, meeting everyone's gaze in turn. 'In the name of the Senate, and for the sanctity and prosperity of all the Evolved, you must all be destroyed.'

'Talon, Rowan, get out of here,' Lana ordered them through her comms.

War drew her sword and pressed the blade to Poser's throat. 'Take us all to your Sanctum.'

Poser raised an eyebrow at her. 'Run? You, War? In all the years—'

'*Now!*'

Poser shot his tentacles out to War, Lana and her team. They all vanished and reappeared inside a candlelit hall.

Opulent was the first word Lana thought to describe what she saw. The high walls were lined with art: scenes of battle. And there were glass domes on pedestals, each containing a model of a world the Collector had torn, collided, fused together.

Miri moved to the nearest window and took in the view of a vast maze, not made of hedge, but of rippling curtains of energy. A Veil, identical to the one that separated her and Lowen's worlds, skirted the perimeter. Her fingers curled in, and she turned on Poser with fury. Her fist struck his jaw, and he fell to the floor.

'Is this where you killed her?' Miri shouted.

'Lady, I don't–'

'My mother!'

Poser stared up at Miri. She looked like the woman who had forced her way into his Sanctum.

'You'd best answer her,' War growled. 'I'll not protect you anymore.' She pointed her sword at him. 'And no tentacle tricks! I will carve you in half if you slither even one of them near anyone again!'

'Fine. No tricks.' He levitated onto his feet and wiped his fingers across his jaw. The bruise disappeared. He met Miri's glare with seemingly genuine concern. 'Your mother came looking for answers.'

'Her name was Ina,' Miri said between clenched teeth.

'Ina wouldn't leave until I agreed to restore her family.' Poser shrugged. 'I said I didn't have the power to. I summoned the Collector. He said the worlds he created can't withstand another dramatic change. Of course, she argued solutions, demanded we restore every world he made. But it can't be done. I told Ina that and returned her to her world.'

Tears welled in Miri's eyes, her fists shaking. She turned and stormed out of the hall. Lana followed her down a corridor.

'He's a monster,' Miri said, when she stopped and turned to face Lana.

'Collecting worlds seems to be a curiosity for Lords like Poser.'

'They must be stopped.'

'The Senate is coming for him,' said Lana, gazing deep into Miri's eyes. 'I think we should take advantage of their interest in keeping their secret safe.'

Miri followed Lana back to the others. Poser was seated at the head of the massive dining table. Saule and Shen were watching for the Senate Guard. Rachel and Lincoln were questioning Poser about his Sanctum defences.

'They're no use,' Poser groaned. 'This place was designed to stop mortals from getting to me, not the Senate Guard. They're probably on the other side of that Veil right now, trying to tear through.' He readjusted his ruffled shirt collar. 'Best we accept it, kids. The Senate want us dead. We're dead.'

'We have a plan,' said Lana, stalking toward him. 'How do we reach the Senate?'

Poser started shaking his head. 'Uh-uh, bad plan.'

'Perhaps I can help.'

Everybody turned to find the Keeper of the Well standing in a beam of light shining through the window. Fear was beside her. He bowed apologetically and said, 'I lied to you, Lana, that day in the village.'

Lana raised an eyebrow with a gesture to the Keeper. 'You know you're the same as her?'

Fear nodded. 'There are many who do, but cannot challenge this caste system.'

'Not until we all take a stand,' the Keeper said. 'With your help, Lana, we can bring an end to this construct.'

'Then we must not delay,' said War, puffing up her chest, her hand on the hilt of her sword. 'Let us assemble–' She paused, blinking as though she were about to black out.

Lana and Miri looked from War to the Keeper. Both Evolved beings were shaking their heads, dazed. Shen was standing closest to Poser, who fell against him. He stepped aside and let Poser hit the floor. Saule gasped when Fear became limp, but his body didn't drop. He instead floated lifelessly. Rachel caught War when she swayed.

'What's happening to them?' Miri asked Lana.

'I don't know.' Out of the corner of her eye, Lana saw the Veil beyond the maze outside parting like a curtain. The Senate Guard flew through the opening wedge in single file until all eleven were inside Poser's Sanctum.

War was regaining her senses. She stood with Rachel's help and spotted the Senate Guard. She opened a translucent gate in front of her. 'Everybody in!' she barked.

Shen took Poser by the back of his suit collar and dragged him through the gate. Fear snapped back to consciousness, and the others assisted the Keeper. The gate closed behind them, leaving Poser's lavish hall empty.

Chapter 25

They all entered Mechtropolis, outside the mansion known as Contrivance. The Keeper was lucid but confused.

'Where are we?' she asked War.

'An alternate version of Earth,' Rachel explained, while typing a message on her ring console. 'I'm contacting the Sedit. Hopefully they're ready to help us out.'

'We should separate,' Lana suggested. 'Shen, Lincoln, contact Talon and portal aboard her ship. I'll text you once we have a plan.'

The two wished the others luck and left to arrange portal travel. The others heard a loud groan, and the Collector sat up from long grass.

'You got out?' Rachel called to him.

'I was jettisoned,' the Collector snapped, while looking for his missing sandal. 'Contrivance thought I died during the time dilation.'

'The what?'

'The Senate must have used the Eye to look into the future,' War grumbled. 'That's why we passed out.'

'It is forbidden to look forward,' the Keeper explained. 'It is meant only for studying the past.'

Poser smirked. 'Sounds like they're onto your little rebellion, Keeps.'

The Collector stood abruptly when he recognised Poser's voice. 'My Lord! You're here!' He hopped toward Poser while putting on his sandal. 'Please excuse this most egregious faux pas. I found this exquisite world for you, but then I was deceived by–'

'Stop talking,' Poser commanded. 'We're in a tight spot, kid.

The Senate Guard are on our tail.'

'Why, my Lord?'

'Because we found out he's not our Lord,' War answered sternly. 'Lords and Minions are made-up titles to create a false hierarchy.'

The Collector shifted awkwardly from foot to foot. 'We can't ascend?'

'There is no ascension, twit!' War shouted, causing him to cower.

Lana raised calming hands to War and turned to the Collector. 'Finding out so-called "all-knowing" people have been perpetuating social oppression for generations is rough, I know. But we need you on board. Now is the time to set things right. This shit has to stop.'

'I have always been told I am not complete as long as I am a Minion, that I am only temporary, that I must become more,' the Collector murmured, his fists clenched. 'This whole time, I have been complete?' He gritted his teeth, his narrowing eyes darting to Poser. 'I have been equal to everyone my whole life?'

'Yes,' War encouraged. 'Use it. Together, we will take it to them.'

'How far forward can they see?' Rachel asked the Keeper.

'Ten, perhaps fifteen minutes ahead,' the Keeper replied, checking the skies for the Senate Guard. Though she was not as anxious as Poser, the Keeper did not like their chances of escape.

'We have a slim advantage,' said Rachel, and set an alarm on her ring console for ten minutes. 'They see us here, panicking, arguing.' She looked to Poser. 'We can jump to somewhere else.'

'If they don't find us first,' Poser whined.

'I'll go back to the College,' the Collector offered, untying his top knot to let his hair fall about his ears. He gave Miri a guilty frown. 'There, I may be able to undo some of what I have done.'

'What is this College, exactly?' Miri asked sceptically.

'We travel to different worlds and collect environments, cultures, people. We plant them between Veils, in sustainable planetary arrangements.'

The air rippled like a mirage above hot ground, and the Sedit woman, Kirin, stepped through. Her Prince, Thulu, followed.

'Can you create a gateway that can shroud all of us?' Rachel asked. 'We need to buy ourselves some time.'

Thulu nodded to Kirin, and together, they created a dome of heat-distorted air over the whole group.

'How many of your people are restored?' Rachel asked Kirin.

'Ten, so far,' she answered. 'What danger do you face?'

'Us,' the Keeper of the Well said. 'Our fellow Evolved are trying to maintain a hierarchy, which they will protect at any cost.'

'Evolved?' Thulu thought for a moment. 'Oh, you are the "Lords" and "Minions" race,' he deduced with a chuckle. 'My kind have encountered you before.' He looked from the Keeper to Poser with disgust. 'You are a troublesome lot. Though I cannot claim to belong to a virtuous race, we never sought to deceive or oppress our brethren. And the evolution of the Sedit and Lustitians took a far more holistic course than yours.'

'What's he talking about?' Lana asked the Keeper.

'Might as well spill it, Keeps,' Poser said, constantly looking to the skies for the Senate Guard. 'We're dead anyway.'

When the Keeper remained silent, Poser did a double take. 'Really? Okay, I'll tell 'em.' He cleared his throat. 'So, our civilisation was only one hundred years older than yours,' he started with glance to Lana and Rachel, 'when our space explorers discovered the Eye, a time device built by an ancient race long gone. We had the technology to create a matter portal. We channelled our DNA through the matter portal and into the Eye. The process accelerated our evolution to what we are now.'

'The Well...' Miri gazed at her hands, changing her skin to demon-red with patterns of black.

'It is the original matter portal,' the Keeper confessed.

War's dark wavy locks swayed when she shook her head, trying to make sense of her existence.

'You cheated time?' Lana asked.

The Keeper sighed. 'Yes.'

Fear nodded humbly. 'I chose my form around the time humans developed the concept of fearing the unknown. I did not want to be immortal, so I decided that I would only exist for as long as the concept. I may have underestimated the irrationality of the human mind.'

'This culture of control is beneath us,' the Keeper stated resolutely. 'It is time it stopped.'

'Gimme a break!' Poser hollered. 'Control is who we are. It's what we do. We've done things to people; turned their worlds into our own playthings.' He pointed at Miri. 'That toothpaste can't be put back in the tube. You want us to stop? You gotta stop who we are.' He looked over Miri's shoulder to the Collector. 'Let's go, kid. We're turning ourselves in.'

The Collector started toward Poser, with his head down, obedient. War took hold of his arm and shoved him back toward the others. An incredulous bellow erupted from her throat. 'You dare command him like nothing has changed!' She drew her sword and whipped the flat side across Poser's stunned expression, hard enough to turn him around. And she drove her boot into his behind, sending him into the grass on his belly. '*Everything* has changed!' she shouted.

'We should turn him in,' the Keeper advised. 'I can get us to the Senate. But we need to get the lead Guard alone.' She caught Lana's pensive glance toward Miri. 'You have a plan.'

'I do.' Lana typed a request to Rowan and asked Talon to return with the Black Heron. She looked to each person in their party. 'The Keeper and I are turning Poser in. Or so they will think,' she added before Poser could object. 'War, you and the Keeper will come and play along.'

Rachel's alarm sounded, and she gazed up at the sound of engines dialling down in thrust. It was the Black Heron descending for a swift landing. It rotated, and the loading bay door came down at the same time the landing gear made contact with the ground.

'We brought the Shifters like you asked,' Rowan called, descending a ramp with an armful of boxes. 'What's the plan?'

'For now, we scatter,' Lana said, taking Shifters from Rowan's boxes and handing them to her team. 'Miri, the Keeper and I will stay. Everyone else, choose a different realm and go there now.'

War grabbed Poser by his collar. 'Come, weakling.' And with an open hand, she gestured to the Collector. 'Come, brother. We go.'

'Ro, you should get back to Fiona,' Rachel advised him. 'We've got this.'

He gave Rachel a knowing look and programmed one of the Shifters to open a portal back home.

'I need to go back to the Portal Hub,' Rachel said to Lana. 'Let me know if you need me.'

Lana nodded and watched Shen, Saule and Lincoln each disappear through a portal, one after the other. Miri took Poser's form and knelt at Lana and the Keeper's feet. Lana drew her side-arm and hesitantly aimed it at Miri's head.

'Better you be unconscious,' the Keeper whispered. Miri slumped down and closed her eyes.

A wide tear rippled through the air twenty metres away, high above Contrivance. The Senate Guards appeared, and ten remained hovering while their leader descended. His cloven feet met the ground with a double thud, and he glowered down at "Poser".

'I have enlightened all of the mortals,' the Keeper explained. 'This one called Lana knocked Poser down. His lies have had no effect on his Minions. The Collector has returned to his duties, and War is doing whatever mongering she does.'

The lead Guard listened, his eyes wandering from Lana to the Keeper.

'The Senate will be most pleased to know of your loyalty,' he stated.

'If this fool is to be executed, I offer my Well as his final doom.'

The lead Guard took hold of Poser's hips and hefted him up over one shoulder. 'His death must be witnessed by the Senate.'

The Keeper was aware of the Guards above, gazing down her cleavage, admiring her athletic physique. She placed her hand on the lead Guard's arm and let her soft skin glide along his bulging muscles. 'Come, follow me to my domain. We can become better acquainted after you toss him in the Well.'

The lead Guard paused and looked down at her hand. He glanced over his shoulder at the floating Guards. 'Return to the Senate. I will send Poser to his doom.'

'Take your time, Tahrin,' one of the Guards called, and garish laughter erupted among the others. They all ascended, created a gate to their home world and disappeared through it.

Tahrin's gaze returned to the Keeper, probing her curves with pale grey eyes, in which she saw the depth of violent centuries, of punishment and execution.

Chapter 26

The Keeper led Tahrin, Lana and Miri as Poser into her Sanctum. Miri immediately fought vertigo when she saw the endless starlit expanse below Tahrin's cloven feet. Then she saw the subtle gloss from the light of the Well shine along the transparent floor.

'Cast this fool aside, noble Captain,' the Keeper said, letting her red gown fall from her left shoulder, exposing her breast. 'The human will knock him cold should he wake. Let's you and I forge some memories.'

Tahrin shrugged Miri off his shoulder, and she tumbled onto the floor. He drew down the Keeper's gown. She took a step back, letting him drink in her naked, athletic physique. His cloven feet trampled her gown, and he took her chin between finger and thumb.

'Before you receive my seed…' Tahrin thrust himself roughly against her. 'Know that if I find this a ruse, to save the lives of those present when the secret was uttered, I will not turn you in to the Senate.'

The Keeper raised an eyebrow. 'You would betray your sacred oath for me?'

Tahrin gave her a toothy grin. 'I would give you to my fellow Guards to make merry with until you die.'

'I don't doubt it, Captain. You will find no subterfuge here.' She glanced to Lana. 'Watch Poser. Put him out again if he wakes.'

Lana bowed, hiding her glowering hatred for Tahrin before he looked her way. She paused when she felt the Keeper connect telepathically to her mind, giving her knowledge to use a new forming ability. She crouched to touch Miri's forehead, sharing what the Keeper gave her.

The Keeper drew Tahrin away from the Well, staring lust into his eyes. 'Come, my winged stallion.'

'Should you survive, woman, I may make you my concubine.'

Miri let her form return and crept to the Well with Lana. They reached into it, and energy surged through them.

'You may break.' Tahrin groaned with arousal. 'But you will know ecstasy in every thrust of my—'

He saw vibrant light washing over the Keeper's dark skin. He turned to see Lana and Miri stalking toward him, the light of the Well reflecting against their demon forms.

Lana's right hand and Miri's left latched onto his throat before he could react. He took hold of their arms, but found he could not free himself. Their grips tightened. He dropped to his knees. The Keeper let out a cry that drummed in his chest, and he looked up to see her rising above him, her fist drawn back at the apex of her leap. His eyes widened as she bore down on him. Her fist broke through the crown of his skull and crushed his brain. Blood dribbled from his nostrils, out of his mouth, down his chin, and dripped down his chest.

The Keeper pulled her hand free from Tahrin's skull, and she held out her blood-soaked palm. The floor moved, carrying him to the Well like dead cattle on a conveyor belt. His body fell into the swirling colours and light, consumed without a trace. The Keeper flicked her hand, and the blood disappeared.

'I am sorry you had to see that,' she said and waved her hand over her naked body. Her gown formed itself over her shoulders and wrapped itself comfortably around her. 'And I appreciate your assistance. Tahrin deserved worse. He has imprisoned countless "dissidents", and he mistreated women.'

After a moment's silence, Miri looked from the Keeper to Lana. 'If the plan was for me to infiltrate their Senate by assuming Tahrin's identity, I cannot. He was too large. And I don't know how to grow as you did, Lana, when you fought Thulu.'

'I can show you how to put yourself inside Lana,' the Keeper offered.

'Excuse me?'

'I think she means you and I can merge to match Tahrin's size,' said Lana. 'We can look like him in one body.' She turned to the Keeper. 'Let's do that.'

The Keeper stood between Lana and Miri and placed a hand on each of them. Her skill and knowledge entered their minds once again.

Miri pressed her palm against Lana's chest. Lana gasped when Miri's hand sank into her. Both their skin tones turned pale, their physiques rippling with muscle. Miri stepped into Lana, and their bodies merged, growing large and masculine in one form. Broad wings sprouted from their back. Tahrin was complete.

'Incredible,' Miri said in Tahrin's deep voice. She turned to the Keeper before Lana was ready to move, and their single form toppled awkwardly. Their combined weight hit the floor with a clap.

'It will take practice.'

'No kidding,' Lana grumbled. 'Miri, let's roll left onto our elbows. Good, now knees under…'

'I hear you both with Tahrin's ears and inside my mind,' Miri commented shakily as they slowly stood back up.

'I know,' said Lana. 'I feel like I'm the only one in this body, until you make a move. Then I feel like a puppet.'

'The Senate is located in the Citadel, our city,' the Keeper explained, circling "Tahrin" to inspect the merge. 'Make mention of our courtship and that you have sent for me. I will organise those I trust to join us and find you once you have entered the world of the Evolved. You can change back to your original forms if you need to prepare before setting off.'

'We do,' said Lana. She and Miri separated out of the winged form.

'Good luck to you both.'

Lana and Miri emerged from a portal at the base of Miri's tree house. A guard announced their arrival, and Lowen stepped out from the front door.

'Are you both alright?' she called down.

'We're okay,' Lana answered.

Lowen looked to the guard, who was stationed on a tree bridge five metres away at her eye level. 'Call the meeting,' she ordered. 'All must attend.'

'I forgot to warn everyone that my mother may start running the entire village,' Miri said to Lana under her breath.

Lowen descended to ground level. 'Lana, I would like you to take us all to my village, after I have addressed Miri's here. All who have suffered the Tear must meet. There is much to discuss.' She paused, checking them over. 'You both look exhausted.'

'Much has happened,' Miri sighed. 'Lana and I will meet you once we are rested.'

'Of course, but before you do, there's good news: the elders have cracked Ina's Rune code. Many of the pages in her books made no sense because she was writing in Rune language. Now, we've determined the location of the Sanctum where she found Poser, and the location of the College, the place where Collectors hone their ability to tear and sample worlds.'

Miri took her mother's hands and looked into her eyes with conviction. 'We are going to make them stop.'

'No more suffering,' Lowen agreed, her eyes watering. 'Go now and rest. I will see you at the meeting.'

Lana woke the next morning, having slept a full eight hours without stirring. She felt Miri's arm draped over her side. She heard voices downstairs, and a spoon scraping the bottom of one of Miri's wooden bowls.

'We have company,' Lana whispered to Miri, stroking her arm.

'Mmm?'

'Sorry, ladies, did we wake you?' Saule called from downstairs.

'We're up,' Lana called back. She rose with Miri, and they kissed.

Miri found white cotton handkerchiefs in her bedside drawer. 'We should practice,' she suggested, binding her and Lana's wrists. They stood in the open space before the double bed, Miri behind Lana. Lana bent down to tie their ankles and Miri gasped at the sudden thrust to her groin.

'I think we should switch,' she giggled.

They switched and started walking together like Frankenstein's monster, with Miri taking the lead.

'Hey, you two,' Rachel called from the bottom of the stairs. 'Stop fooling around and have some breakfast.'

Lana and Miri fell over, landing on their left side with their heads overhanging the top step. 'We are engaged in important training,' Miri said and laughed with Lana.

'Saule,' Lana called. 'Could you come and untie us? Please and thank you.'

They ate breakfast with Saule, Shen and Rachel, laughing about recent events, like when Rachel tricked the Collector into getting trapped in Contrivance. Shen cracked a smile at Lana's mimicking of Poser's dumbfounded expressions when he knew he was done for.

'Where did you put that idiot, anyway?' Lana asked Saule. She paused when Saule didn't answer. 'He's behind me, isn't he…'

Everyone nodded.

'I'll let all that slide, kid,' came Poser's voice, while his gateway closed. 'Seeing as you guys saved my skin. So what's the plan?'

'The less you know, the better,' Rachel answered, with an untrusting eye on him.

Miri glanced at the sunlight beaming across the floor through the window. 'My mother will have begun the meeting by now,' she said. 'I must attend.'

'Diplomacy is preferable to violence,' Shen offered sagely.

'Says the guy who butchered a dozen of his army's top brass,' scoffed Poser. 'That's right, War's not the only one who set the Eye on you people and your chequered pasts. Except for yours, kid.' He glanced to Saule. 'Even becoming a rock star didn't sully your straight-edge living, huh?'

'Latvian upbringing.' Saule shrugged innocently.

Shen returned the conversation to Miri's mother. 'Lowen is wise and very brave to take on such a responsibility. To discuss taking your people's voice to the so-called "Evolved" is–'

'Your ma's going to *what?*' Poser spun to face Miri. 'The Senate can't be reasoned with. They do what works for the hierarchy.'

'You want us to go in guns blazing?' Lana asked in retort.

'More like bombs exploding, cannons blasting,' said Poser, his eyes wide. 'You think those guys with the wings are the scariest thing we have? We didn't just hit fast forward on our evolution for intellectual enlightenment. We evolved our watch dogs, our soldiers, and our monsters.' He looked around the room. 'Speaking of, where's that cute yet bloodthirsty pilot of yours, Lana?'

'She said she had to go back to Rome.'

Chapter 27

Talon was surveying Chinese ghost towns from Earth's orbit when her ship sensors detected a trade freighter entering Earth space. She gently pulled the thrust lever, tailing the gigantic vessel. After inverting the Black Heron, she engaged the magnetic anchoring and latched her ship onto the underside of the freighter's hull. It landed at a domestic airport outside of Xi'an, China. Talon and Bell unbuckled their harnesses, flipped down and steadied themselves on the rubber ceiling of their ship.

Talon filled a bowl of water, turned on some music and inverted the security camera feeds for Bell to keep an eye on. *I'll be back soon,* she signed.

A portal opened once she input the coordinates she was given by the Peace Keeper network. She entered and was in pitch darkness when the sphere closed behind her. Motion detectors turned on an overhead lamp. A wall panel automatically slid aside, revealing a walk-in wardrobe, which Talon inspected; clothing and disguises on one side, weapons opposite, tactical gear at the back.

Once dressed in a cami summer dress and matching sneakers, Talon adjusted her black wig and pushed a heavy door open. A barrage of street noise filled the room. She closed the bookcase door behind her, left the furnished apartment through a rear exit and found a bicycle in the alley. She departed on her memorised route, joining a stream of busy traffic.

Deep booms sounded from the inner-city Drum Tower as she

approached the roundabout. She took a left, parked the bike and walked to the Muslim Market. She received cheerful greetings from the first stall owners, and soon she was weaving through the crowd of marketgoers, embroiled in the cacophony of haggling and the delicious smells of sweet and savoury food.

'I invite you into our sanctuary,' a middle-aged woman said, beckoning Talon. 'Come inside and learn of our ways, child.'

Talon glimpsed the woman's hand sign. *She's a Peace Keeper Operative.* Talon smiled and followed her to a high-walled monastery.

The woman gestured to a chair in the shade. 'Rest, while I fetch tea and a sister who will speak to you about our way.'

The walls reduced the market's volume by about half. Talon shifted her chair into the sunlight. She gazed across the monastery courtyard, at the swaying trees, their leaves a bright yellow. Her moment of reverie was broken by a man pacing to and from the monastery wall – a tourist, by the over-practical way he was dressed – watching American news on his wrist device.

'*There is no Council, sir. And until new members are officially elected, political authority has reverted to the old ways. First on my agenda as acting President is singles. Singles are untrustworthy, irresponsible delinquents living in an unhappily temporary and available state.*'

A different voice countered the woman's rhetoric, stating, '*These are adults you're vilifying, not juvenile criminals. They show remarkable resilience against people like you and the adversities you represent. Singles are UC Citizens who have the same rights as you and me.*'

'*They have to earn those rights by taking part in human culture,*' the President argued. '*All singles have two weeks from today to enter a relationship and pass a probationary period of couple-reporting. Anyone found to be single after this fortnight will be detained by our ISE agents and evicted from Earth. They can go join that culture-killing rabble of "social freedom" fruitcakes for all I care.*'

'*Acting President, is it true your International Singles Eviction agency is funded by InvEstir? This is what they wanted, wasn't it? Sever ties with our allies, make Earth vulnerable? Sabre Company wanted the same thing; to revert everything back to what you call "the old ways".*'

'*We're done here.*'

The tourist looked up from the screen with a grimace when a rotund woman wearing almost the same outfit as him exited the building.

'What the hell took ya so long?' he hollered. 'I've been out in this stinkin' heat… What is that?'

'I'm sorry, babe,' the woman said. 'I was buying tea.'

'You're spendin' my money on piss-water?'

Talon stood abruptly. She felt a gentle hand on her arm.

'Tea for you, child,' the woman said, having returned from inside. 'Do not engage,' she advised, in a low English accent. 'Your targets are the last of InvEstir.'

Talon accepted the cup of tea, and felt a paper note under it. She watched the operative leave before reading two names: Sheik Bagher and Father Anatole, each sub-headed with the coordinates and name of a Xi'an hotel.

'Out of order? What a surprise,' the irate husband complained.

Talon followed him to the back of an outhouse he'd tried, and after making sure no one was looking, she opened a portal and pulled him through it.

Bad singing came from an en-suite shower, while Talon held the tourist's mouth from behind. Intermittent streams of his urine slashed a white suede couch. Talon glanced around for bodyguards. Satisfied that they were likely in the hall outside, she choked the man until he fell, unconscious, face-down in a puddle of his own pee. She hacked his wristwatch, transferred the entire substantial sum of credits from his bank account to a new one she created in his wife's name, locked him out and then sent her a text message with the account details. *I've had enough. I'm leaving you. Here's a chunk'a credits. Go buy all the piss-water you want. Don't look for me. I've got someone else, and more credits than you ever knew about.*

Talon opened another portal and dragged him through to a Kuru space port. She stomped his watch and stripped him down to nothing, while hot swirling wind whipped off her wig. She stepped back into to the hotel room before the portal closed, ears pricked to the singing still coming from the bathroom. The shower turned off. Talon entered the bedroom, took off her shoes, hitched up her dress and reclined on the bed. A naked man in his seventies stepped out of the bathroom, drying his grey beard. *Sheik Bagher*, she assumed.

'What do we have here?' He grinned, tossing the towel. '*Hulw alkaramil!* My boys know me well.' He touched her pink hair. 'Tsk, tsk, tsk, kids these da–'

Talon grappled him and pinned him to the bed, opened a portal to Father Anatole's room and dragged him through it.

'Oy!' a man's voice cried out behind Talon.

A teenage boy ran past her, hastily unlocked the door and ran out. Two bodyguards gave chase.

'Leave him, you idiots! In here!' the man within the room called out, too late.

Talon watched him pull his pants back up and replace his skull cap. *Father Anatole.* She opened a portal behind him as soon as her previous one closed, swung Bagher and threw him at Anatole. The two of them tumbled through the portal and onto a tiled floor. The sphere closed, and the men breathed heavily, looking all around themselves. They were in a dusty but new-looking apartment. From a window, they guessed they were on a first or second floor.

'InvEstir?' Bagher asked, as they recognised each other.

Father Anatole nodded gravely. 'The girl is known as Talon. She is a killer.'

'No more hiding,' Bagher fumed, grabbing at Anatole's wrists for a comms device. 'There will be no Universal Council ever again. I'll call the others.'

Anatole slapped Bagher's hands away. 'Call *who?*' he shrieked. 'We're the only ones left! The others were found dead this morning.' He sobbed, sliding his cap from his balding head. 'Why do you think we were put up in those rooms, where no one would look for us?'

Bagher shook his head in disbelief. 'Not possible. W-we have fifteen syndicates, bodyguards.'

'What good are paid goons with no one alive to pay–'

A distant popping sounded above them. The floor shook. Wall decorations fell as the popping became deafening booms, closer and closer, until the ceiling collapsed in on them.

Concrete dust rose from the demolished apartment building, among a forest of weathered, abandoned high-rise housing estates.

Everyone in Lowen's village filed toward the main longhouse. Children played outside, while the grown-ups and seniors stood at the doors and windows of the already packed meeting hall. Words spoken inside were carried to those leaning in to listen at the back and huddled outside in the cool air.

Lowen hosted the meeting. Each representing elder of all the different peoples affected by the Tear had spoken their piece. Orin, the Mountain Folk shaman, sat in attendance with the elders, but he had elected not to speak.

'Thank you all for coming,' Lowen started, waiting a moment for everyone to settle and for murmurs to fall silent. 'As many of you know, my brave daughter and her fellow world explorers broke through the Veil to find me. Thanks to them, I have new information to share with you. Those responsible for the devastation and loss we have suffered are called the Evolved. They have done to others what they did to us. Many others. Many worlds.'

'Why?' a woman in the middle of the seated crowd asked.

'From what my daughter has seen, it appears the Evolved do this for the curiosity of collection.'

The crowd murmured angrily.

'We are confident that we will be able to reach them and–'

Lowen paused at the sound of electricity crackling. Light distorted in the one-metre space between the podium and the crowd. A man and a woman stepped out of the gateway. The villagers rose. Some were fearful and turned to flee, but most stayed, shouting, 'Seize them! They took our families!'

The Evolved gazed upon the crowd with disdain.

'Everybody please return to your seats and calm yourself,' Lowen called, thumping a wooden gavel on the podium. She stepped down and approached the man and woman. 'I assume, by your entrance, that you are Evolved,' she said calmly and with dignity. 'Do you represent your Senate?'

'We are, and we do,' said the man. 'We would like to address any here who would listen.'

Lowen gestured to the podium and nodded. 'Proceed.'

Orin watched the white-robed man step up to the podium, then leaned to get a view of the female. She remained on the floor, level with the crowd. White silk ribbons bound her breasts. A single length was tied around her waist, with a wide length hung behind and another in front. Her elbows were bent and her hands closed, as though she were holding something invisible.

'Treasured mortals,' the man began. 'I am Senate member Dol'Nane.' He touched the golden torc around his neck, assuming everyone knew the symbol on it proved his identity. 'My counterpart, Bastet, and I have travelled here from the Citadel to deliver you all a message of peace.'

Orin's palms began to sweat. He approached Lowen and whispered in her ear, 'We are all in great danger. You must stop the meeting. Everyone must evacuate, now.'

Lowen saw fear in his eyes. She did not know him, but Miri did, and she trusted her daughter. She stood and opened her mouth to speak to Dol'Nane, but the crowd erupted, no longer able to hold back their anger.

'Reverse what you have done!' one woman shouted. 'Give back those we have lost!'

'Monsters!' another called from the back.

Dol'Nane glared at the angry crowd while the villagers vented their anger and called out emotional pleas. He raised his hands and lowered them with his fingers pointed down.

Steel bars dropped over each window. The only doors to the hall swung closed, knocking down everyone standing in the passage.

Lana and her team ascended the ramp to the Black Heron once Talon landed outside the Fyrst Born forest.

'How can the meeting be under threat?' Lana asked Poser, opening the armoury doors. She paused, noticing that most of the C4 packs were gone. 'It's not like the Evolved can watch our every move like the freaking Gods of Olympus.'

'You hit the nail on the head, sweet cheeks.' Though his tone was calm, Poser was holding Lana's gaze with wide eyes. 'I can't tell you any more here.'

'Fine.' Lana holstered her side-arm and hand axe, then programmed a portal to Mechtropolis. She turned to Rachel, Talon and Shen. 'Everyone ready?'

They nodded and walked through the mercury sphere when it opened and expanded.

'I can meet you at the longhouse if you need to go,' Lana said to Miri.

'I want to hear what Poser has to say.' Miri shouldered her bow and quiver. 'He has not fed us false information yet. When he does, I will be there to deal his punishment.'

'I'll hold him down,' Lana agreed.

When the two of them emerged in Mechtropolis, Poser wasted no time.

'The Senate can see everyone in any of the worlds that have been made by a Collector like my Minion.'

'They will be watching the meeting in my mother's village.' Miri used her ring console to activate a portal. 'I must warn her.'

'We're all coming with you,' Lana pledged. 'If the Evolved—' She turned to Rachel, who'd tapped her shoulder. 'What?' Her eyebrows shot up when she saw an entire acre of exposed dirt where the mechanical mansion used to be.

'Contrivance is gone,' Rachel murmured, turning to the city. Smoke rose from the buildings. 'I better go check on Ken and Hedy.'

Saule followed her gaze. 'I'll come with you.'

'Good luck,' said Lana. She stepped through the portal with Shen, Miri and Talon.

Bastet turned to the gateway that remained open to their world and clicked her tongue. A growl sounded from within when she gave an invisible length of rope in her hands a single tug. A pale, beastly head emerged from the gateway, hairless, tiger-like in shape, but with a hooked goblin nose instead of a feline snout.

Gasps and cries of fright rolled over the crowd, and everyone moved back. They panicked when they realised there was no escape. The beast stalked in, thumping the wooden floorboards with its heavy, meaty paws. It was twice the size of any jungle cat. Its long, narrow ears were folded back, its golden eyes darting to its closest prey.

'If you would all hear what I have to say,' Dol'Nane continued, 'there is a good chance you will survive.'

Lowen put herself between the crowd and the pale beast. She held her arms out, motioning for everyone to sit down. And she turned to Dol'Nane. 'Did you come here to threaten us?'

'We came to offer you a chance to pledge your fealty to the Evolved.'

'Fealty?' Lowen uttered incredulously. 'You take everything and everyone we hold dear, and now you dare–'

The beast roared at Lowen. Men and women in the crowd screamed and whimpered.

Dol'Nane raised his voice, leaning over the podium, his bushy eyebrows slanted menacingly. 'Pledge yourselves and become honoured subjects of the Evolved.' He flicked his hand to Bastet. 'Or be destroyed.'

Chapter 28

Rachel and Saule followed the path of destruction on foot. The first magnet-drawn cart they came to was inactive. The driver sat motionless at the wheel. They found more of Ken's robot citizens further on, frozen in stride. Most had fallen over. Rachel looked among the women, dressed in their meticulously crafted spring dresses. She half expected them to resume gossiping at any minute. A southerly wind was blowing debris from Contrivance's destruction, coating these machine people in fallout.

Thumping vibrations and falling concrete echoed against the tall buildings, cutting into the silence, shaking Rachel from her reverie. And she gasped when a small hand touched her side.

'Mummy, I'm scared.'

She looked down at the mechanical boy, a life-like manikin reaching for her hand. The left side of his face was coated in dust. His right was scratched, his ear crumpled.

'I'm not–' Rachel saw a slender metal arm under a slab of concrete. *Likely his mother*, she thought.

Rachel took the boy's hand. 'I'm not going to leave you.'

'We will give you all a moment to decide,' Dol'Nane told Lowen's people.

Lowen broke her glare from the pompous man long enough to speak with the elders from Miri's village. 'My daughter is on her way,' she whispered to them.

'Clearly, they can attack us anywhere, at any time!' one of the elders cautioned. 'Many lives will be lost. We will have to surrender to their will eventually.'

'We must pledge to them,' another advised.

Lowen's fists were clenched, but she lowered her head. 'Very well.' She walked back to the podium and glanced up to Dol'Nane. He looked down his nose at her and raised an eyebrow expectantly.

'We…' Lowen started with a gesture to the elders. 'We have decided–'

'I understand,' Dol'Nane stated sympathetically. 'This is a difficult choice to make. Let me make it easier for you.'

He clicked his fingers, and Bastet commanded her beast to attack. It leapt and closed its mouth over the arm of the nearest civilian, chomping it off at the man's elbow. He cried out and the crowd screamed.

'Stop!' Lowen shouted.

'You are next, if you do not pledge!' Dol'Nane barked at her.

The beast swung around to Lowen, chewing the severed arm, blood oozing from its lips and down its pale skin. It took two thumping steps toward her, paused and turned its ear to the wall left of the crowd. There was a hiss before four burning lines appeared in the shape of a doorway. A thump from the other side toppled the log wall.

Lowen peered through the smoke to see Miri step in wearing her waist sash and white cotton shirt. She had a bow over one shoulder and quiver over the other. Her skin was fading from demon red.

'I am Miri, daughter of Lowen and Ina,' she stated powerfully, while taking off her bow and nocking an arrow. 'The Fyrst Born will not bow to the Evolved, or to any other.'

'You insolent wench,' Dol'Nane growled.

Miri loosed the arrow before he could utter another sound. It stabbed through his forehead and hit the wall behind him, coated in blood.

Dol'Nane staggered back from the podium, his eyes crossed, jaw slackened. The hole in his head closed, leaving a trickle of blood. Shaking his perception back into focus, he shouted, 'Kill them all!'

The beast advanced. Shen entered the hall and stood in the creature's path, holding his staff before him. It dove through the air, mouth wide open, roaring, a trail of saliva flowing from its gums. Shen stepped aside, pulled the concealed blade from his staff and chopped at its neck. The enormous weight of its body hit the floor and slid against the wall, while its head tumbled behind Shen. Bastet cried out in horror, staring at her fallen pet.

'You think a mere arrow can kill me, girl?' Dol'Nane scoffed at Miri.

Lana strode into the hall, turned her hips and shoulders and swung her arm with a fiery shout. Her hand axe sailed horizontally, sliced through Dol'Nane's neck and thudded into the wall below Miri's arrow.

Dol'Nane slumped sideways against the podium. His head slid off his shoulders like food off a dinner plate. His body sank, and the golden torc rolled across the floor to Orin's hooves. The bars on the windows faded, and the doors to the wall opened. Bastet backed away from Lana and Miri and turned to run through the gateway.

'Seize her!' someone called from the crowd. Three people gave chase and tackled her to the ground. She watched Dol'Nane's body fade and the gate disappear.

'See to that man's arm,' said Miri. 'This meeting will now resume. We must set out terms.'

'The Senate will not comply with the terms of any mortal,' Bastet stated. 'Especially now that you have murdered one of us! How did you know our weakness?'

Lana shrugged. 'I didn't, but thanks for telling us that taking your head off works for all of you.'

Poser entered the hall through the burnt-out doorway. 'Best do whatever these people tell you, kitten. I count two worlds wise to our collecting. How many more collected worlds of pissed off people do you think they're gonna get to and collaborate with?'

'How in the blazing suns are you still alive?' Bastet exclaimed. 'I dispatched the Senate Guard personally.'

'I bet you did.' Poser couldn't resist a smirk. 'Your boyfriend Tahrin is dead, by the way.'

Bastet spat at the floor. 'Good riddance.'

'Can the Senate hear as well as see us?' Miri asked Poser.

He shook his head. 'Long as we don't mime this out, your plan is golden.'

'We're going to escort you back to the Senate as Tahrin,' Lana said to Bastet, and exchanged a glance with Miri. 'We can take his form.'

'Fine,' Bastet said, struggling against the villagers holding her. 'Strike me, you weaklings. They are watching!'

One of the women backhanded her without hesitation.

Lana drew her side-arm on Bastet. 'What do you get out of cooperating with us?'

'I will tell you my conditions once we are in my world.'

Poser looked from Talon and Shen to Lana and Miri. 'So, just us? I thought I was pretty clear about the need for bombs and cannons.'

'Miri and I are going in first. Get War and your Collector.' Lana turned to Shen and Talon. 'I'll send you guys entry coordinates when I can.'

Good luck, Talon signed.

Reinforcement bars jutted from broken chunks of concrete. Rachel and Saule followed the ground-shuddering thumps over the rise of the street. They were both shocked and amazed to see Contrivance mobile on six mechanical legs. Mechtropolis had been brought to a standstill, and now Rachel knew why.

'Contrivance must have breached the Faraday cage and shut everything down.'

'Everyone is sleeping,' the mechanical boy murmured, gazing along the street.

'The Overseer will wake them up,' Saule assured him. 'We just have to stop the bad house first.'

The mansion had lengthened itself to fit through the city streets. With cables and arms connecting each of its three sections, it snaked over carts and around corners like a mechanical centipede.

'How do we stop it?' Saule asked Rachel, out of her depth when it came to fighting a giant robotic house.

'No time for explosives,' Rachel said. *An EMP?* she thought. *No, it has an independent power source, the core we copied to help the Sedit.* She knelt beside the boy and looked into his lenses. His metal eyelashes closed intermittently to simulate blinking.

'We need you to stay here and keep these sleeping people company. Can you do that for us?'

'Can I nap with them?'

'Sure.'

Saule patted his metallic yellow hair and walked on with Rachel.

'Back door,' Rachel told Saule, when she saw double doors at the rear of the mechanical centipede. 'That's how we get to its core.'

They broke into a run, snaking around debris and hurdling inert machine people lying in their way. Saule, being younger and spryer, reached the doors before Rachel. She jumped against them, holding a knob and balancing one foot on the ledge. She turned the other knob and yanked the door open so Rachel could enter.

As soon as Rachel was in, she tumbled from the floor to the wall when Contrivance tilted, climbing over a cart, machine legs crushing it down. Saule followed Rachel in, steadying herself against the sudden sway when the mansion levelled out. Furniture slid across the hardwood floors, and the crashing of other loose objects could be heard in the rooms further up the centipede.

Hedy had located the power source that animated Contrivance in a tunnel beneath it. Rachel assumed that to become mobile, it must have hoisted the core up into its hull. She found the trapdoor Hedy had told her about, and Saule followed her down into the dark space below the floorboards. Both women had to crouch, and their eyes adjusted to the red hue emitted by the core. Contrivance came to a lurching halt. Rachel thought it had detected intruders. Its hydraulics churned loudly when its legs shuffled, aligning its entire length. There was only a moment of pause before Contrivance accelerated, creating enough inertia to throw Rachel and Saule onto their backs. A dramatic tilt caused them to slide past the glowing core and hit the back wall of the hull, breaking the apparently hasty cladding Contrivance had applied. Daylight poured in, and Saule took hold of a ledge with one hand and caught Rachel with her other.

Rachel gasped at the vertiginous view, the cascade of debris being shredded from the side of the building. They were ascending the Overseer's building roughly two feet per second.

Saule used her forming energy to levitate herself and Rachel back into the core compartment.

At the top floor, Hedy, Ken and the mechanical maid, Rosalie were evacuating the last of the Sedit. They sent the equipment and a crate of gyro hearts with the Sedit so they could continue transplanting and save their race.

Thahl was standing at the gateway to his world. Everyone was through save Hedy, Ken and Rosalie. 'Come!' he called over the shuddering and groaning of the distressed building.

'We have to stop Contrivance,' Hedy replied. 'Go! Save your people!'

Thahl bowed and disappeared through the gate.

Hedy opened a window and looked down. The mansion was digging its legs into structural supports before lifting its immense weight. It was only ten metres down.

The rogue machine's voice rang out through external speakers, echoing through the streets. 'I am more advanced than anything you have created! I will rule this city as I see fit, without you, without human control!'

'We have to get to its core somehow,' Hedy called back to Ken. She felt Rosalie's hand on her shoulder.

'*Por favor*, step aside, madam.' Hedy had not only upgraded Rosalie's motor control strength, but had also built an independent signal receiver inside her head, preventing Contrivance from shutting her down.

'Rosalie, what are you going to do?'

'This.'

Rosalie stepped through the open window and let her body drop. She heard Hedy gasp before wind battered her audio receivers. Rosalie oriented her body with the help of her wide metal skirt. Air rushed between her legs and became trapped, creating enough resistance to land her body feet-first on the mansion. Its nose was reinforced with steel plating, with no access to the inside. Rosalie had to climb down the wriggling centipede to its midsection. Her skirt was too wide for her to fit through the cables tethering the two sections of the building. She tore it off, slipped through a narrow gap and landed on her back. She felt a doorknob under her, so she took hold of it and gave it a twist. Rosalie swung down when the door opened into the rear section of the mansion. Dangling, she looked for the floor panel Hedy had used to access the core. It was already open. She let go of the door, slid against the vertical floor, caught the ledge of the trapdoor and climbed in.

'Rosalie?'

She turned to see Rachel and a younger woman holding onto what they could, three metres down the basement, poised to remove the glowing red core.

'Do not touch,' Rosalie cautioned. '*Incendio*. It will burn you.' She looked past Rachel and saw light coming through the rear of the basement. 'Step aside, *por favor*.'

'What are you going to do?'

'This.'

Rosalie inverted her body, braced her powerful legs against the inner hull of the basement and pushed off, combining the fall of gravity and her forced descent. Arms in front of her, Rosalie took hold of the core. The cables holding it gave way, and she and the core sailed through the opening at the rear.

Contrivance came to a grinding halt.

Rachel and Saule watched the robotic maid plummet, the red glow of the core fading. They barely heard the impact before a small cloud of rubble plumed from the street below.

Chapter 29

Saule and Rachel entered the Overseer's building through a broken door. Contrivance was shut down, frozen, latched onto the side of the building like an ugly brooch. The signal it was emitting to shut down all other machines, including those maintaining the city power supply, stopped the moment Rosalie ripped out its core. Power was restored, and Saule and Rachel rode the elevator to street level.

Machine citizens were picking themselves up and helping others get on their feet. Saule raised her force field like an umbrella over Rachel and herself while they went in search of Rosalie, shielding them from falling glass and steel that continued to dislodge from Contrivance's vertical path. The two of them rounded a tall mound of rubble. There she was, her body broken in two, the extinguished power core still gripped firmly in her arms.

Saule and Rachel carried her into the lobby of the Overseer's building. There, they were met by Hedy and Ken.

Hedy knelt down beside her friend, gazing sadly over her broken body. 'So brave. So very brave.'

Saule took a knee opposite Hedy and reached over Rosalie, her palm stopping an inch above Rosalie's forehead. 'Kim says Rosalie is still in there, but she can't activate.' Saule looked from Hedy to Ken. 'She says there is a vast amount of room in Rosalie, in your other machines as well. Room to grow, to learn.'

Ken tilted his head, intrigued.

'Let's get her up to the workshop,' Hedy urged.

Bastet entered the Citadel, the world of the Evolved. Lana and Miri followed as Tahrin, and they walked side by side across what appeared to be a common space before the Senate buildings. Humanoids and creatures Lana and Miri had never seen before socialised. Some were seated on park benches, others were hovering in the air, legs crossed, too engaged in discussion to notice Tahrin and Bastet's return. There were two suns in the cloudless sky, but the air was cool. East and north were the directions of light, which created curious shadows.

The main entrance to the Senate chambers was an enormous marble archway sculpted like twisting vines. Flowers circled an opulent fountain with male and female nudes meeting with hands raised in the centre circle. Miri gasped inwardly when the stone statues changed position in a fluid motion to hold hands at the fountain edge.

Bastet gestured to a staircase to her left. 'My affairs are conducted–'

'Affairs?' Miri interrupted in Tahrin's deep voice. 'Is that what you call terrorising innocent civilians?'

Bastet gave her a blank stare. 'Tahrin and I usually meet on the balcony on the east side. You never enter here. You detest what we do.'

'Something we and your late lover have in common.'

Bastet didn't show how much Miri's words stung. 'I will summon the other Senate members.' She paused. 'What of Tahrin's men? They are sworn to protect the Senate.'

'My friends and I will deal with them.'

'Good. I will meet you on the balcony in an hour.'

Lana and Miri watched the immortal woman sashay through tall doors.

'You cannot trust her,' a sage voice said behind them.

Tahrin turned awkwardly. Lana and Miri were still learning to move in unison. The Keeper stood before them, draped in a gold-speckled blue gown. She wore a headdress of blue feathers set in a golden circlet.

'Her help is a risk we have to take,' Lana replied.

'I have called for all who wish to dismantle the current order to gather,' the Keeper informed them quietly, scanning to her left and right. Satisfied they were not being monitored by anyone, she continued. 'They wait among the population, remaining inconspicuous, ready for my signal. What is your plan beyond confronting the Senate?'

'Treaty is preferable to violence,' Miri answered. 'But if they do not capitulate, then we must use force.'

'It'll probably come to that,' Lana predicted.

The Keeper found listening to this version of Tahrin amusing. 'Quite fitting that such a beast now be puppet to the very gender he took pleasure in abusing. Speaking of...' She nodded to a tall, grey building about two hundred metres from where they stood. 'We had better deal with the rest of the Senate Guard while we have the element of surprise. Where will you meet Bastet?'

'A balcony on the east side of the Senate chambers.'

The Keeper glanced at Tahrin's folded wings. 'It is high. Do you know how to use those?'

'Um…' Lana started, while Tahrin's eyes widened.

'No,' Miri answered.

'You will manage. We must first deal with Tahrin's Guards.'

'My friends are waiting for a gateway,' Lana whispered, giving passersby a sideways glance. 'You'll have to open it inside the guard house.'

The Keeper nodded and beckoned Tahrin to follow. 'To be clear, we are not all the same as Poser, his sponsors and the Collector College. Everyone here has storied reasons for their ambitions, be they good or bad.'

'We're yet to hear Bastet's story,' Lana commented.

'What little I know of hers is painful,' the Keeper admitted. 'Whatever she tells you, do not let it weaken your guard. She is very dangerous.'

'Keeper, what do you call this world?' Miri asked.

'The Citadel. It is where the Senate is, where there is commerce, where there is learning…' They arrived at the guard house. 'And where there is law.'

The guard house doors were a few feet taller than Tahrin. Lana and Miri raised his hand to knock and paused at the Keeper's gentle touch.

'This is Tahrin's house,' she reminded them, arranging her gown so that it plunged, revealing her cleavage.

Lana and Miri shoved the door with a masculine grunt. It swung wide and hit the interior stone wall. This caused all seven of the winged Guards to look up from their meal, their ale and their card games.

Tahrin placed his hand on the Keeper's buttock, pushed her roughly inside and barked at the top of his voice, 'Your Captain returns with a body that does not relent!'

The Keeper staggered in with dainty steps. She panted and darted her eyes fearfully at the approaching Guards. They were all laughing and leering intently at her.

'What of Poser?' one of them called from the back. 'What part of him did you take as trophy?'

'None,' Tahrin replied. 'Once I set him alight, he smelled like roast pig.' He slapped his toned stomach. 'I could not resist.'

The first Guard to reach the Keeper flicked her gown off her left shoulder and then her right. It cascaded over her breasts, down her hips and crumpled about her feet. She felt Tahrin's strong arms take her from behind her knees and lower back, and he carried her a few feet away from the salivating demons.

'Close the doors,' he commanded.

'Rules are rules,' one of the Guards resigned happily. 'Captain first!'

Tahrin set the Keeper down on her feet. 'Now,' Lana whispered.

Softly spoken words came from between the Keeper's lips, and she moved her hands and twirled her wrists. A sliver of light distortion appeared to Tahrin's left and widened.

A Guard who was leaning back to swig the last of his ale caught a glimpse of the gate opening. His eyes narrowed, and he wiped his lips. Before he could open his mouth to alert his comrades, a jet-black figure of similar size and build to himself stepped out of the gate and launched itself at him. Two more entered, and they rose into the air, flapping black wings and forming bright molten rock in their hands.

Kirin entered beside Thulu, stuck out her arm and clotheslined a Guard that made a dash for the exit. Prince Thulu breathed a long gout of blue flame into the chest of another, pinning him to the back wall and incinerating him in seconds.

'We have this under control!' the Keeper called to Lana and Miri over the shouts and battle cries. 'Go and confront the Senate!'

Chapter 30

Bastet excused herself from the Senate meeting and closed the balcony doors behind her. She looked about the space, puzzled to find it empty. 'Tahrin!' she hissed. Laboured breathing came from the ledge, and a hand gripped the marble rail. Tahrin's other arm reached over, and he lifted himself up.

'What are you doing?' Bastet exclaimed.

Lana and Miri were gazing over the rail at the four-storey climb they had achieved. 'Do we have an audience?' Lana asked Bastet.

'Most of our members are already here.'

'Then let's go,' Lana said between breaths, waving Tahrin's hand at the door, though she and Miri were still holding onto the rail.

'Before we do this, I have a condition,' Bastet stated firmly.

Lana and Miri stood upright and composed Tahrin's intimidating build. 'You mean apart from being able to live?'

'What I want in return for my help will become evident once the meeting starts.' She turned and opened the doors.

'Manifested by a master crafter,' a thin woman announced, showing a woven silver ring on her finger to two lavishly dressed Senate members.

'Divine, Mrs Wedly, simply divine,' the twin ladies seated across from her complimented.

Wedly gave Bastet a judgemental smirk. 'That was quick. Tahrin usually gives you a good long…' She stammered when she saw him enter the room. 'Oh, good day to you, Captain.'

Tahrin crossed his muscled arms over his broad chest and gave the jewelled woman a cold stare.

'I called this meeting,' Bastet began. 'The matter relates to the collection of certain worlds.'

'My steward told me *you* summoned the meeting,' one twin said to the other.

Lana judged them both to be aged around thirty, though their behaviour suggested superiority, and their attitude toward Bastet indicated they were high up the Evolved hierarchy.

Three more Senate members arrived, and one of the men grumbled, 'This had better be important. My Collector and I were about to seal the deal on a human planet.'

'Which world, Mr Barbodere?' Wedly demanded, with a glance to the man's Collector, who had tagged along. 'I wasn't informed that Uni-Earths are back on the table.'

'Earth is the most coveted world, due to population density,' Bastet whispered to Tahrin. 'Versions of it vary in price. Our society is based on a hierarchy similar to the caste system used by some of your human cultures on Earth. Only the highest caste can afford to bid for a version like yours where there is no war. These versions are called Unified Earths. Luckily for your Earth, the bidding never ends, and no one has been legally eligible–'

'Have you forgotten your place, Bastet?' Barbodere spat. 'You do not speak while the Senate is in session, until you are spoken to. As I was saying: yes, the Uni-Earths are back on the table, but my business took me to a rather barren one.' He raised his double chin and smiled proudly. 'The desert-like terrain will compliment my jungle world quite nicely.'

'You speak of the one with the little town on it,' one twin deduced, while the other prompted, 'Stone River? That's a backwater planet, Mr Barbodere. You don't want that.'

Lana took two stomping steps toward the man who was buying her parents' home. All of the Senate members fell silent and stared at Tahrin.

'Collecting is the reason I called this meeting,' Bastet stated.

'You called us here?' Barbodere exclaimed indignantly. 'Bodyguards cannot summon the Senate. How dare you pull me away from my affairs?

Dol'Nane summons, not you!'

'You will all stop taking worlds,' Miri commanded angrily in Tahrin's deep voice.

'He believes there is a risk to our security that must be attended to,' Bastet clarified. 'Until the matter is resolved, all collecting must cease.'

The Collector sitting at the table was shocked. 'Wh– For how long?'

'What is the security risk?' Barbodere questioned, his big belly folding over the table as he leaned toward Tahrin. 'Come on, you big oaf, out with it! You don't scare me, demon. Harm us and I'll have your head.' He jabbed a finger at Bastet. 'And your little mummy will be tortured to death.'

Before Lana or Miri could react, Bastet stepped forward. 'Dol'Nane is dead.'

The corpulent man's mouth opened in shock, and the others gasped.

'That is the security threat,' she continued. 'Dol'Nane and I were delivering the usual offer to people in one of Poser's worlds. Their champions assassinated–'

'You were his charge!' one of the Senate members yelled. 'You were supposed to protect him!'

Bastet gave the member a cold stare. 'We must stop collecting.'

'We do not bow to threats from peasants on worlds we own!' Barbodere shouted. He glared at Tahrin. 'Hunt down these "champions" and crush them!'

'They may already be here,' Bastet warned, further seeding fear into the Senate.

'You must assemble the Guards and – and… guard us!' Mrs Wedly stammered.

'They have been dispatched,' Miri answered flatly.

Bastet's eyebrows shot up, unprepared for how coordinated mortals could be.

'They are patrolling the city,' Lana clarified. 'And I have recruited a new guard force to escort you all to the College.'

'Who?' Bastet asked, finding herself out of the loop.

'The Sedit. They are waiting downstairs.'

'How in the abyss did you convince them–' Barbodere started with incredulous suspicion.

'Does it matter?' one of the twins exclaimed. She and her sister tapped at slim metallic panels attached to the lapels of their silk jackets. 'Somebody knows how to kill us, and they won't stop with Dol'Nane.' Collars formed around their necks as gorgets.

Mrs Wedly applied her neck armour too. Lana could see that it was flexible and her axe probably couldn't penetrate it. Glass clinked noisily when Wedly raided a drinking cabinet. She opened a bottle of wine and drank deeply.

Miri leaned Tahrin to Bastet and nodded to Barbodere. 'Why is he sweating?'

'He fears death,' Bastet whispered back

'But you can all choose how you look.'

'Our memories of how our mortal body looked and functioned dictate much of how we exist,' she explained. 'Only the most creative minds developed the ability to override such memories as perspiring and temperature variance.'

Lana waited until Barbodere ushered the three ladies out of the room and their nervous chattering could be heard in the hallway. 'Were you abused when you were mortal?'

Bastet looked up into Tahrin's eyes. Lana and Miri were unsure whether the two of them were looking at this beautiful woman as her late lover or her tormentor.

'I am going to kill them.'

'What?' Lana and Miri uttered in unison.

'That is my condition,' Bastet answered flatly. 'I will destroy the Senate, and you will not stop me.'

Chapter 31

After Hedy restored the original signal, instruction for all automatons to resume their routine was emitted across the city, and work crews were assigned clean-up and repair duties. Rachel watched on while Saule worked with Ken and Hedy to repair Rosalie. Kim's expertise was hampered by having to instruct Saule step by step: *Fuse this wire, connect that housing there.*

Dust particles caught the sunlight beaming in from the tall windows. The familiar clink and clang of citizens in their carts going about their business below comforted Hedy. There was no indication of any other anomalous intelligence in her and Ken's machines, though the two of them would stay vigilant and tread carefully when building anything new.

'Almost done,' Ken whispered, wiping sweat from his brow. 'Mechanically, she'll be as good as new.'

'Now comes the hard part,' Hedy murmured. She and Ken looked to Saule.

'Give me a minute.' Saule was leaning on the table, staring down at the maid's peaceful face. Her body was all copper-plated housing with chrome joints. Her metal lids covered her eyes. *Are you sure you want to do this?* she asked Kim.

I have burdened you far too long, Kim assured her. *I thank you, Saule Rocobi, for letting me in and allowing me safe harbour. You are a good friend, and I am forever in your debt. If something goes wrong—*

'Don't,' Saule blurted aloud. She wiped tears from her eyes. 'Don't let it go wrong.'

Hedy placed her hand on Saule's shoulder. 'She is a brave woman. I hope she knows what she's doing.'

Saule moved to the end of the table, leaned over Rosalie's body and placed her hands either side of her head. Kim used her Forming ability through Saule, causing her hands to glow blue. Rosalie's body trembled. The transfer was complete.

Saule felt Kim go, and a void was left inside her. Loneliness crept in. Her heart clenched. She took hold of the table as though it were all that kept her from falling, from drowning.

Hedy and Ken watched a monitor reading electrical signals in the body's core processor. The spectrum line remained flat.

Rachel touched Saule's shoulder, offering comfort. 'Take her hand,' she whispered.

The machine hand felt cold in Saule's when she held it.

A rise in the spectrum line caused Hedy to gasp. The machine's eyelids fluttered and opened.

Saule smiled, tears streaming down her cheeks. 'Kim, are you in there?'

'It's me, Saule. I can't move.' Her voice sounded distorted.

'Give it time,' said Ken.

'Rosalie is talking to me,' Kim murmured. 'She's showing me how.' Her voice became clear, and her fingers closed over Saule's. She raised herself and swung her legs off the table.

'Slow, slow,' Rachel cautioned, helping Saule keep Kim's new body steady.

Kim held her metallic hands in front of her, looking at her palms and turning her wrists.

'You're warm,' Saule told her, holding her side.

Kim pressed her hand against her chest. 'The gyro is permeating heat through the copper, and the copper is heating the tension cables.' Her feet met the carpeted floor. She could feel her joints being aided by cables installed where human muscles are. 'This is amazing.' Kim looked from Ken to Hedy. 'Thank you.'

'This is ridiculous,' Lana grumbled as she and Miri trudged carefully down the steps of the Senate building, moving Tahrin's legs in unison. 'Why is it so long and heavy all the time? Isn't it supposed to retract or something when it's not, you know, being used?'

'I understand you're frustrated,' Miri chided, 'but please focus or we will fall.'

They found all of the Senate members waiting when they rounded the corner to the foyer.

'Where are these Sedit you promised us?' one of the twins demanded. 'We're not setting foot out there without protection.'

'They're waiting for you outside,' Lana said patiently. 'Follow me.'

'Where's Bastet?' asked Mrs Wedly, swaying groggily from too much wine. 'Lover's quarrel?' She staggered against Tahrin, fed her arm around his and drew close. 'Her loss.'

'Lady, you are barking up the wrong–'

Lana stuttered when Miri took over Tahrin's vocal cords. 'Madam, this is not the time.' Miri opened the door and gestured for everyone to exit.

'By the skies, these Sedit do look formidable,' Barbodere exclaimed with relief.

'Come now, Tahrin,' Wedly purred. She waited for Barbodere to exit after the sisters and closed the door. 'If this is to be my last hour…' Her voice echoed in the large foyer. She pulled Tahrin's loincloth aside and stroked his member.

'Woah!' Lana exclaimed and held her back, but she moved Tahrin's hand to her breast.

'Take me now, demon,' Wedly cooed.

Lana and Miri saw a bright red flash pass through the woman's gorget. A thin glowing line in the metal sizzled. Her hands fell to her sides, her body dropped and her head rolled away from her shoulders. The metal ring clattered in two pieces onto the marble floor. They wobbled like hi-hats before settling with a double clap.

Bastet stepped out of her marshal sword-wielding stance. Her weapon was a khopesh-shaped blade of pure energy. She pressed a button on the hilt, and the blade sizzled and vanished. She pushed the ornamental handle into a sheath on her lower back.

'Why did you do that?' Miri breathed through Tahrin's lips.

'These people should not be leading this world,' Bastet stated coolly. 'I thought I would be serving a great cause, serving innovation and creativity. Like the Pharaohs of old on your planet, these "Lords" built magnificent structures, a beautiful city, but always to the detriment of their people.' She retrieved Wedly's neck armour from the floor. 'They established their hierarchy, and they kept others from realising their potential.'

'Did you kill the Pharaohs?' Lana asked in wonder.

'I did not have to.' Bastet opened the door. 'Those who did not die from inbreeding-related illnesses killed each other.'

The Senate members gasped when they saw the gorget in Bastet's hand.

'There was an attack,' she explained. 'We killed the assailant, but not before…'

Lana and Miri stepped out as Tahrin and nodded to Thulu, who was standing in the light of the two suns.

'Assume escort formation,' Lana ordered, and she turned to the Senate members. 'We need to move quickly. You, lead us to the College,' she said to Barbodere.

Feeling exposed and frightened, he didn't attempt to correct Tahrin's tone. He walked with surprising speed, setting the pace for both the group and their Sedit escort.

'Oh, thank the stars,' he said, after rounding a corner to see three Minions standing at the entrance to the College. 'War is here. The greatest warrior has come to protect her Senate.'

Lana and Miri saw the twins roll their eyes at the lust in the man's exuberant tone.

Poser's Collector stood with War, looking nervous, as he had not yet heard word of Thulu's victory over Tahrin's Guards.

'Where is the Keeper?' Lana asked Thulu.

'She was injured during the fight, and has returned to the Well to heal.' Thulu nodded to the tallest among the three figures standing at the College gates. 'She has sent Fear in her stead.'

Thulu was responsible for the death of Kim's entire Lustitian crew. And Lana had witnessed his warriors give their lives to literally build him into a giant version of himself in their attempt to take what they needed from Earth. She could accept this creature as an ally, but she could not yet trust him as a friend.

The College building looked Grecian in design. It was two stories in height, with columns supporting the domed roof. The exterior walls were patterned with a relief of cascading vines. The Senate members filed in through the doors, led by Poser's Collector. He gestured for everyone to enter, waiting to move to Tahrin's side.

'Poser is hiding close by,' he whispered. 'Are Tahrin's Guards dead? Did you get them all?'

'They're dead. We're almost done.'

'We must speak to the Headmaster,' one of the twins told a teacher inside the College.

Once everyone was inside, War picked up a tall, unlit torch holder and slid it through the handles to bar the doors. Thulu commanded two of his warriors to stand guard.

Lana and Miri stared up in wonder. A view of space beyond the two suns was somehow projected against the domed ceiling. Students who had the ability to levitate hovered in different areas of the stars. Others stood on floating disc platforms. Grids appeared across the dome, and areas of the cosmos could be zoomed into and sectioned off so other students' study was not interrupted.

The Headmaster of the College arrived, wearing black robes that met the floor. His bushy, greying eyebrows were slanted in a frown. And though he was very tall and broad-shouldered, his commanding build was offset by his poor posture. 'Why are my doors barred?' he demanded. 'Who are these creatures?'

'We are in grave danger as long as the works of this College continue,' the twins explained in unison. 'Stop everything!'

'This is preposterous,' the Headmaster retorted. 'Who would dare threaten you or any of our great institutions?'

'Sir, we command you to shut this place down!' Barbodere shouted, pushing his way through the twins. 'Who cares who dares? We are being killed one by one! They even got Dol'Nane. Can't you see? Only three of us remain!'

A red-hot flash passed through his neck gauntlet at the end of his last word. He leaned, and his head slid away from his body. The Headmaster caught the man's lifeless head with a gasp. He stared down at the bloated face looking up at him, frozen in horror.

'Two remain,' Bastet corrected, raising her blade to the twins. 'And it is I who dare.'

Chapter 32

'We have been deceived!' the twins shrieked and hid behind the Headmaster's bulk.

The third-last Senate member's head and body disappeared, leaving the Headmaster's hands empty.

'Tahrin, seize her!' the ladies cried.

Tahrin's form slowly shortened and bifurcated until Lana and Miri appeared, standing beside one another.

'I order this school closed!' the Headmaster called out. 'There's no need for more killing,' he pleaded. 'We will do as you command.'

Miri reached up and roughly took a fistful of his gown collar. 'Permanently.'

'Wh– but…' the Headmaster stammered.

'Your College took my world.' Miri's teeth sharpened when she pulled him close to her face. 'You tear entire families apart.' Her eyes turned orange. Her skin turned red. 'Never again.'

'I am confused,' War stated evenly. 'Why is Bastet killing off the Senate?'

Poser's Collector was standing next to her. 'Bastet was their protector,' he explained. 'Poser once told me she was sleeping her way up the ranks to get close to them, but he never knew her motives.'

'Devious minx,' War commented approvingly.

The Headmaster was now sweating profusely. 'We – we would have to destroy the core, the power source.'

'Take us to it,' Lana demanded.

'Not until Bastet is restrained,' the Headmaster retorted. And he added, in low tone that gradually rose to an operatic crescendo, 'If she kills all five members of the Senate, the Well will implode, and the matter surging through it will deliver us to oblivion!'

Lana turned her furrowed brow to Bastet. 'Really?' She pointed through the open College doors. A crowd of citizens had gathered to see what the commotion was about. 'Your scorn's so hot you're willing to wipe everyone out?'

'Really,' Bastet stated dispassionately.

Thulu broke out into laughter before containing himself enough to ask the Headmaster, 'Why would you tie the fate of your world to the lives of five people?'

'If our democracy fails, our world must be made new,' the Headmaster explained. 'Tahrin and his Guards are supposed to stop any threat like the unrest among Minions. Their dreams of achieving Lord status were deemed a threat to our hierarchy.'

'Because eventually we would all become Lords,' War deduced, 'over no one.'

'It is not about lording over others!' Bastet snapped. Her voice was harsh, her eyes never leaving the twins.

Lana noticed the ribbons crossing Bastet's chest were bunched while her sword was raised, revealing a tattoo on her left breast: two blue circles, one higher than the other.

'It is about their selfish, motherless disdain for youth, and the erasure of any future generations,' Bastet said.

One of the twins spoke nervously with a shrug. 'It was a necessary sacrifice we made to—'

A sharp intake of breath between Bastet's teeth silenced her. 'It was *murder*,' Bastet seethed, tightening her grip on her blade.

'If I may explain,' the Headmaster offered, hands raised. 'When our original world, our solar system, entered the path of a black hole, we had the means to escape it. We started building ships to escape the system, find another home. But first tests were carried out to see what was on the other side of the black hole. We waited while the animals jettisoned through it were monitored remotely. Two years into their journey, our readings indicated their cells never aged a day. When they returned, all but two recommenced aging. The adults had become immortal.

The young aged rapidly and died.'

Bastet lowered her blade, speaking to Lana and Miri. 'The black hole was going to tear our planet apart. The Senate had a limited number of ships, and only two avenues of escape: travel through the black hole or flee into outer space.'

The Headmaster nodded solemnly. 'The Senate committed all ships to transport the adult population of the entire planet through the black hole.'

The crying of those who had lost their children could be heard among the growing crowd.

'It was genocide!' a woman shouted.

'There were not enough transports even for us!' one of the twins pleaded to the crowd. 'There was not enough time to build more!'

Bastet swung her blade to the woman's face without looking, close enough for her to feel the heat of it. 'Our young could have found another planet.' Tears welled in her eyes. 'They would have continued on for generations somewhere safe. Instead, it is now only us. Ageless, we sap our existence from a dead world.'

'None of you can reproduce?' Miri asked.

The Headmaster shook his head, staring fearfully at the glowing blade.

Lana stepped close to Bastet, placing a hand gently on her sword arm. 'Use your experience. Help younger worlds like mine make better decisions.'

'I walked that path once. I tried to heal my sorrow by helping mortals. Your people did not listen.'

'Your world is made from the Well,' Miri said. 'It is the other end of the black hole you travelled from.'

'The matter used to create everything comes from our solar system,' the Headmaster confirmed. 'The planets have been broken down over thousands of years, and will be for thousands more. We built the Well as a funnel, a safe way to syphon matter. If it is destroyed, all is lost.'

'So be it.' Bastet faced the twins and drew back her weapon. 'Feel my pain.'

Shocked murmurs rolled through the crowd when Lana caught Bastet's elbow, halting her swing. 'Don't do this.'

Shouts came from those who supported Bastet, followed by retaliatory arguments.

'No?' Bastet snapped. 'Dol'Nane and I were demanding her people pledge fealty to us.' She glanced at Miri. 'Her world was not the first. Our numbers were once in the millions. But too much matter was being used too quickly.'

'It is forbidden to speak of this,' the Headmaster protested. 'Everybody out! Close the doors!' Two of his students carried out his order quickly.

'Hierarchy was introduced,' Bastet continued. 'We fought each other for the highest position. There were assassinations every day.' She gestured impatiently to War. 'She was chosen by the first Senate to fight the wars of Lords overthrowing Lords to become Lords! We took the worlds of mortals, took their warriors, and pitted them against our enemies.' Bastet's piercing eyes returned to Lana while the twins whimpered. 'I will exact my revenge and end this madness. And I will fight you all if necessary.'

Lana stepped away from Bastet. Her eyes wandered to Miri, seeking her guidance.

Miri looked to the Headmaster, to the students standing and floating, stunned. 'I only want you to stop taking worlds, hurting families.'

'Again,' the Headmaster stated, 'I will tell you where the core is, and how to shut it down, once Bastet has been restrained.'

'He's lying,' Bastet said. 'The core is the Well. Everything we are, all that we take, is drawn from the Well. Your worlds will be free,' she told Miri. 'Go now. Your work here is done.'

'It is true.' They all turned when the Keeper spoke. The gate she had opened to enter the College closed behind her. She gazed upon Bastet calmly. 'I am sorry, child. I cannot allow my people to meet oblivion.'

The sword fell from Bastet's hand, and she was raised from the ground.

'I will assume control of the Senate,' the Keeper announced, regarding the twins with disdain, 'until better leaders are elected.' She addressed Miri now with a promise. 'This College will never interfere with other worlds again.'

Miri and Lana saw Poser's translucent tentacle imbedded in Bastet's back. She was fighting against his control, and she turned her head and followed the length of the tendril up.

'Gateways will be built between your worlds, so that all may travel freely,' the Keeper continued. 'Families will be reunited, and aid will be provided until you no longer need us.'

Poser descended from the map of the galaxy. 'Don't everybody thank me at once,' he gloated. 'Only saved the world just now.' Nobody paid him any attention. 'You're welcome.'

'Our worlds must be joined permanently,' Miri demanded, looking from the Keeper to the Headmaster.

'Repair the damage you've done and leave them alone forever,' Lana added with equal conviction.

'It will be done,' the Keeper assured them. And she locked her eyes on the Headmaster, causing him to flinch. 'No one will oppose my will.'

'It will take some time to bind the worlds and safely remove the Veils,' the Headmaster stuttered. 'But the gates can be put in place immediately.'

'Do it now,' the Keeper commanded.

The Headmaster moved, tripping on his robe. He clapped his hands and signalled his students. 'You heard the Keeper. To work, my Collectors!'

'We cannot undo what we have done.' The Keeper looked from Bastet to Miri. 'But we can change our ways. Return to your family; I will monitor progress here.'

'What will happen to Bastet?' Lana asked, while Miri used her ring console to program a portal home.

The Keeper gestured to the twins. 'Once these two are taken to a secret location, Bastet will be free. I will keep a close eye on her.' Her tone became heartfelt. 'Thank you. Without you, this coup would not have been possible.'

The portal opened, and Lana went to say goodbye to Thulu. 'Come and visit us sometime.'

Thulu nodded and turned to the Keeper. 'I will stay and assist you.'

Lana followed Miri through the portal. The second it closed, one of the Sedit warriors standing guard at the College doors cried out and then fell silent. They lifted the bar from the great doors and swung them open.

Thulu saw the tendrils in the backs of his warriors and assumed a martial stance. 'Release them at once!' he shouted at Poser.

'Sure.' Poser released Thulu's warriors and strode confidently to the door. 'You all did me a favour by killing Tahrin's Guards. So I'll give you a chance to leave. Hurry, though. It's about to get crowded in here.'

Behind him were hundreds of men and women, all armed with bladed weapons. They crowded outside the College doors.

The Keeper could hear the cries of civilians being attacked, maimed and killed. Shock and anger darkened her expression. 'What have you done? This was not part of our agreement!'

'I didn't agree to you running the College. How am I supposed to do what I do with you looking over my shoulder?'

'What you do must stop,' the Keeper commanded. 'Other worlds will retaliate. We should never have interfered–'

'Save it, sister,' Poser interrupted. 'You've had plenty of opportunity to close the College. We all need the Well. You have the power to shut it down. Something goes wrong, and all of a sudden you grow a conscience?'

'I was assured no one was being harmed,' the Keeper growled. 'That only people of the same kin were being sampled. Families were always supposed to be whole when moved.'

'Have you got any idea how long that takes? And how the heck was War supposed to stir up conflict if everyone in the world was the same? I wouldn't have the sponsors I do now if I'd followed the stupid rules!'

'And how do you justify this?' The Keeper gestured angrily at the fighting outside.

'I'm glad you asked.' He gave her a wry smile. 'This is gonna make up for battle I lost against Lana and Co, losing War and my Collector. Everyone'll see this. When there's nothing left to break out there, this College is gonna rebuild the city, and all new folk will be invited to enjoy fresh real estate. The headline there, in case you missed it: *real estate.*'

The Keeper's eyes widened. 'You are insane.'

'I'm a businessman. Speaking of which…' Poser raised a finger. 'I'll be dropping by your ever-givin' Well a little later for some patronage. My boys and girls'll need a more permanent upgrade. The crap running through their veins is killin' 'em.'

'It doesn't work that way,' the Keeper said. She was hesitant to reveal information that could help Poser, but she couldn't withhold a potential threat to human life, even if those lives were forfeit. 'The energy is too much for mortals.'

Poser scowled at her. 'If my army can't use it, no one will.'

'I am the Keeper of the Well. You cannot–'

'My sponsors are already there with the mojo to lock off energy flow to any hero types like Lana and her hung gal pal.'

The Keeper watched Poser turn his head and give a mental command to his fighters waiting outside the doors. Two entered, took hold of Bastet and dragged her away. The men were heavy-set, their veins coursing over bulging muscles that looked hideously inflated.

'Pull up a chair and grab some popcorn, people,' Poser called over his shoulder while he walked in the direction that the Headmaster had gone. 'You're in for one heck of a show!' He stopped abruptly and turned around. 'And, Keeper. Breathe a word of any of this to Lana and Co, and… well, think of something I might do to you, and then think of something a heck of a lot worse.'

Chapter 33

Lana and Miri arrived in the village outside Lowen's house. A gentle breeze carried chill air. The first ray of sun was melting the frost. Chimneys puffed smoke, and the smell of wood burning filled the streets.

Lana pulled out her tie and let her hair drop to her shoulders. 'Such a relief.'

'Yes,' said Miri. 'My people will finally be able to see their loved ones again.'

'I meant us not having to be Tahrin anymore, but absolutely.'

'Oh.' Miri chuckled. 'That was ridiculous.'

Lowen opened her door, having heard them. 'I'm so glad you're alright. What happened?'

Miri hugged her mother. 'They will build gates in the Veil and eventually take it down altogether.'

'And leave us be?'

Miri exchanged an uncertain glance with Lana and allowed her to answer.

'The one called the Keeper is in control now. I trust she'll see it done.'

Lowen ushered them both inside. 'Let me get you something to eat. Go and bathe. I won't be long.'

Lana and Miri both sank into Lowen's hot tub. Lana closed her eyes and breathed in the steam. She felt Miri move to her side, head on her shoulder. Sunlight beamed through the window when the clouds cleared. Miri gazed upon Lana's toned body, lit golden in the steamy water.

Her hand caressed Lana's curves and shallows.

'What was that?' Lana turned to the street-facing wall of the bathroom.

Miri's ears pricked to a commotion outside. A second later, a man fell through the thatched roof. Riding his back was Bastet. She landed next to the tub, straw and broken timber falling around them. The man heaved himself up with her on top of him. His tattooed arms strained, veins coursing over his enormous muscles. Lana and Miri jumped out of the tub when he staggered over the rim.

Bastet pressed one hand over the other at the back of his man bun and pushed his head under the water. He raised himself, head out, gasping and crying out as though lifting a weight greater than he ever had before, grim determination in his eyes.

'Foul beast!' Bastet growled.

'Bastet, who is this meat sack?' Lana asked, while she and Miri towelled themselves.

'Poser has betrayed the Keeper of the Well,' Bastet explained between breaths, her chest heaving. 'The city is overrun by these animals, fuelled by unnatural—'

'Anabolic steroids,' Lana prompted, covering her nose at the bitter whiff of the big man's sweat, made all the more pungent in the steam-filled room. 'He's a gym junkie. We've fought these guys before.'

Bastet slid over the man's shoulders so her legs were in the tub. She held him under, while his legs kicked, his large hands gripping Bastet's tightening thighs.

'Poser may still allow travel between the collected worlds as per your demands, but his business relies on variation, on spectacles of violence performed by different cultures.' She stepped over the drowned man. 'He will continue to sample worlds.'

'We must stop him,' said Miri.

Lana pointed to the hole in the ceiling. 'How did you know we were in this house? In this room?'

'I scouted this village with my cat before Dol'Nane and I were scheduled to speak with your people.' Bastet nodded to Miri. 'I needed gravity on my side to best my captors. There is another in the street, impaled on something, I think.'

Lowen burst into the bathroom and gasped at the body on the floor. 'What in the stars!' She saw the debris and looked up to the light beaming through the ceiling. 'There is a large man with bulbous arms,' she said, gesturing for Lana and Miri to follow her. 'He lives, but not for long.'

Lana and Miri dressed themselves and followed her outside. Lana tapped a message through her ring console, asking Sam O'Conner for assistance.

Iron spikes protruded from a man's chest. He'd fallen back-first on a row of pitchforks. By the time Lana approached, he was choking on his own blood-filled lungs, and he died within seconds. A crowd formed, and what began as murmurs became raised voices.

'That witch used her beast to attack us!' one villager yelled, pointing at Bastet.

Lowen attempted to calm them down by assuring them that this was not an attack, but an escape, and that Bastet was now aiding them.

Sam arrived ten minutes later and took blood samples from the two men before their bodies were carried away by the villagers to be burned. She let her equipment run diagnostics on Lowen's front porch. Lana and Sam sat across the dining table from Bastet, while Miri and Lowen prepared tea in the kitchen. Miri explained the gist of how the Well was a black hole through which Bastet's people had travelled, leaving behind their young, who would not survive the journey due to a rapid aging affect.

Lowen could not even begin to comment on the selfish decision they had made. *Surely fleeing with their families on vessels capable of traversing the stars would have been the only moral option*, she thought, and merely shook her head. She and Miri returned to the others and poured them each a cup of an infusion that smelled like pomegranate.

'You had children?' Lana asked Bastet, and watched her lips press together, a sudden sadness glazing her eyes. Lana immediately regretted broaching the subject, but she was no less curious about what drove Bastet to try and eliminate every member of the Senate.

Bastet's hand wandered to her chest. She pressed two fingers against her tattoo. 'I had two beautiful boys, three and five years old. I bribed the enforcers, gave them everything of value that we had, and they stowed the three of us on board one of the ships.' She drank some tea, set the cup down and swallowed. 'We went through the black hole. My boys began to appear gaunt and frail.'

'Cell degeneration,' Sam prompted quietly.

'I knew the agony they would suffer. So I gave them something to make them sleep, one last time.'

Lana reached across the table and took Bastet's hand.

Miri's posture straightened when a thought occurred to her. 'Could you not reverse the Senate's decision?'

Sam's eyebrow rose. She hadn't expected a sci-fi theory to come from Miri.

'The Eye,' Miri clarified. 'The Senate used it to find Poser by looking into the future. Can it not be used to change the past?'

'Many of us wished to use it for that very purpose,' Bastet replied. 'We have not been able to dial back time at all, let alone by thousands of years. We can only manage a brief glimpse into the near future, and even that small feat causes mass disorientation.'

Lowen was gazing out her dining room window with deep concern. 'The people of this village have suffered so much.' She turned to Bastet. 'These encounters we've had with your people have frightened families into leaving. Should we expect more violence?'

'Perhaps it is best if the young and infirm go to a safer camp,' Miri suggested.

'Poser is a narcissist and a sociopath,' said Lana.

'Add intelligence, and you've got one dangerous prick,' Sam mused.

'But he's also predictable,' Lana continued. 'He'll escalate conflict whenever he is opposed. He'll meet any show of force with something bigger and better.'

Bastet nodded. 'A frontal assault will only spur him on and serve his needs.' Her expression darkened. 'Perhaps it has been Poser's intention this whole time to appear the entertainer, while he builds a force great enough to achieve total domination.'

'I doubt self-assured, wankerish bravado has won Poser any allies,' Sam stated.

'Nobody came to his aid when Tahrin and the Senate Guard hunted him,' Miri agreed.

'He has angered your Sedit friends,' Bastet added.

Lana stood and walked to the window to gaze at the street.

'Poser has control over fighters, but he has no advisors,' Lowen offered, watching Lana's pensive stare.

Lana saw a gate open in the middle of the street. War stepped through, followed by Fear and Kirin.

'He has no one,' she said finally. 'We have everyone.'

Chapter 34

Lana was pleased to see Kirin, the Sedit woman who had fought Tahrin's Guards. Her form had changed since Lana last saw her. Her face was now human in shape, her nose no longer a cat snout. And her obsidian body had become smooth.

'My Prince briefed me on the latest,' she told Lana. 'What is your plan?'

'Miri and I will go in unnoticed.'

'Hopefully,' Miri prompted.

'We'll create a distraction,' Lana continued, 'while everyone else will take Poser's army by surprise.'

'I welcome the chance to rend that fool's head from his body,' War said with an intense glare.

'Poser will return to the Well,' Fear warned.

'That's our first problem,' Lana agreed.

'I've finished analysing their blood,' said Sam. 'They're already incredibly strong.' She looked Bastet's athletic but small frame up and down. 'I don't know how you escaped, let alone drowned one of them.'

'They are encumbered by their bulbous limbs,' Bastet stated.

Sam gave everyone a run-down of her findings. 'There were fatal amounts of creatine, erythropoietin and androstenedione in their blood, as well as a cocktail of methamphetamines and opiates. Any pharmacist will tell you these people should not be alive.'

'You're our way in, babe.'

Everybody turned to see Rachel closing the door to Lowen's house behind her.

'Sorry I'm late,' she said and opened her arms in time to receive Sam's hug.

'Are you alright?' Sam asked. 'Lana told me Contrivance attacked Mechtropolis.'

'Rosalie sacrificed herself to kill it. Hedy, Ken and Saule rebuilt her and transferred Kim into the machine body. She's not in Saule anymore.'

'Incredible,' Sam murmured.

Lana approached and hugged Rachel. 'Glad you're here. Sam's our way in?'

'Sure,' Sam agreed nervously. 'Poser's army must have dozens of medics keeping them dosed up and alive. If we turn up with drugs, they'll let us in.'

Lana looked to Miri for her opinion.

'It is a risk we must take.'

Lana nodded slowly, taking in her three closest friends, their fearless determination and unwavering support. Then she addressed Fear. 'I need you to go to the Keeper now. You're our eyes and ears at the Well until we can get there in numbers.'

Fear bowed his bald head and disappeared.

'War and Kirin…' Lana handed each of them a ring console and accessed her own to show them how to use it. 'I need you to find Shen and Talon. These are their coordinates. The four of you will rendezvous with Commander Lincoln. I'll brief him before we leave.'

War committed the coordinates to memory and opened a gateway. Kirin followed her through before it closed.

'I must go,' Bastet said to Lana, opening a gateway behind herself. 'I will return with Syoja. She will make short work of Poser's fighters.'

'Who?'

'My eldest cat. She is trained to hunt and kill only those with a specific scent. I will give her the foreign chemical odour these barbarians emit.' She turned and stepped through the gate.

Lana opened a portal to the Black Heron and went through with Rachel and Sam. Miri gave her mother a hug goodbye and joined them. They outfitted themselves in the armoury, with thigh and waist straps that allowed them to carry their weapons concealed beneath clothing.

Miri changed her form to look like one of the robed College students. 'I will enter first and find robes for you all.' She opened a portal and stepped through. Only two minutes later, she sent them her coordinates.

When Sam, Lana and Rachel arrived in a secluded area beside the College, the portal closed behind them. Miri nodded discreetly at two women smoking cigarettes under a tree. They both wore blue medical scrubs. A handled box of pharmaceuticals lay at their feet.

'I could only find one robe,' Miri whispered, handing it to Lana.

The two women were facing the street leading to the guard house. The taller one flicked her butt to the ground and blew her last lungful of smoke.

'Excuse me,' Miri said, approaching them side on. 'Have either of you seen our great leader?'

'Buzz off, College nerd.'

Lana and Rachel knocked them both out simultaneously. They dragged the women into the bushes behind the tree and stripped one so Sam could take the disguise.

They approached the guard house and were shocked to find a pile of dead, roided-up soldiers heaped outside the door. There was chanting coming from inside. *'Amrap! Emom! Gain on gains!'*

The door swung open, and a muscled woman stepped out, chanting over her shoulder. She shouldered past Sam. 'Move. I gotta ass to grass.'

The four of them entered and watched a group of men and women, all large and grotesque in build, standing in a half circle. 'Drop set!' they chanted, cheering on a man no older than twenty preparing to lift an enormous amount of weight.

'That's gotta be at least thirty kilos more than he weighs,' Sam whispered to Rachel.

The bar strained under his pull. His eyes bulged, and he dropped the weight with a loud clang. He clutched his chest, staggered and fell to the floor.

'Weak! Weak!' the crowd jeered.

'What happened?' Lana asked Sam.

'He tore his aorta. His heart stopped.'

'That's why back home, only licenced Olympians are legally allowed to lift more than their body weight,' Rachel explained. 'Let's call Poser's army "Roiders" from now on.'

The dead bodybuilder was carried outside, while a woman, who seemed to be the leader of the group, was handing out syringes, tubs of powder and packets of tablets.

The air rippled above a table in the middle of the guard house, and Poser stepped out onto it. He took off his suit jacket and altered his appearance to appear muscled beneath his business shirt.

Miri spotted Poser first and gestured for the others to follow her to the back of the crowd.

'Bros,' his voice boomed, silencing the crowd. 'Congrats on taking the city. I've got a small group roughhousing where you're all going next, to give our sponsors a little preview of the main event. Who wants to join 'em?'

Poser received a rowdy cry from all of them. He spaced his next words like a boxing announcer. 'Are… you… ready!?' And he stepped aside while they cheered, ushering the crowd through a new gateway he opened.

Miri, Lana, Sam and Rachel followed amongst them, heads down as they passed by Poser. They emerged in sunlight, at the top of a hill, in the middle of a road. Lana gasped when she recognised the cityscape.

San Francisco.

Chapter 35

Lana used her robe to conceal her ring console display while she sent a message to update everyone about Poser's location. Police and other emergency service sirens wailed in the distance. Those of Poser's Roiders armed with blunt objects were smashing cars and breaking into houses.

Lana felt someone take her by the arm, and she was pulled into an alley between two Victorian-style buildings. Miri alerted the others and followed.

The Keeper pulled back her hood and greeted them. She was wearing the same College robe as Lana and Miri. She glanced back at Poser's army and drew them deeper into shadow.

'In order to save your world, you must find Poser's sponsors,' the Keeper explained quickly. 'They channel their powers to him whenever they wish to see a spectacle such as this. That is how Poser is able to amass armies.'

'That's why they vanished before,' Rachel deduced. 'His sponsors pulled out.'

'Even with their combined powers, they can only use the Well to essentially borrow people in such numbers. All of those people are tethered to wherever they were sourced from.' The Keeper looked to the street again, before continuing. 'Poser is trying to change them, fill them with chemicals, in order to break the tether and keep his army. But it isn't working. To keep them, he must transform these people completely. My spies tell me there is a creature hiding somewhere in your city. This creature has DNA which can infect and take over any living thing.'

'The Warden Mutagen,' Lana said, her eyes widening. 'Talon and I tracked a Warden to Stone River. There've been reports of others…'

'I have no idea where this Warden they seek is. But I know where the sponsors are. They have each taken vantage points, in person this time. If we can get to them, we can eliminate all three, and their tether to the army will fail.'

Lana and Miri exchanged an uneasy look, but they arrived at the same reasoning: if these sponsors were not stopped here and now, they would continue creating conflicts in other worlds, purely for entertainment.

'I spoke to someone when I assumed Poser's form,' Miri offered, and changed her appearance to become a middle-aged man wearing golden robes and jewelled rings on every finger.

'Brilliant.' The Keeper smiled. 'He is the sponsor called Rich, "The Libertine". The guards protecting the other two will not stop you if you appear as him. But Rich always has a slave with him.'

'That'll be me,' Lana volunteered.

'We should head to the Shifter Facility and prep some drones,' Sam said to Rachel. 'They'll cover more of the city than we can.'

'Let's go,' Rachel agreed and looked to Lana and Miri. 'Good luck, you two.'

Lana also wished them luck and asked the Keeper where Poser's sponsors were located.

'King is up in the Unity Building, Rich is on the island Alcatraz, and Duke Cia is atop Coit Tower. They watch in separate locations, because they are in competition for the most wealth and power.'

Lana gazed up at the Unity Building, previously known as the Transamerica Pyramid. It was closest. 'Let's start there.'

The Keeper held out her arms, and a short robe materialised. 'Slaves wear a tunic.' And she handed it to Lana before opening her exit gateway. Anger clouded her expression. 'The sponsors have also locked off energy flow from my Well to all mortals. It will take me some time to undo this.' She paused. 'One more thing before I leave: Bastet escaped. She will no doubt—'

'We know,' said Lana. 'She came to us.'

'Good. Where are you holding her?'

Lana raised an eyebrow. 'She left. I don't think any cell could hold her.'

'True.' The Keeper stared at the ground, as though a solution was there to be found. 'I will see that my people protect the twins.' She bowed to them. 'Good luck.'

Lana typed another blanket text message, feeding everyone the Keeper's intel. 'I don't have the exact coordinates for the Unity Building, so we'll have to leg it.' She took off her robe and inspected the belted tunic. The material was cotton with a plunging V-neck.

'We must move quickly,' Miri urged.

Text responses came through to Lana's console. 'War, Shen, Talon and Kirin are coming to engage Poser's Roiders, while Lincoln and Jolie coordinate evacuation.'

When the two of them stepped out of the alley, somebody collided with Miri. A young man stammered his apology when he saw Lord Rich. 'My deepest apologies, sir.'

Lana saw that the tunic he was wearing was the same as hers. 'Where are you headed?' she asked.

'The Tower of Coit. And you to the Island of Alcatraz?'

'We wish to visit King, actually.'

'I see.' He gazed off to the Unity Building, and back at the Lord in his lavish robes. 'I was about to open a gate to my master, but here, I will open one for you.' He used what looked like an ordinary stone that fit snugly in his palm to open a gate.

'Well done, son,' Miri complimented him. 'Say 'ello to Lord Cia for me then, eh?'

The slave bowed while Lana and Miri disappeared through the gate. When they emerged on the other side, Lana barely recognised the observation room. Granted, the last time she was there, she was fighting a bat Warden, but the space was now darkly furnished, with dim lighting. Guests of the sponsor sat in black satin chairs that were raised and rotatable, so each could follow the action below in comfort. At the furthest wall was an open gateway. Slaves carrying trays of food and drink emerged from it, setting their cargo at a buffet table. They then returned through it. To where, Lana thought she should find out.

'You honour our master with your presence, Lord,' said an approaching slave to Miri. 'This way, please.'

Miri nodded and followed.

'To what do I owe the pleasure of your visit, Lord Rich?' the sponsor, King, queried. The chubby-faced man wore a double-breasted black uniform and dark eyeliner, making his pale skin look even more ghostly. 'I hope you're not here to argue over this spot.'

'Nah, mate. Just wanted to see the start from this angle,' Miri answered confidently, watching the Black Heron swoop down to the street below and fire plasma blasts at Poser's forces. 'You don't mind the comp'ny?'

King smiled arrogantly and gestured to an open chair. Miri glanced from the exit gate to Lana. 'Slave, fetch me my favourite drink.'

Lana bowed, and a slave with a tight hair bun ushered her to the far side of the room and through the gate.

'The kitchen is here,' the slave stated bluntly, then pointed to a door. 'Don't go in there. Our master has people searching for the creature he wants.'

'Searching how?'

The slave shot a warning glare at Lana. 'Fetch your master's piss and be off, girl.' She turned to walk away, stopped and faced Lana. 'The gall the two of you have, showing up uninvited. Honestly, is your Lord a complete idiot, or is he actually trying to start a war?' She turned and stormed off before Lana could think of a response.

Lana found a glass and reached for a random decanter of liquid, among a tray of half a dozen. In her peripheral vision, she saw that the remaining two slaves were about to leave. Once they were gone, Lana went through the door she was told not to.

She padded barefoot along a two-metre-wide corridor. The cold floor was a glossy black. Light shone from shoulder-height windows further on. Lana spotted an armoured guard on his way out of a well-lit room. She quickly judged her distance from him and leaned into a sprint. The guard exited, glanced right and gasped when he saw Lana running horizontally, her feet thudding across the glass, her body fully lit. She crossed him, striking with her knee. His head and shoulders swung, and the rest of him twirled like a rag doll before he hit the floor.

Lana rolled into the shadows.

'What was that?' came a voice from the room.

Lana heard heavy boots and guessed the owner to be the first guard's patrol partner. With only a second to react, she threw herself into a cartwheel. The guard left the room, saw bare legs out of the corner of his eye and grunted when Lana's foot clapped the side of his head. He fell sideways against the door, and the last bit of consciousness was knocked out of him when his helmet slammed into the door frame.

A hand fell on Lana's shoulder as soon as she rose from the floor. She slapped her hand down on her assailant's, trapping it while she buried her free elbow into the body behind her, a woman, by the pitch of her angry cry. Lana felt a vicious grip at the back of her head, and pain shot through her scalp as her hair was pulled taut. She drew back her elbow, but instead of striking, she turned her hips and shoulders, pushing the floor with all the strength of her legs. Her jump threw her opponent against the window. Lana arrived behind the female guard, gripped the back of her helmet and forced her forehead into the glass, creating a radial break. She released the guard, but the helmet was stuck in the sharp splinters. Lana left her there with light shining through her spiked halo.

Lana entered the well-lit room and found multiple holo displays on each wall. They were chest cams, which were, she assumed, attached to the leaders of separate groups of Poser's forces. Audio came from a feed behind her, and she turned her attention to what they had found.

'Possible target location. Signs of scavenging.'

By the feed, they looked to be beneath San Francisco. Lana tapped at her comms. 'Rache, Sam, I'm in some kind of situation room one of the sponsors has set up. Looks like Poser is getting close to finding the Warden in a tunnel, not sure where.'

'Copy that, Lana,' Sam replied. 'We could flush the tunnels while Lincoln and Jolie are evacuating the city. AM units are on standby in the air around the bay. They'll spot whatever's flushed.'

'Good plan. I've got an idea on how to take down the sponsors. Miri and I will meet up with you once I've got it in motion.' Lana sent a message to Talon, waited thirty seconds and opened a portal to the Black Heron's loading bay. She stepped through the mercury sphere and snatched a C4 timed explosive from the armoury. As soon as she left, Talon resumed diving through the streets of San Francisco, sending surgical strikes of plasma fire into Poser's soldiers.

Lana set the C4 timer for two minutes, returned through the kitchen, picked up a drink and threw a cloth over her other hand holding the bomb. She was about to step through the gateway when someone grabbed her roughly.

'Lord Rich sent you to steal information on the creature's whereabouts!'

the slave with the tight bun cursed, and backhanded Lana across the mouth. 'King will have your heads!'

Lana licked her split lip and spat blood on the slave's chest. 'Duke Cia sent us, bitch. So enjoy your last hours in servitude. King's wealth will be ours!' She drove her foot hard between the woman's legs. The slave dropped to her knees, groaning, while Lana stepped through the gateway. She strode toward Miri, and upon handing over the drink, Lana made skin contact with Miri and spoke into her mind.

Miri's eyes darted to the cloth-covered lump in Lana's hand. She took a sip of the beverage and immediately spat it to the floor. 'What in the bloomin' heck is this?' She grabbed Lana roughly and drew her over her knee.

While Miri slapped Lana's behind, Lana yelped and dropped the bomb under Miri's chair.

'Stupid girl!' Miri yelled, pulling Lana off her to stand. She bowed to her host apologetically. 'Goin' now, King. See ya round.'

'Always a pleasure, Libertine.'

The two of them walked quickly. As soon as they were clear of the room and prying eyes, Lana used her ring console to open a portal to the Shifter Facility just outside the city.

Chapter 36

King watched the screens that magnified the chaos playing out in the streets below. His thin smile widened now and then, and he laughed at a group of Poser's gargantuan men and women flipping a car onto its roof.

'My Lord!'

He turned to see his senior servant taking short steps out of the kitchen with one hand clutching her groin.

'Rich and Cia are plotting against you,' she reported.

King stood and opened his mouth to speak. The C4 timer reached zero. The room exploded.

Lana and Miri joined Sam and Rachel in the portal hub, and they watched the feed from one of the probes searching the city. Sam had set it to hover and record the explosion at the top floor of the Unity Building. The windows had burst, and smoke plumed. King and his servant most likely survived and would heal in seconds.

Miri touched Lana's arm while pulling on her bow and quiver, having changed back to her original form. She whispered, 'Sorry about the spanking.'

Rachel's postured straightened while she was clipping on a belt. 'What did you say?'

'Sorbet and sparkling,' said Lana and cleared her throat with a blush. 'Celebrating tonight.'

'Right…'

'How goes the fight out there?' Professor O'Conner enquired, leaning in the doorway.

'The plan is in motion,' Lana replied, eyeing him with concern. She had not visited his facility for months, and he seemed to have aged years. She exchanged a worried look with Sam, and they both helped him down the few steps to the portal room's floor.

'Dad, you look terrible.' Sam pressed her palm against his forehead.

'I'll call the nurse,' Rachel offered.

'Unfortunate that the people of San Francisco should have to suffer two attacks on their city in such a short space of time,' Pete commented, ignoring their concern. 'The navy and military protected the bay from 1850 right through to World War II. Alcatraz was a military base, Angel Island too. No enemies came.' He looked wearily to the screens showing the probe observations of the combat in the streets of San Francisco. 'Now this.'

Lana found a chair for Pete and drew it behind him. 'Professor, I think you should be in bed.'

'I'm sorry to have to tell you this, girls…' Pete started, sitting himself down.

'What?' Sam asked hesitantly.

Lana was speechless, her eyes darting from Pete to Sam.

Pete placed his frail hands on Sam's shoulders. 'I'm old, Sam. And I'm lucky.' His eyes were bright under the lights of the portal room. 'My specialist said… Well, it's not good. But I'm okay with it.'

Sam hugged him close. Tears spilled down her cheeks. Rachel's arm slid over her back as she hugged them both gently.

When Miri took Lana's hand, she could feel Lana trembling.

Sam could only manage a whisper. 'How long?'

'Long enough.' Pete drew Sam back and looked into her eyes. 'I know it's hard for you. I want you to know that whatever happens, when it happens, I'm proud of you and I love you.'

Rachel's console sounded an alert, and she turned to a monitor. One of the drones watching the city irrigation exit tunnels had zeroed in on a creature trapped in a filter cage. Its humanoid physique looked female, and it had four arms and a scorpion tail.

'I'll stay with Dad and feed you intel from here,' said Sam, watching the screen.

Rachel and Lana were hesitant to leave her, but they knew the entire city was depending on them to combat this threat.

'Go,' said Pete, and squeezed Sam. 'I'm in good hands.'

Lana opened a portal and followed Miri and Rachel through it.

Poser arrived at the top of Coit Tower to find King sheathing his sword. He held the severed head of Duke Cia over the wall and let it go.

'Now for the Libertine,' King announced, wiping his black gloves against the servant standing next to him. The lady with the tight bun stood diligently rigid while he did so.

'Hell of a time to settle a score, don't you think?' Poser exclaimed.

'The iron could not be hotter,' King proclaimed. 'They think their bomb destroyed me. I will–'

'You're killing my army!' Poser shouted, gesturing with both hands to the streets below. 'No army, no show! Isn't the whole point of this alliance so you can watch other people kill other people, instead of you guys killing each other?'

King watched whole clusters of Poser's fighters vanish into thin air. He turned back to Poser. 'That was the originally purpose of this arrangement. And you have served us all well.'

'Okay, and the hairy *but*?' Poser prompted impatiently.

King opened a gateway beside his servant and nodded for her to go. 'Retribution takes priority in this instance. Turning a blind eye to such treachery as was done to me today would be a sign of weakness.' And he followed his servant through.

King arrived at the tallest building on Alcatraz Island, and greeted the real Lord Rich cordially.

'Blimey!' Rich exclaimed, standing abruptly. 'You alright, old boy? 'Ell of a pop from your den up there.'

'Shut it, Rich,' King spat. 'Fool isn't your part to play, you conniving old cock.' He looked the grey-haired but muscled man up and down, from his silk slippers to his red-dyed fur coat, which matched the maroon carpet beneath his gem-studded golden throne. 'No, your part is the clever co-conspirator.' King gestured to the sea before swiftly drawing his sword. 'And mine, on this island stage, is executioner!'

'You 'aving a laugh?' Rich giggled. 'Duke put you up to this, did 'e?' His grin gradually faded. 'Alright, then.' With a click of his fingers, all four of his servants drew swords.

King's servant drew hers and lunged at them. She beheaded three before the last swung at her neck, a second after her own back-swing. They fell against each other, and both their heads toppled.

'Bloody Nora,' Rich murmured, watching on. He drew a concealed dagger and turned on King. A flash of steel stopped him in his tracks. He dropped to his knees. King booted him in the chest and caught his severed head. He heard clapping behind him and spun to point his sword at War. She clapped twice more, smiling broadly.

'Ah, Poser's battle hound,' said King, glancing to Lana and Miri either side of her. 'And the troublesome mortals.' He approached until the tip of his sword was snug between War's breasts. 'I've observed many of your feats. You are a cunning creature.'

War smiled frankly. 'Observed while cuffing your carrot, no doubt.'

King glared and pressed hard on the hilt. 'You would do well to—'

Faster than he could flinch, War swatted away King's sword, grabbed his throat and lifted him with one hand. He kicked and clawed, cursing between his teeth. Lana and Miri looked away before War's other hand took hold. A sickening twist of bone and a tear of flesh ended King.

'It is done,' War stated, tossing the Lord's head aside. 'And may I say, Lana of Casal: well played.'

Lana gave War an appreciative glance, and checked her ring console when a notification sounded. 'Lincoln and his team have captured the Warden,' she told Miri. 'They're going to fly to a holding facility.'

'Where is Poser?' Miri asked War.

'Right behind you, sweet pea,' Poser announced, standing behind them with his arms crossed over his chest. He turned his furrowed brow to Lana. 'So you tricked my most stab-happy sponsor into killing the others and then you killed him. Now their power is gone and my army is fading away. How very human.' He shrugged and pushed his hands into his pockets. 'What now? You gonna have War twist my head off too?'

'He will find other sponsors,' War cautioned Lana and Miri.

'Correction: they'll find me.'

'You have saved your city, but battle will be sparked in other worlds, if not yours,' she added, ignoring him.

'The College will amend the damage they have done,' Miri said to Lana. 'Poser is the only threat that remains.'

Lana took in War and Miri's counsel, but she was also watching Poser's body language. He was not able to hide a slight smile. 'You should be angry,' she said finally, remembering her own words. *He'll escalate conflict whenever he is opposed.* 'You're not.'

Poser's wry smile grew wide. 'You got me, fair and square.'

Miri detected a different kind of arrogance in Poser. A self-assuredness, even in the face of certain death, that chilled her to the bone. 'What have you done?'

War backhanded him across the mouth. 'Speak!'

Poser spat blood on the ground and casually smeared it with the toe of his polished shoe. 'You live in a collected world,' he said, and looked up at Miri candidly. The intimidating glare she returned did nothing to dent his confidence. 'A world that wouldn't exist without us. *Won't* exist without us.'

War drew back her hand, preparing to deal Poser another blow.

'Dead man's switch,' Poser said, raising his hands defensively. 'I implanted information in Bastet's head. My will hides it. I die' – he clicked his fingers – 'total recall.'

'What information?' Lana demanded.

'We have access to the Eye that can show us the future,' Poser explained. 'The twins know the location of another one, the Eye of Atlantia. Atlantia shows you the past.'

'Is this true?' Miri asked War.

'Such a place does exist,' War confirmed. 'No one has found it.' She took a fistful of Poser's shirt collar and lifted him inches off the ground. 'Bastet would have spent every waking moment searching for it, to get to her children.'

'Only the Senate knew,' Poser continued, his shoes scraping the ground. 'They told me to use my ability to hide any knowledge of it from Bastet.'

'Lies!'

'Atlantia is on an inhabited planet,' he insisted. 'The people there know how to travel through the Eye into the past.' His eyes darted to each of them. 'How would I know that?'

'So if we kill you, Bastet will know this was kept from her and she'll stop at nothing to kill the twins,' Lana deduced.

'And my world will cease to exist.' Miri gave Lana a defeated look. 'He must live.'

'Mayday, mayday!' Lincoln's voice sounded over Lana's comms. 'The Warden has broken loose. Our ship is going down.'

Poser neatened his collar. 'I think it's fate, us butting heads like this. Eventually, you're all gonna realise we should be working together.' He saw a transport ship over the bay, banking with a dramatic tilt. It performed inverted flight for a couple of seconds before lurching to one side again. Poser raised a finger while taking a few steps back. 'You know what? Seeing as you can't kill me, I'm just going to leave.' He tried to open a gate, but War took hold of him again.

'For you, I will find a prison far worse than this island ever–'

War heard the ship's engines, and she, Lana and Miri all turned around.

The wing ploughed through the top floor of the building they were standing on, and the nose struck War head-on before she could evade it. The ship cut through the roof, throwing metal and concrete into the air, before grinding to a thudding halt.

Chapter 37

Poser lifted himself onto his elbows. Blinded by concrete dust, he raised his hand to create a gateway, but someone grabbed him roughly.

'You're not going anywhere,' said Lana. She cleared her lungs and called out to Miri and War. Crumbling debris was all she could hear. Dragging Poser along with her, she followed the underside of the ship, the left wing pointing to the sky. The bay door had been ripped off. Sparks illuminated the interior. Lana drew her side-arm and entered. Only during the flashes of electricity could she see the dismembered bodies of AM units. They looked like they'd been impaled, their gaping wounds cauterised by acid. The poisonous smell of the acid burned in Lana's nostrils as she stepped further in. It reached her throat, and she immediately retreated to the open air, coughing and spluttering. She flinched at the sudden sound of footfalls and aimed her weapon at the opposite side of the trench the ship had dug into the building.

'Lana?' Miri called, emerging from behind the wreckage.

'Miri, are you hurt?' Lana could see minor bruising on Miri's left cheek, and a tear in her shirt revealed a graze across her abdomen.

'I'm okay. And you?'

Though her clothes were shredded, Lana had armoured her skin before the crash, and had suffered no injuries. 'I'm fine,' she called. 'Can't find Lincoln, though. The Warden is loose.'

'I'm fine too, by the way,' Poser said, patting down his torn suit.

The dust had settled, and Lana scanned the rooftop while typing a message on her ring console to Rachel. 'No sign of War.'

'Let's get the heck outta here,' Poser urged. 'Before whatever did this—'

Lana and Miri looked to Poser when he cried out. They watched his tie rise over a bulge in his chest before it exploded. Acid mist was taken by the wind, leaving a crater in Poser's chest. He tucked his chin, his eyes wide with terror.

A female Warden spliced with scorpion DNA emerged when Poser dropped to his knees. Sunlight gleamed off her black carapace armour. Pincer jaws opened to reveal razor-sharp teeth, and two lidless, domed eyes stared at Lana.

Lana aimed her handgun and fired over Poser's shoulder. The Warden flinched and covered her face after a bullet busted her left eye. Miri drew her bow, pulled hard on the string, and loosed an arrow. It flew over Poser's crown, parting his hair before thudding into the scorpion's chest. While Miri prepared another arrow, she saw three UC ships flying from the mainland toward them in her peripheral vision.

Lana emptied her clip into her target, but the bullets were not of a high enough calibre to penetrate the Warden's carapace. She ejected the clip, reached to her side and realised her ammo belt must have been torn off her.

Miri loosed her final arrow, having lost her reserves. The scorpion staggered back, using her pincers to snap each protruding arrow.

Poser watched debris passing and squinted through the blinding light of day while Lana dragged his limp body out of the ship. He could see her lips moving.

'Gateway! Open a damn gateway!' she shouted, sitting him up like a doll.

Though his chest was healing, Poser's arms were limp by his sides, his legs numb. Half a lung of air afforded him his last words, 'Fun while it lasted.'

Lana saw a brief flash of a stinger behind his head. She was staring into Poser's eyes when his jaw dropped. Bone cracked inside his skull. She dropped to her elbows and armoured her skin. Searing heat blew over her back, followed by cool wind.

Lana rose to see Poser slump to one side. Headless. Acid vapour drifted from his neck.

The scorpion woman arched her long body into a charge. Miri ran to intercept, dropped her shoulder and committed her speed to a jarring collision with the Warden. Landing on her side, the scorpion lashed Miri with her tail. Lana caught Miri, and they both fell into rubble.

Tail curling over her, the Warden's intimidating silhouette blocked the sun. She puffed her chest and roared at Lana and Miri. She dropped, catching the roof with all six limbs. Her frighteningly swift legs covered the few metres between them in half a second. She tracked Lana and Miri's scrambling retreat, knocked them down and pinned them together.

The Warden lifted her rear high. Her back formed a curve, pressing her chest against Lana. Though she'd armoured her skin, Lana cried out when the Warden's jagged carapace pinched the nerves beneath her skin and compressed her muscles against her ribcage, forcing air out of her lungs. She saw the stinger coming down. It was an inch from her nose in the blink of an eye. The scorpion shrieked when the muscled arms that had caught her tail lifted her stinger and drove it into her neck.

Burning venom gas expanded violently. Hot vapour exploded out of the Warden's throat and severed her spine. War lifted the lifeless monster above her head like a victorious titan, freeing Lana and Miri.

Lana gasped in air while Miri helped her to her feet. Hot air blew over them as downward thrusters slowed the ships landing either side of the craft imbedded in the roof. Lincoln stumbled out of the wreckage, holding his broken arm. He watched War drop the Warden and chop off one of its pincers.

Miri looked from War to Lana. 'Poser is dead. We must find Bastet.'

'Her fury will be reignited,' War stated darkly, tearing a strip of her waist sash to tie her trophy onto her belt. 'She will find the twins and end them.'

Jolie descended the ramp of her ship and called to them, 'Come aboard. I'll treat your wounds.'

'You should evacuate the people of your world,' War advised Miri and turned to Lana. 'The threat to collected worlds is not over. I will seek out the Keeper and send you the location of the twins.'

Lana drew War into a hug. 'Thank you for saving our lives.'

Once aboard Jolie's ship, Lana sent a message to Jess and Anook in the Forest Realm, requesting asylum for Miri's people.

'Mountain Folk, Raekeem, Vess and humans... so many families are in danger.' Miri did not wince while Jolie applied ointment to her abrasions before bandaging her.

Lana programmed a portal to the Ether Realm, and followed Miri through the mercury sphere. The air was cooler on the other side. The last of the evening sun shone through the trees as they ascended a wooden elevator to the tree home of Miri's sister. Lana could smell braziers being lit in the neighbouring homes. She could not contain her smile at the sight of Miri's niece when she ran up to them, calling their names, arms outstretched for a hug. She was growing tall like her mother.

'I'll prepare supper,' she told her mother, striding off to the kitchen.

Miri's sister listened to Lana and Miri's news. She wasted no time. Snatching a whistle arrow from a quiver hanging on the wall, she stepped outside with her bow and fired it into the air. It sailed out of the canopy, whistling a tone that all in the village would hear.

'You both look like you have tumbled down a mountain,' she remarked gravely when she returned. 'Wash, eat and then take my bed. I will send runners to the Raekeem, Mountain Folk and human tribes.'

Bastet stood atop the Senate building, gazing out at the city. People were using their forming abilities to repair broken structures. Poser's Roiders had fired their guns at buildings, swung sledgehammers, thrown Molotov cocktails. It was all matter that could be renewed from the Well, the black hole through which the Evolved had travelled so many thousands of years before. Now, preparations were being made for Rebirth, the annual celebration of escaping annihilation.

Twenty members of the rebel force that the Keeper had assembled stood behind Bastet. She gestured to the citizens below. 'They escaped their fate as able adults, mortals, selfishly abandoning their young. Now they are gods, immune to age and disease. The sacrifice they made is all but forgotten.' She turned to the men and women who all shared her pain. She made a fist, and spoke loudly. 'The Senate never erected a monument to that time of loss, never announced an annual day of mourning. Instead, an annual day of festivities. They celebrate that vain, reprehensible act of cowardice.'

Four gateways were open wide, showing like-minded people standing in anticipation, all from lands created with the Well. And through one of the gates, Bastet could see the Well itself, guarded by her followers.

Bastet looked into their eyes and saw their anger. 'So many noble mothers and fathers stayed behind, died holding their children, obliterated, reduced to matter. Matter we now breathe, build with, use to prolong our existence. They deserve to be honoured and remembered. And we do honour and remember them.' She gave an inclusive sweep of her arm. 'We few who braved the journey with our children, only to lose them to the cruel ravages of age, will not forget. We will not forgive.'

Bastet's eyes gleamed with both rage and sorrow. 'It is time to end the suffering.'

She turned to gaze down on the people raising colourful decorations for Rebirth.

'It is time to join those brave souls. Time for all to become matter.'

Chapter 38

Lana and Miri woke to the aroma of steamed vegetables, bean dumplings and herbal tea. Miri's niece ushered them to the table and then went to help her mother pack. Miri's sister had returned home and was filling shoulder bags and backpacks with essentials.

'The elders are meeting in the hall,' she said hurriedly. 'Mother as well. She will help coordinate. There is no need for us to attend. Everybody is being told to evacuate.'

There was a knock at the door, and Miri opened it to find Jolie holding an armful of spare backpacks. 'We've programmed portals to the Forest Realm to open at each village. Our units are deploying tents now.'

'I cannot thank you enough.' Miri drew Jolie into a hug.

Jolie saw Miri's niece and sister packing, and what could be their last home-prepared meal on the table. 'Eat,' she insisted. 'I'll help them pack.'

Lana rubbed Miri's back reassuringly while she ate. On the opposite side of the table, the air rippled, and the Keeper stepped into their world and sat down.

'How do you know where to find us?' Lana asked, finished the last of her meal.

'You probe worlds with the eyes of tiny aircraft. My people probe as well, only we detect a particular person's presence like a scent or a feeling.'

Miri read the Keeper's eyes, her slackened shoulders. Defeat was not something Miri thought she would ever see in this woman.

'Bastet has rallied many of my comrades, those I secretly gathered to overthrow the Senate,' the Keeper explained. 'It seems many among them were more frustrated with our way of life than I had imagined. They will defend Bastet while she executes the twins.' The Keeper shrugged. 'I suppose our existence was always temporary. All existence is temporary. Though your efforts may be for naught, I know you will try to stop Bastet anyway, so I will give you this gift.' She cupped her hands and produced a lump of what looked like terracotta clay. After separating it into two pieces, she handed them to Lana and Miri. The moment the clay made contact with their skin, it turned fluid and slipped through their pores. Lana and Miri gasped at the warm sensation that coursed through them like a blood transfusion.

'It is all I could extract from the Well. It was not locked off by Poser's sponsors as I suspected. Bastet's people have been spreading the word; the majority of my people are now convinced that we have lived too long. The Well, it seems, welcomes this. It wants it.'

'You mean to say the people who think Bastet will succeed are causing the Well to close?' Miri questioned.

'Perception is a powerful thing,' the Keeper explained. 'It is how we built our world during the time of rebirth. We will things into existence. We manifest our lives through will and perception. All of it can be undone if we are convinced that all is lost.'

'Bastet is creating that perception,' said Lana. 'She might not need to kill the twins, if everyone thinks doom is inevitable.'

'What was it you gave to us?' Miri asked, looking at her arms and seeing no change.

'You will not be able to change like before,' said the Keeper. 'You can equip yourselves with small things, like a chest plate, gauntlets, or claws for combat.'

'Bastet won't let anyone or anything kill the twins but her,' Lana thought aloud.

A narrow column of sand started pouring from the ceiling. Granules danced on the table and formed a mound. The three women gazed up at the continuous stream.

'It's a tiny gateway,' the Keeper said, reaching with one hand to close it. The sand stopped. 'This would never happen, unless–' She stood abruptly. 'I must get back to the Well.'

The gateway re-opened, wider. The table was covered with sand in seconds. Another opened facing Miri. Sea water gushed out, knocking her to the floor. Both new gateways opened so wide they joined.

'I will try to slow what is happening!' The Keeper called over her shoulder, disappearing through a gate before it closed behind her.

'Everybody out!' Lana shouted over the high-pressure roar of water and the hiss of sand, which were quickly filling the room. Miri coughed and gasped for air. She took Lana's hand and they followed everyone out of the door. Ice-cold water tackled their legs before the wave shot out, snapping the door frame and bursting through the windows. Lana and Miri were blown from the tree, carried by white foam, while the others made it down the ropes. Holding Miri tightly, Lana turned mid-air, armoured her skin and took the full impact of the neighbouring tree house. Their combined weight sent them crashing through the wall. Lana collided with the centre column and was knocked unconscious before the two of them hit the floor.

Jolie led everyone to the open portal that was linked to the Forest Realm. A curtain of sea water rushed down from the house they had escaped. She wiped her soaked hair away from her eyes and looked up at the hole in the neighbouring tree house. She was opening her mouth to call out for Lana and Miri when she paused and her eyes widened. A gateway was stretching twenty metres wide behind the base of that very tree. As the height of the gateway rose, Jolie could see a sunlit mountainside moving like a river. Boulders tumbled at speed, rolling faster on their descent.

'Lana, Miri! Get out!' she yelled. 'Get out now!'

A boulder the size of a van broke course when it exited the gateway and hurtled toward the Forest Realm portal. Jolie ran full tilt through the mercury sphere and collided with Miri's sister and her daughter. 'Get back! Everybody back!' She shoved as many people away from the portal as she could while tapping through menus on her ring console. She hit "Close Portal" three times before it began to shrink. A tree stabbed through the portal like a spear. The boulder rolled over it, crushing its branches. The tumbling weight shook the ground, throwing dirt in its wake. Splinters of wood and bark exploded, and leaves drifted down while everyone listened to the hulking mass of rock travel through the bushland, flattening everything in its path.

The twins were chained by their necks and surrounded by Bastet's followers atop the Senate building. Bastet's back was turned to them, and she gazed down at the citizens below. Many were staring up at her, but most were either holding each other or looking forlorn, resigned to their fate. By now, word had spread of Bastet's intentions. Any not sharing their last moments with their loved ones were those who believed they could escape to another world. Angry chanting was approaching from the road to the College.

There was a battle brewing. And Bastet welcomed it.

Hundreds had stormed the College to demand a solution. The Headmaster knew there was only one way to survive this, so he'd told them to take up arms and stop Bastet from executing the twins.

A gateway opened at Bastet's side, and snow poured out before one of her followers emerged. He shrugged ice from his shoulders. 'It seems you may not have to execute the twins,' he reported. 'Perception has become a driving force behind our cause.'

Bastet spun around and glared at him. 'What?'

'All of the collected worlds are bleeding into each other,' he explained.

Another gateway opened over the roof, and a follower tumbled out, covered in dirt. Rocks came through and hit the roof until a pile formed, and a child rolled out, crying out for his mother.

Bastet breathed out in frustration and shoved the man out of the way. 'All of you, go to the collected worlds and open more gates to wherever they are evacuating!' She grabbed one of her followers roughly and pointed to the child. 'Take the boy with you, and find his parents.'

Bastet watched them all disperse through gateways. One of the twins laughed at her. 'Is the end not working out to your liking, "Protector"?'

Bastet shot a warning glare at her.

'All worlds failing, all at once?' the other twin said before Bastet could utter a rebuke. 'What do the citizens down there care? They're upset about the end of their own lives, not those of villagers in collected worlds.'

Bastet's expression darkened when she realised what the twins were saying. The angry chanting below was growing closer. She drew her sword and turned slowly toward it, her grip tightening audibly around the handle. Her eyes, ears and teeth changed shape until they became feline. Her calves bent into a cat's hind legs. She crouched and sprang over the ledge. Wind whipped against the fur that grew over her skin.

She landed deftly in front of the chanting mob.

'Headmaster!' Bastet shouted over the crowd. 'Show yourself!'

'Yes, you heard correctly!' the Headmaster called. He emerged, hunched while unbuttoning his long black robe. He raised a bushy eyebrow at Bastet and straightened until he stood eight feet tall. 'It is I who have caused the worlds to fail.' His robe slid off his hulking shoulders, and he pushed out his broad, deep chest. Though he was aged, he was powerfully built. 'While you were being carried off like a common criminal, my students and I were preparing something that might dissuade you from killing the twins.'

Bastet glared up at him. 'Go back to your College,' she commanded. 'Stop the worlds from breaking, and you may keep your head.'

'It is too late,' he said, pushing his chubby fingers into spiked knuckle dusters.

Bastet assumed her fighting stance and pointed the tip of her sword at him. 'Fine. Your head. Bring it to me.'

'Oh, this is not a duel, Bastet.' The large man gestured to the angry mob of citizens and students with him. They each took a broadsword from their belt. 'This is a lynching.'

Chapter 39

Miri wiped splinters from her face. She heard Jolie call out somewhere below for her and Lana to get out. The tree house shook, and a rumbling sound grew to a thunderous pounding. Rocks were slamming into the tree trunk, and a second later, a violent collision snapped its midsection. The house toppled into rolling boulders. Furniture and cutlery were thrown everywhere. Miri wrapped one arm around the centre pillar and held onto Lana's waist with the other. The pain from her injuries, coupled with the exertion of taking Lana's weight, was almost unbearable. The tendons in Miri's neck bulged when she swung Lana's limp body and locked both legs around her.

Miri looked down to see that the wall below them was being carved away by the rush of sharp rocks. With both hands now on the centre pillar, she was able to program a new portal. Miri shrieked when the house dropped another metre into the boulders eating it away. She summoned the power given to her by the Keeper, formed claws and gripped the pillar. The portal to her home opened beneath them a second later. She released, and she and Lana fell through the sphere and hit the lounge room floor. Breathing hard through clenched teeth, Miri closed the portal and rose to her knees, hovering over Lana.

Lana's eyes fluttered open, and she bolted upright, clutching Miri.

Miri guided Lana's face to hers. 'We're okay. Deep breaths.' She waited a couple of seconds while Lana calmed herself. 'We are not sa–' A lump formed in her throat when she thought of the words she was about to say about the place that was not just their home, but where their love for each other had blossomed. 'We are not safe here. You need to open a portal to the Forest Realm. My ring does not have the coordinates.'

Lana did so quickly. A tremor shook the floor, and she saw through the window that neighbouring trees were swaying. 'I'm so sorry, Miri.' Lana winced at her injuries, new and old. 'Your home.'

Miri placed her hands either side of Lana's face and touched their foreheads together. 'You are my home.'

Lana kissed her, and they both rose at the sound of rippling mercury. Miri paused before the portal and ran to the winding staircase. She stumbled up the first few steps until she realised her legs had turned to jelly and clambered up to the bedroom. The house shuddered, and the staircase rails snapped.

'Miri, there's no time!'

Miri returned to the stairs and hurdled the rail. Lana caught her and toppled backward through the portal, onto rocky dirt. The portal retracted, and they both got to their feet.

A smile spread across Lana's lips and tears welled in her eyes when she saw what Miri had risked going up to the bedroom for.

'You have been friends since birth,' said Miri, and she held out Lana's plush red panda teddy for her to take. Lana embraced them both.

'Lana! Miri!' Rachel called, jogging over to them.

'Is everyone out?'

'The last of the Raekeem are coming through now,' Rachel assured them. 'But there are other groups unaccounted for.'

Miri gazed at an open portal, where Raekeem men, women and children were filing out. This desperate scene reminded her of the day her home world was torn apart. She had searched the wandering souls, finding her sister and only half of the people they knew. Everyone else was gone.

'The Keeper opened all these gateways?' Lana asked, looking to six different gates that varied in size. People were filing out, followed by debris according to the environment they came from: water, dirt, sand, snow.

Rachel had to raise her voice over the cacophony of traumatised survivors calling for their loved ones. 'Bastet sent her followers when she heard this was happening.'

Lana saw a man dressed in ornate robes, obviously one of the followers. He was guiding a dirt-covered boy through the crowds. A man and a woman cried out when they saw their child. The man let the boy run to them, and he met Lana's gaze. He approached her and nodded to the others. 'We are sorry there was not enough time for you all to evacuate,' he said quickly. 'But, please, can you help Bastet? She is facing the Headmaster and his horde alone.'

Miri winced as she lurched angrily at him. 'You expect us to aid someone who would destroy these people's homes?' She jabbed her hand toward a family she recognised, the people who gave her and Lana refuge in their cabin during the snowstorm. 'You people make me sick!'

The volume of the crowd died to quiet murmurs when they turned to watch Miri.

'You tore apart our families, our homes!' Tears streaked her dirt-covered face, stinging cuts down to her chin.

The man stood hopelessly, fingers absently bunching his gold and white robes.

'Now you want your world to end,' Miri croaked, dry-mouthed. 'And in so doing, end ours.' She drew in a sharp breath, and screamed at him while Lana and Rachel held her.

'How *dare* you!'

Chapter 40

The Keeper knew the open square in her city where the fight would be raging. She looked from Rachel to Miri to Lana. 'Bastet will not last long against so many.'

The four women were sitting in a marquee, at one table of several that had been arranged as a mess hall. Food was being prepared, and refugees from the different worlds were forming a line to pick up a plate and fork. Both Miri and Lana had been treated by Jolie, but they were in no condition to fight.

'There is more at stake than just her survival,' the Keeper continued. 'The twins are the only Senate members left, and they alone cannot rule our people. I was to assume leadership before Poser launched his attack. Now the Headmaster threatens that transition. If he succeeds in defeating Bastet, in front of everyone, the people will choose him. Under his rule, he would seek out new worlds to collect.' She gestured to the forest and then to Rachel. 'This world, your world, it won't matter to him; the Headmaster will take new land, segregate its families, and my people will love him for it. Because it will be a reassuring sign: "Business as usual".'

'And under your rule?' Miri asked. 'You will stop world collecting?'

'I will do more than stop it,' the Keeper answered without hesitation. 'I will force the College to restore the worlds that are being devastated right now. They have the ability. I will make them replant every tree, repave every road and install permanent gateways between all worlds.'

Miri winced and held her ribs when she rose from the table.

'Then the Headmaster must die.'

Ship engines could be heard approaching from the sky. Lana left the tent to watch the Black Heron descend from the clouds.

Talon had found the coordinates to a naturally forming portal to get her ship from Home Realm to the Forest Realm. The loading bay was packed full of supplies for the refugees. General Lincoln and his AM units were all occupied in San Francisco, restoring damaged homes and businesses.

The bay door opened as soon as the ship touched down. Shen and Saule rolled large packs of food, clothing, tents and sleeping bags down the ramp.

'Captain,' Shen greeted Lana.

Saule winced at how Lana was carrying herself. 'You're in bad shape.'

'Yeah. I don't think Miri and I will be much help this time.'

Bell was pulling a crate of supplies down the ramp and across the ground, seemingly on her own, until it stopped and Talon emerged from behind it. She surprised Lana by placing a hand on her shoulder. Talon never made physical contact with anyone outside of hand-to-hand combat.

'Wuff!' Bell told Lana confidently, wagging her tail. Talon nodded and signed to Lana, *We'll take it from here.*

Bastet ducked under a blade swung by a College student, turned and threw out her leg, sweeping her assailant off the ground and onto his back. She drew her burning blade through his neck, slashing the ground with a hiss, and parried the next attack that bore down on her head. Another swing severed her ear before she could avoid it. Gritting her teeth, she head-butted the man in front of her. He staggered, and she used the gap to launch a kick into his chest. This move drew her away from those swinging their swords at her rear, and brought her closer to an opening she had spotted moments earlier.

Bastet parried attacks while pushing forward. She dove and slashed the last opponent in her way while in mid-air, lopping the woman's head off as she broke free of the horde, rolling to her feet and taking quick backward steps, her eyes darting to those running to flank her.

All of the deep cuts running along Bastet's back, arms, rib cage, legs and face finally had time to heal. Her missing ear reformed, but blood still soaked her fur at every wound site.

She had not been lynched yet. But it was only a matter of time before someone would strike true and take her head.

A rumbling sounded above her, and Bastet saw a ship fly out of an open gateway. The Black Heron swooped and fired an arc of blasts across the horde, causing them to back away from Bastet. It dove behind her and landed. The bay door opened, and Shen, Saule, Talon and the Keeper stepped down the ramp to join the outnumbered cat woman.

'We are here to defeat the Headmaster and restore the collected worlds,' the Keeper assured her. While the Headmaster stood at the back of his horde, Bastet had fought alone. Though her ideals endangered entire worlds, including her own, Bastet had sent her only defence away to help evacuate the displaced.

Before Bastet could utter a word, the Headmaster shouted, 'Take them all!'

Saule used the powers Kim had left with her to create a flat force field beneath the closest people running at her. She flipped it sharply, throwing them all to the ground. Shen swung his staff over his head, widened his stance and struck a man down. Talon was armed with a crossbow, each bolt tipped with explosives. A man not wearing a black robe took the first hit. In a burst of red mist, his skull was gone. As per the Keeper's instruction, she avoided the College students. They were the only ones with the skill to undo the damage being done to the collected worlds.

A woman running alongside the Headmaster took Talon's next shaft to the head, and the explosion sprayed blood against him. He grabbed two of his students by the back of their collars and used them as shields while he ran at Talon. A few metres before he closed the gap, he threw the students at Shen and Saule.

Saule caught them both mid-air with a force field and swept them toward the Keeper, who opened a gateway. The students disappeared through the gate, and she closed it.

Talon fired her last bolt. The Headmaster ducked under it. Shen advanced on him, and he caught Shen's staff and swung him into the horde.

Saule and the Keeper circled the horde, taking College students singularly or in pairs with a force field and sweeping them through a gateway, where Fear waited on the other side to subdue them.

The Headmaster bore down on Bastet and Talon, hammering with his fists like a raging gorilla. Talon dropped on her back and locked her legs around his right arm. Bastet deflected his other hand with the flat of her blade, sidestepped and chopped off his right arm. Talon grappled him and threw him onto his side while he howled in pain. He kicked Bastet in the gut when she attempted another swing, sending her into the horde.

Chips of wood flew off Shen's staff while he parried attacks from all directions. Finally, he found an opening to strike a blow. Just as his staff caught the woman in the forehead, he was thrown sideways by the impact of Bastet's body. His staff clattered across the ground. Bastet rolled off him, but as soon as he rose to his feet, he was knocked down again by Talon when she came hurtling through the air.

All three of them were surrounded by swinging broadswords. Talon leaned back to avoid a blade. She spun her body low and swept her attacker's legs out from under him.

The Headmaster charged Bastet, knocking down everyone in his path. He stopped abruptly when he realised he was standing in shadow. He looked up to see the Black Heron hovering above and snapped his glare to Talon. She was tapping a command into her ring console.

'Kill the pink-haired one!' he shouted.

Shen defended Talon while she completed the remote sequence. The Black Heron extended its wings, tilted its nose to the horde and fired.

Saule and the Keeper managed to remove four more College students before the blasts reached them. Saule quickly formed a force field dome over the Keeper, Shen, Bastet and Talon while they huddled together. Weapons clattered to the ground and death cries rang out over the pounding blasts. The barrage was sustained until no targets remained. The Black Heron completed an elegant reverse descent, landed and powered down.

The smoke cleared, and Saule lifted the force field. Light shone through a hole in the Headmaster's chest. It closed slowly, but his legs would take longer to reform. He propped himself up on one elbow and groaned through the searing pain. A shadow crept over him, and he saw broadswords either side of a pair of furred legs. His vision climbed up Bastet's torso as she raised her weapons.

'I yield,' the Headmaster croaked.

Bastet held his pained gaze. She swung both blades across her body.

The Headmaster's jaw dropped. His tongue rolled to one side, and his head slid off his neck.

Slowly lowering the blades to her sides, Bastet gazed across the burnt bodies of those who had come to lynch her.

The Keeper stepped through a gateway atop the Senate building. The twins flinched when she arrived beside them.

'That gateway leads to the College and its students,' she said to them in a commanding voice, with a nod to the gate. 'Go there and await my instructions.'

The twins stumbled through. A portal opened, and Lana and Miri joined the Keeper. The Black Heron swooped down behind them and landed. Saule, Shen and Talon descended the ramp.

Lana was glad to see none of them were injured. She felt Miri's hand take hers, and could sense that her partner was unsure if all of the immortals below were capable of what the Keeper was about to demand of them.

'Brothers and sisters,' the Keeper addressed the crowd below, her voice loud and inviting. 'Together, we have entered a new era. A new way of life. A new purpose.'

Uncertain murmurs rippled through the masses. Most were afraid of what Bastet might do next. They respected the Keeper of their Well, of the essence that sustained them. But they were also looking at Bastet, who still stood while so many of their fellow citizens were slain trying to stop her from ending their existence.

Bastet could feel their eyes on her, and she met their uneasy gazes. Despite her anger toward their ignorance and the false virtue they held on to, she saw potential for change.

'Listen to your leader,' Bastet said in a restrained tone. 'Heed her words.' She breathed through what she hoped would be the last of her anger. Finally, she dropped the broadswords she had used to execute the Headmaster, and gazed up at the arches and balconies around the city decorated for the day of Rebirth.

'I will stand with the Keeper of the Well as her protector,' she said.

'But on one condition. We will no longer celebrate Rebirth, for we had no right to sacrifice our children. This day marks the beginning of our redemption.'

The Keeper nodded. 'From this moment forth, we will live in service to those from whom we have taken so much. Together, we will rebuild the collected worlds as their people wish them to be. Our future is their future.'

The crowd was rendered speechless for a full minute. Murmurs started. Light clapping erupted. Somebody called out 'Our future, their future!' and the crowd began to chant, rising to a cacophony of celebration.

The Keeper raised her hands in salute, and the crowd roared. She turned and spoke to Miri. 'They may only be happy because they are now sure their world is not coming to an end. Either way, I will make sure everyone contributes to the rebuilding of your worlds.'

'You have all made the right choice,' Miri said. She followed the others back onto the Black Heron. The ship rose and flew to intercept a naturally occurring portal. They entered the Forest Realm, greeted by the familiar view of Earth and the moon. Talon took the Black Heron down to the refugee camp and landed. She and Bell joined the others in the loading bay, just as Rachel was walking up the ramp.

Saule and Shen opened separate portals and stood at their respective exits, hugging Lana and Miri goodbye.

'My band and I are going back on tour in a few days,' Saule told them. 'Come and see us.'

'I will gladly attend with my son,' said Shen and added, bowing to Lana, 'Thanks to you, he and I have many memories to make together.'

Lana's trembling lips spread to a proud smile. 'It was an honour,' she managed, swallowing her emotion during this seemingly sudden farewell.

'Thank you both so much,' Miri said, her eyes tearing.

When Saule and Shen left and the portals closed, Rachel guided the others back to the marquee.

'Everyone insisted on coming to lend a hand,' she told Lana, gesturing to a group of people who were unpacking aid packages from a crate.

'Everyone?' Lana asked. 'Who—'

'Hey, they're back!' a girl shouted. 'Lana! Miri!'

Lana's sister Brody came running between stacked boxes. Lana crouched in time to receive her colliding hug, which lasted a moment before it was Miri's turn.

Lana stood in amazement as her gaze wandered over the group, who were paused, turning toward her and smiling. *Mum, Dad, Theresa, Rowan, Lincoln, Jolie, Hutch, you're all here.* Sam emerged from behind them, pushing her father in a wheelchair. Anook and Jess were walking by with baskets of fruit. They stopped and smiled. Lana felt Miri press against her, and they looked to each other, both crying. A purple-skinned figure arrived beside Miri, and she glanced around to see Jihna, the Kiyola warrior, and three other Kiyol arriving with supply crates.

'My…' Miri wiped her eyes, and tried again to speak. 'My deepest gratitude to all of you for coming. Thank you.' Her sister, Lowen, other Fyrst Born, Amir the Blacksmith and other Vess came to express their gratitude.

Lana helped Brody climb onto a crate, where she handed out aid packages to approaching families, bringing a smile to those in need.

Preview to
SONIC HOWL

Cold and wet, grass prickled against her skin. Murmurs grew to words she could understand.

'Lana? What are you doing here?'

She flinched at a hand on her shoulder and rolled onto one knee. Light shone in her eyes, but she could see two men, a house behind them. Getting her knees under her, she prepared to make her escape, only to find her path blocked by garden gnomes. They stood against the perimeter of the yard. Each had a shovel in hand, their bearded smiles glazed wet.

'Lana, it's okay. It's us. You're safe.'

'Wh-Who are you? Where am I?' she asked the man who touched her.

'It's me, Paul.' He gestured behind him. 'This is Ted. We're your friends. La–' He paused and took a step closer. 'You're not Lana.'

Ted went back inside, returning a moment later with a towel. He and Paul wrapped her in it and helped her into the house. She stopped when she caught her reflection. Paul watched her in the bathroom mirror. Now, he could see her hair was a natural dark blonde. And her eyes were green.

'I'm not her,' she murmured, as though speaking his thoughts.

She raised her shaking hand and followed the curve of her lower lip with her fingers. 'Who am I?'

'It'll come to you,' Paul assured her. 'Here's a shirt.' He gestured to the shower. 'Go ahead and wash up while Ted and I make your bed.'

She stepped in, and the door closed behind her. After testing the knobs and the temperature of the water, she found comfort under the constant stream of warmth. She emerged some time later, dressed in a long pink shirt. She stopped before entering the lounge when she heard the two men engaged in a heated discussion.

'There's no way I can get us in,' Paul grumbled. 'We'll have to take our pitch to a smaller company.'

'Which will be bought by a Sonic Howl team for double, triple the price,' his partner argued. 'We have to find a way. We need this.'

Paul let out a tired sigh. 'I know, I know. First, we have to get the prototype to run.'

'It runs, just not… for long.'

'Yeah, twenty seconds, that's–' Paul followed Ted's gaze to their guest, standing in the doorway. He greeted her and gestured to cushions he'd laid on the lounge floor. 'There's a spare blanket if you need it. Sorry about the engine,' he added with a nod to a toaster-sized machine sitting on the lounge room coffee table.

When she didn't respond, he clapped his palms together awkwardly and stepped out with Ted.

An hour later, the digital clock in the kitchen read 1 a.m. She couldn't sleep. Thumping noise from across the street vibrated through the floorboards. She rose and approached the window, a scowl forming on her brow when she drew the curtain aside. People were drinking, swinging to the music coming from a stage obscured at the rear of the house opposite. She left through the front door, padding barefoot across the road. The cool wind pressed her shirt against her body. She snaked through the crowd of young men and women. The stage came into view. It was set in a partially built shed, tall speakers either side, emitting noise that hammered her eardrums and thumped in her chest. She moved to the back of one speaker and took hold of the wires.

'Hey! What do you think you're doing?' People jeered and shouted at her.

She tore the wires out. The singing stopped, the drummer lost pace.

Somebody shoved her away from the speaker. She took his wrist, turned her body and threw him onto the stage. Another man approached. She pushed him aside and stalked on to the next speaker.

Her shirt tore when somebody pulled her against the stage. She jammed her thumb under her assailant's rib cage, and he cried out. Doubled over, the lanyard he was wearing fell. She read *Sonic Howl* printed on it and the letters *V.I.P.*

Following the rapidly dispersing crowd, she walked back across the street with a generator from the party under her arm, through the front door of Paul's house, into the lounge. She put the motor under the coffee table, climbed under her doona cover, lay down and went to sleep.

She was stirred by low voices that rose to argument, then hushed to a compromising murmur. She sat up, feeling the warmth of the morning sun beaming into the lounge.

Thudding footsteps, and then the door to the bedroom opened. Paul's partner, Ted, stopped with a gasp, hand to his chest.

'Good morning,' he breathed out, and with a courteous half turn, he strode to the kitchen in a huff.

Paul walked by briskly, as though giving chase. He paused to greet her and saw that the old pink cotton shirt he'd given her was torn.

'You went out last night.'

'Couldn't sleep.'

Paul sat down on the edge of the couch and faced the kitchen. 'The neighbours have parties all the time. They stopped early.' He looked watched her curiously. 'Know anything about that?'

She shrugged and looked away.

Paul saw even less of Lana in this woman than he had the night before. 'You can't stay here. Not unless you're a registered resident. The country is overpopulated, and there's a strict refugee policy. I won't bore you with the politics. Basically, you need an identity. My aunt passed away this year. She was leaving our old faith to live here with me, before I met Ted. I never registered her death, and I know a guy who can doctor our relation status from aunt to niece. If you want to stay, you can be her.'

'What was her name?'

Paul opened his mouth to answer, but pressed his lips shut instead. 'We can change that too. Have a think about who you want to be.'

He stood from the couch. 'Fresh towels in the bathroom. Make yourself at home.' And he left to join his partner in the kitchen.

After a two-minute discussion, Ted arrived in the door to the lounge and looked down his nose at her. 'You'll have to earn your keep around here, sister.'

Those words reminded her of the lanyard she took last night. She retrieved it from under her pillow and dangled it for him to see.

'Is that…?' He paced over to her and snatched it. 'Paul, get in here!'

Paul saw the lanyard and recognised what it meant. He raised his glasses onto his forehead and brought the tag close to his face to inspect the clearance level. 'Where did–'

'Who cares?' Ted exclaimed 'We're in!' He cleared his throat, regained some composure and leaned closer to her. 'You've earned your keep and then some, mystery girl.'

She smiled for the first time. It was small, but Paul saw it. He held her gaze and spoke to his partner. 'I'll get the registration papers.'

'I'm taking this one clothes shopping after breakfast,' Ted announced. 'That colour looks good on you,' he mused, but raised a disapproving eyebrow. 'We'll find you something less… torn.'

Paul was still holding the lanyard as though it were a precious object. 'You think yourself up a name while I fix you some eggs.'

She took the fourteen-gauge speaker wires out from under her pillow and pulled the electric generator she'd stolen out from under the coffee table.

Whistling a tune from the kitchen to the lounge, plated breakfast and orange juice in each hand, Paul stopped with a frustrated stomp. 'Cripes! I forgot to move the engine to the garage. Ted, honey!' he called over his shoulder.

Ted strode in, saw his partner nod to the coffee table and huffed. 'I just cleared a spot for it in the… Paul, how long?'

'How long what?'

Paul's ears found the answer to his own question. A low hum. Then he glimpsed an indigo light, stepping closer to see a full ring of plasma arcing in the engine's transparent cylinder.

'How long?' Ted repeated and then raised a hand as if to say *nobody move*. 'Coming up on twenty…'

Paul was so transfixed by that light he didn't notice his house guest